PRAISE FOR KEN MACGREGOR

This latest collection provides such a comprehensive slew of creative and wildly inventive kills, I'm not sure whether I should fear Ken or whether I should ask for my own creative death at his hands. Given that they're all so much fun, I know what I'm leaning towards. Best get my affairs in order!

— ZACHARY ASHFORD, AUTHOR OF
POLYPHEMUS.

I laughed, and then was horrified that I laughed, as I read Ken come up with the most fiendish ways in which people volunteered to die. I think we would all be lucky for Ken to write how we were going to die."

— MATT BRANDENBURG, AUTHOR OF ...
AND OUT COME THE TOYS

The horrors in *Some People I Have Killed* are divinely inspired, the irony wickedly twisted. Yet, these delightfully sinful morsels still shine with a sense of humanity that can only come from Ken MacGregor. Grab this collection and prepare to savor!

— DOUGLAS FORD, AUTHOR OF *LET'S CUT UP DAD!* AND *WHO DIES FIRS*

Some People I Have Killed is a fun collection from the man who makes your worst nightmares come true. And by 'fun', I mean 'twisted.' If I could pick anyone to bump me off, it'd be Ken MacGregor: inventive, funny, and just the right side of sick.

— LINDA NAGLE

Some People I Have Killed is a twisted therapy session where Ken MacGregor exorcises his demons by creatively offing people you might know. If you've ever wondered what would happen if your deepest anxieties were weaponized, this anthology is your dark and humorous field guide."

— GABY TRIANA

SOME PEOPLE I HAVE KILLED

SOME PEOPLE I HAVE KILLED

KEN MACGREGOR

Dragon's Roost Press

Some People I Have Killed is published by Dragon's Roost Press.

This anthology is © 2025 Dragon's Roost Press and Ken MacGregor.

Artwork by Milo MacGregor

Printed in the United States of America

Ingram ISBN: 978-1-956824-60-5

Print ISBN: 978-1-956824-64-3

Digital ISBN: 978-1-956824-59-9

Dragon's Roost Press

2470 Hunter Rd.

Brighton, MI 48114

thedragonsroost.biz

No AI was used in the creation of this book.

To all my victims. You are such good sports!

CONTENTS

FOREWORD

In 2021, I was signing books at a local outdoor event in Ypsilanti, Michigan. Every month, at least when it's not Winter, there's a celebration of cool stuff called First Fridays. My friend Holly Schoenfield—also the cover artist for my anthology *Stitched Lips*—suggested that I find a hook to bring more people to the table. Something I could do in real-time. Something personal to me. Something no one else was doing.

Thus was "Killed by Ken" born. And, after more than two years, I finally have enough of them to share the results with you.

This has been a uniquely challenging process for me: not only did I have to work on a tight deadline (initially a week, though over time I pushed it out to a month, while also focusing on making them longer and more involved), but I had to operate within very strict parameters. I had to use the information the clients gave me, stay as true to it as possible, while still making the story fun and unsettling. Based on the feedback I've gotten from nearly every person who hired me to do this, I have done a fairly good job of that. It's been challenging, but also a *lot* of fun! I've learned so many things I never would have known otherwise, from all the different kinds of centipedes there are to the fact that there's a rare disease that makes you age prematurely. I've had to stretch my own imagination to accommodate the stories in ways I've never had to before, and I believe I'm a better writer for it.

So, a heartfelt thank you to everyone who has hired me to do a "Killed by Ken". You have not only helped me fill a void in the fiction industry that nobody knew needed to be filled, but you have also pushed me to improve myself, which I deeply appreciate.

Let's get down to the nuts and bolts of the thing.

I developed a questionnaire, with things like "What is your current job or artistic passion (or both)?" and "Name something you dislike or find distasteful." There are only nine questions. From the answers (and for a small fee), I created a completely original story, not using a template or anything, and emailed it to the purchaser. Oh, and I would kill them, or do something equally horrible that left them wishing they were dead. Fictionally, of course. I would have charged an awful lot more to do it for real.

In the following pages, you will find all the people I have killed…so far. You will likely notice that many take place in and around Ypsilanti, Michigan; that's because I live there, and so do several of my victims. I will include the answers folks gave me that sparked the idea, so you can see how I got where I did. In every instance (except the first, because Holly asked me to keep her name, and one other, which I will explain when you get there), I have changed the names of the participants, to protect their identities.

So, without further ado, please allow me to introduce you to Some People I Have Killed.

INTRODUCTION

Ken MacGregor is every bit the wild man you think he is from seeing him at cons, on social media, or in indie horror films. He's a writer at the razor-thin juncture of the absurd and the macabre, a Shirley Jackson Award nominated editor, a theatrical and film actor, family man, friendly neighborhood bookmobile driver, and oh-no-really *contract killer* with more notches in his belt than you have teeth in your head.

This collection you hold in your hand (or on your Kindle or on your phone) wouldn't exist if not for one crazy, glorious idea he had in those weird twilight days of the early pandemic. What if, he wondered, he could leverage his position as a *regular* selling his books at horror cons and fan events around the greater Ypsilanti, MI area to get people interested in *personalized* stories? Stories not just written *for* them, but written *about* them. As a writer of horror and the weird, well informed by the history of science fiction and fantasy, the possibilities for a client's demise would be limitless.

One fateful Saturday, a sign-up sheet with a short questionnaire was planted on a table flanked by his books, and *Killed by Ken* was born.

The world of the publishing genre writer has a dark side, whether you're in it for the horror, the mystery, the sci-fi, or the fantasy. It's part of the American hierarchy of pay: those who work the hardest often go elbow-to-elbow under the table for scraps, while a small handful of "big name" authors eat their fill.

Oh, but writing is *fun,* you say (presumably with a belly full of fun). Yes, writing a story can and should be a great experience, but that doesn't mean you don't often have to carve its essence right out of your guts. And then you send it out into the world with hope, to a web zine, magazine, or anthology, and wait for that letter from the editor, one that probably has a bloody "unfortunately" glistening somewhere near the top, a rejection that feels, inescapably, like a rejection of your personhood, your humanity, and most especially your life choices, rather than what it most likely is: an editor (also a creative soul, one hopes) not seeing your story as the right fit with their vision for what *their* creative baby should be.

If you live in this world, you'll appreciate the genius of the concept: instead of submit-and-reject, why not begin with a willing audience? Doesn't hurt, either, that they've got a vested interest in the main character and what happens next. That they're that much more likely to lose themselves in the dream we writers weave, when the story is their own.

You lose yourself to reading too, right? (You're one of us.) So when a book is open and your eyes are moving rapidly, like they do in your dreams, you are not just rooting for the main character. You *become* them. As a reader, you're in this to live different lives, right? To be everywhere and be everyone (a soldier, a scientist, a queen). Well, you've come to the right place.

Now get ready to die.

Again and again, and in unimaginable ways (raves and apocalypses, flesh eggs and giant beavers). Don't say it's hopeless —it's all in the contract: to live, one must die. You'll see dozens of new faces looking out of the mirror, and you'll feel the teeth of every greasy demon and the claws of every murderous best friend, every accidental plunge and impossible terror.

But don't worry, you're in good hands. MacGregor will catch your essence on its way into the Abyss and sprinkle it over a new life, get you settled in for a brand new ride.

Okay, if you're Ken, that's the end of the intro. Everybody else, gather 'round.

As Ken's co-editor-in-crime at *The Midnight Zone,* I was lucky enough to be able to look over his shoulder as he wrote many of these wildly imaginative stories, and was luckier still to be the very first to read and experience a number of them.

One of the biggest surprises along the way was when the parameters of the project made the stories produced feel more and more like they belonged to an unexplored genre, one wherein the protagonist always dies, but the protagonist is also only one step removed, peering down at the pages to learn her or his own fate. When you ask a real person to acquaint you with them as quickly as possible and then get down to the business of killing them in a story, the truth about *you* is what quickly comes to light.

Ken does the job he was hired to do, and does it with gusto (alligators, mud slides, sexy spiders, and bug cults), but he'll also put a smile on your face, and maybe make you feel that, even with all the times you yourself have to go elbow-to-elbow under the table for the scraps, you are special. You live, and someday you'll die, and it matters.

Don't tell him I told you, but dude loves his victims. As I said, you're in good hands.

Douglas Gwilym

Stoker-nominated author

Pittsburgh, April 21, 2025

THE END OF HOLLY
2021

The very first one of these was quite short. As I did more of them, they got longer. Enjoy!

(Favorite color: Black; Passion: Painting)

"Black 3.0 isn't dark enough!" Holly railed against the proverbial heavens. She was actually yelling at the ceiling, and whoever else might be listening.

Someone was.

Holly was painting yet another skeleton in a long line of them. To call her obsessed would perhaps be unkind, but totally accurate. This particular skeleton was playing the ukulele, wearing a plum-colored beret and a leather choker (the choker dangled loosely on the neck bones, because...no throat. The background was supposed to represent the emptiness of the void, and how music was the only bright spot in an otherwise bleak universe. Or something. It was a work in progress, this theory. That was the trouble with doing things on your own; when it was a commission, you could just *ask* what they wanted. When it came out of your own head, you really had to give it some thought.

The person listening was a woman in Holly's store, *Stardust*, an art gallery featuring local artists, including Holly herself. The woman was gazing about, examining the art, clucking to herself. It was hard to judge her age: somewhere between Mother and Crone.

The woman turned to her, eyes bright and dancing with mischief. "I have something blacker than 3.0," she said. "I doubt you can pay the price though."

Holly sized her up. "If it's that good, I'll try to figure out a way to pay it."

The woman reached into a purse the size of a paperback book. Her arm disappeared up to the biceps.

Holly stared. This was the first impossible thing of the day, but the day was young.

The woman withdrew a tube of paint. No brand. Just the word 'noire' in lower-case letters, typewriter font, black on a white background. She handed it to Holly, who unscrewed the cap and squirted a dab on her palette. The bristles, when she dipped the brush, vanished. She applied some of the paint to her background and whistled low.

"This is incredible," she whispered, and kept painting. Numbly, she swept the brush across the canvas, slathering the black. Before she realized it, she'd used it up, and her painting was perfect. The skeleton in the foreground popped like it was in 3D. No other black had even come close. Unable to tear her eyes away, she asked, "How much?"

"Touch it," the woman said.

Holly stretched out her finger to touch the painting. Her finger rested on the black background, just to the left of the skeleton's pelvis. Instead of wet, it was cold. She reflexively tried to pull away but was stuck. The darkness drew her. "Hey," she yelled. Her hand was gone, icy in the void.

"I told you," said the woman. "You can't afford the price."

The painting pulled her all the way in, and Holly floated, freezing, hugging herself to keep warm, trapped, in the formless void for eternity.

She spent much of it thinking, *I suppose Black 3.0 really wasn't that bad.*

COBRA NAZIS TRY TO TAKE CHICAGO

2021

(Dislikes: Snakes; Favorite food: Matar Paneer; Finds repugnant: Fascists)

Lenore walked out from the annual axe-throwing competition in Naperville, Illinois, head held high from taking fourth place overall. It was her first time in the top ten. She'd been practicing all year. The dead tree behind her mother's house was barely a stump now.

Her phone alerted her to an Indian restaurant in town that Yelp said had excellent Matar Paneer. She would've driven thirty miles out of the way for good food, but this was right off 55. She parked outside and went in. The smell of curry and other spices made her salivate.

It was not the *best* Matar Paneer she'd ever had, but it was close. The curry had just the right amount of heat. Leaning back in her chair, Lenore rested her hands on her deliciously full belly and smiled: the cat who'd had the canary.

The door burst open so hard the glass shattered. The restaurant employees and customers stared, in shocked silence, as four large bipeds slithered in. They wore the black uniforms of the 1940's SS, even sporting the swastika armbands, like extras from a B-grade World War II movie. They had human-sized snake heads, with yellow and black scales, and tiny, shining, hypnotic eyes that stared coldly around the room. Black machine guns hung from shoulder straps, loosely held in their scaly hands, looking ready, looking deadly.

"Great," someone murmured a couple tables over. "Fucking Nazi snakes. Again."

The leader of the SS serpents glared at the man who'd spoken. Above the iron cross insignia on his collar, his hood flared out to reveal oversized false eyes, and he bared his fangs.

The manager stepped out from the swinging kitchen door. She addressed the cobra Nazis. "Look. We don't want any trouble."

The Nazi bastard shot her. For a moment, everyone just stared at her body. Blood pooled out from under her and blossomed on her white uniform from the tiny holes in her chest and abdomen.

Then, some guy threw a beer bottle at the snakes. It hit one in the face and bloodied an eye.

Chaos ensued. The guns popped loudly. Humans dove behind tables and counters. A cook burst out of the kitchen and drove a carving knife into the leader's chest. Another Nazi snake bit the cook on the face, and he quickly turned purple and dropped heavily to the floor. The cobra leader was hurting but not dead. The customers threw whatever they could find at the fascist snakes: saltshakers, plates, sweet Modak dumplings—not a super-effective weapon, if we're being honest—drinking glasses. There were a lot of minor injuries on both sides and a couple more probable fatalities.

Lenore had been taking advantage of the confusion to ease along the wall, keeping low and out of sight. She had spotted the back emergency exit by the restrooms and was heading that way. Finally, she made it to the hallway and stood up, bolting along it. The alarm screamed when she hit the exit bar and she ran to her car, unlocking it with the key fob as she got close.

Once inside, she quickly called 911 and told them there were active shooters in the restaurant. They told her it would be at least five minutes, and to stay out of the line of fire.

"Five minutes," she said, staring through her windshield. "How many will die in that time?" On the passenger seat, her gym bag sat there. Inside it, were five sharp, perfectly balanced throwing axes. She unzipped it. *Five minutes. Five axes. Must be fate.*

Moments later, Lenore stood outside the shattered glass door of the Indian restaurant. She held in axe in each hand, and the other three were held against her ribs, trapped by her left arm. Without a word, she hurled one into the back of a Nazi cobra soldier's head. The second was dead moments later, as she threw another axe. The remaining two dove for cover, spraying bullets behind them as they did. Lenore stepped through the doorway. Her shoes crunched on glass fragments. She had dropped one axe but still had two. One she launched into the Nazi leader's chest. It sunk deep, in almost the exact spot he'd been stabbed before. He fell ignominiously on his ass.

The other one snaked out from behind her, grabbing her ankle and sinking his fangs into her calf.

She cried out and swung, left-handed, connecting with his throat. Blood gushed forth and he yanked away, tearing his fangs from her. The leader was still alive, gasping for air, scaly fingers clutching at nothing.

"Why?" Lenore asked. "Why are you like this?"

The Nazi cobra hissed in response. His eyes were filled with pain and hate.

She lifted her throwing axe high over her head and brought it down, killing him.

The crowd gathered around her, thanking her, calling her a hero.

She sat down hard, suddenly unable to stand. Her left leg had dangerous purple lines radiating along her veins from the twin punctures. "Uh oh," she said.

"You'll be okay," someone lied.

"Earlier today," she said, "I took fourth place."

"Okay," they said.

"Just now," Lenore continued, "I think I took first."

The people around her were talking, but she couldn't hear them. The axe slipped from numb fingers. Her eyelids were suddenly very heavy. She closed them for the last time.

UNRESTFUL BONES

2021

(Favorite food: Taco Bell; Weird fact: found human remains in her yard)

Naomie pulled into the driveway. The smell of hot Crunchwrap Supreme tortured her from the Taco Bell bag on the seat next to her. It had been doing that all the way home. She snagged it and got out.

Her husband was standing by the back door, arms crossed, frowning. She blinked at him. "What the absolute *fuck*, Naomie?" he asked.

Her mind raced. He hadn't asked for anything from the drive-through. She hadn't run up any crazy-ass charges on the credit card lately. She hadn't been sleeping around. "What the what-the-fuck?"

Chester gestured at the chicken coop. *Oh yeah,* she thought. *I forgot about that.* She had, perhaps impulsively, brought another nine chickens, bringing their total to seventeen. "It's not my fault," she told him. "I went to the tractor supply place unsupervised. Look how cute that one is!"

He glared at the chicken in question, then back at her. "We're going to have to expand the damn coop and probably move it further back in the yard. That is, if you still want me to build that deck. Unless you've changed your mind."

She smiled angelically. "Nope. I still want the deck. Thanks, honey! You're the best." Taking her Taco Bell inside, she wolfed it down. She could hear Chester swearing quietly as he drove the shovel into the ground out back. It was going to be so nice having a back deck. And a bigger chicken coop. All the fresh eggs she and her friends could ever want. She might have to get some more chickens. Maybe not. She didn't *have* to keep buying them. It's not like she had a problem.

Four days later, Naomie was handfeeding one of the squirrels that she had basically tamed. She had bought a giant bag of peanuts for this purpose and it was almost half empty.

Behind her, near the house, Chester jumped back, dropping the shovel. "Holy shit!"

She stood up, spilling peanut shells everywhere. "What? Are you okay?"

He didn't answer her. He pointed at the ground. Where he'd been digging, prepping for the eventual back deck they'd been dreaming of for a few years, in the churned-up dirt, was a human skull.

"Holy shit," she echoed.

Naturally, they called the city police, who came out. The police called in the coroner, who confirmed it was definitely human. They brought in a crew to dig up more of the yard (incidentally moving the chicken coop further back in the yard; Chester, watching them do this job he didn't particularly want, nodded in satisfaction). They found the remains of four people total. They speculated that it had been decades since they were interred, and said they'd let Naomie and Chester know if they could identify the remains. Also, that they could go back to whatever it was they were doing when they started digging in the first place.

Naomie texted her five closest friends to tell them they found dead bodies on her property, that she now lived in Murder House, and that they were already planning the First Annual Murder House Party for the coming summer.

For a time, things were quiet. The back deck slowly came together. The chickens (twenty-three now) grew larger and some were excellent layers. The sun was out until nine at night, and the temperature hung close to ninety several days in a row. They had filled the pool and spent a good deal of time in it.

One night, in mid-August, Naomie was sleeping to the soothing sounds of crickets and cicadas. She woke suddenly, vaguely aware of something being wrong. She lay, eyes open, listening hard. Something outside was click-clattering, like dice rattling across the driveway.

She eased out of bed, careful not to disturb her sleeping husband. Pulling on a light robe, she stopped in the kitchen to draw a carving knife from the block. It made a satisfying *shing* noise. Slowly, to keep it quiet, she unlocked the deadbolt on the back door and eased it open. In the distance, she could hear traffic on Michigan Ave. She looked for the source of the strange noise.

There, by the chicken coop. Something was moving. Something large. *Damn it*, she thought. *Coyotes? Bears? Are there bears in Ypsi?* She was pretty sure it wasn't bears. But it was definitely tall enough. *Too skinny though.* Pulling her phone from the pocket of her robe, Naomie thumbed open the flashlight app. She pointed the phone toward the coop and turned it on.

Four skeletons, blood dripping from their jaws, feathers caught in their teeth, turned to her as one. Behind them, most of her chickens were dead or wounded.

"What the fuck?" she whispered. The beam of light wavered with her shaking hand.

The skeletons advanced on her. Naomie turned to go back inside, watching them over her shoulder. The door had locked automatically. "Damn it!" She pounded on it. "Chester. Wake the fuck *up*!"

The skeletons closed in, moving to surround her. Dropping the phone, she lashed out and stabbed on in the eye with the knife. It thunked into the back of its head. It clacked its jaw open and shut. Two more grabbed her robe and played tug-of-war with her.

"Chester! Open the goddamn door or I'm divorcing you right now!" She threw a left hook at one of the skeletons holding her. She broke several of its teeth and split her knuckle open. She kneed one on the pelvis to no great effect. She fought hard, but they overwhelmed her. One sank its teeth into her throat. Hot blood fountained from her carotid artery.

As she was sliding down the wall, onto the brand-new deck, staining the wood with her blood, the door opened behind her. "What the absolute *fuck?*" Chester yelled. He reached back in for the baseball bat they kept there and came out swinging. He bashed in their skulls and shattered their limbs. He lifted Naomie's head, pressing his hand firmly over the wound in her neck, trying to staunch the blood flow. "Fuck. I'm so sorry. I was so tired. Took forever to wake up."

"It's okay," she gurgled. "Sorry I got blood on the new deck."

Somehow, this struck them both as hilarious and they laughed. Naomie cringed at how much it hurt and quickly stopped. "Chester?"

He stroked her hair with his free hand. "Yeah?"

"I think maybe we should move."

"Yeah. Okay. You bet. As soon as you're all better."

She gave him a weak smile. "I don't think that's gonna happen."

"Shut up. Of course, it is."

"I'm sorry. About all the damn chickens. I may have a problem."

He was crying. "Doesn't matter. I love you, in all your crazy, chicken-buying ways."

She couldn't talk. She was too weak. But, in the last few seconds, her eyes told him she loved him too. Overhead, the stars twinkled serenely. *Stupid fucking skeletons,* she thought. *Ate my chickens, you bastards. Ate me too.* The stars went out.

THE RAVE
2021

(Job: Doctor; Favorite music: Trip hop)

Sarah put her feet up on the chair and took another several swallows of coffee. The clock on the wall, unkindly, reminded her that she still had four hours left in her nineteen-hour shift.

A couple tables away in the lounge, a colleague she didn't know lay across three chairs with one arm thrown across her eyes.

"You awake," Sarah asked quietly.

"Barely."

"I feel that." Her jaw creaked in a yawn, and she fought fatigue by finishing the coffee. "I have two days off in a row this week. I'm going to sleep through both of them."

The other doctor moved her arm enough to expose one eye, which looked at her. "Which days?"

"Thursday and Friday."

The doctor sat up. "I have Friday off too. I'm going to a rave."

"Did it suddenly become the 90s when I wasn't looking?"

"Ha! I think it's a reaction to the pandemic: now that we *can* go out again, people are nostalgic for better times."

"Or," Sarah said, "people are bored out of their minds."

"Either way, I'm going. Be nice to cut loose, drink a few, and dance to electronica."

"Tell me, Doctor…"

"Hiller. Call me Carol."

"Where is this rave? Maybe I'll go."

F riday rolled around. Sarah really did sleep for most of Thursday. With no small amount of self-consciousness, she dressed all in black and wore exaggerated makeup. She picked up Dr. Hiller—*Carol. She said to call her 'Carol'*—and they drove down to a farm near Milan. A large barn pulsed with music and multicolored lasers.

Inside, throngs of people danced. A full bar occupied one whole side of the space run by four bartenders who were in constant motion. The speakers pumped out "Teardrop" by Massive Attack.

She leaned in to shout in Carol's ear. "I *love* this band!"

They secured drinks and walked around, taking it all in: no one was masked—it still felt weird not to wear one, though the danger was allegedly long past. A very attractive couple offered them Ecstasy, which might have been tempting if both doctors didn't have to work another long shift tomorrow. They politely declined.

Cage dancers in sparkling bikinis floated above the crowd, suspended from the foot-thick wooden rafters, gyrating to the beat.

A live alligator thrashed in a tank, smack in the middle of the room, splashing water up over the sides, and getting those dancing nearby wet. They seemed to thrill to be so close to such power and ferocity.

Carol followed her wide-eyed gaze. "An *alligator?* That's insane!"

I couldn't agree more, she thought. They found a tall table across from the bar.

The DJ was spinning The Chemical Brothers on actual vinyl. The two doctors took turns refilling their drinks and dancing whenever they were empty again.

Sarah had a pleasant buzz going. She danced among sweating, grinning 20- and 30-somethings blissed out on X. The music throbbed through the crowd, pulsing, thumping, cracking, and splashing.

Wait. What? Splashing?

Cold water hit her feet. Several people near her screamed. The DJ shouted over the mic, causing horrible feedback: "Holy shit! The Gator!"

The tank had ruptured. Twelve feet and seven hundred pounds of alligator surged out, riding the wave of water.

For a moment, it seemed suspended in air, frozen in time. Then it landed on the guy next to her, crushing him under its weight. It whipped around, jaws snapping. They closed around Sarah's thigh, teeth ripping into her flesh. It was the most intense pain she'd ever felt.

Someone large and muscular—she presumed he must be a bouncer—hit the alligator with a heavy wooden table, and it hissed, letting her go. When it spun to face its tormentor, Sarah backed away on her hands as fast as she could go. She left behind an alarming amount of blood.

Dr. Hiller—*Carol, damn it!*—was holding her head, talking to her in that voice: the one Sarah herself used to calm people who are in serious trouble. "It's pierced the femoral." She was applying pressure, but there were so many punctures she couldn't stem the flow. "I'm so sorry I dragged you here."

Sarah smiled weakly. She could feel herself going into shock. "I drove, remember? I wanted to come. Next time we do this, though? No alligators, okay?"

The reptile in question had left the barn. It was outside somewhere, among the cars. She could make out distant sirens and hoped one was an ambulance.

"Definitely," Carol said. "No alligators. Promise." She kept talking but Sarah could no longer hear her. Just lips moving without sound. Everything behind Carol's face was in soft focus. The speakers had gone silent but she could still hear Massive Attack: they were playing "Angel".

"I really do love this band," she tried to say. But her mouth refused to cooperate. Her body was still and getting quite cold. *I guess that's it then,* she thought, and she was gone.

CAUGHT
2021

(Passions: Supporting local artists; Shibari)

E velyn strolled past the first few vendors, a neutral smile of polite interest in place. This served as armor against the inevitable aggressive sales pitch. She *would* buy something—supporting local artists was important—but she would do so in her own time, on her terms.

So far, nothing had leapt out at her, demanding to be bought. If she wasn't inspired, she'd still pick up something small from a couple of artists, at random, to be nice. The glass figurines almost got her: they sparkled in the afternoon sun. Though, they were, perhaps, a trifle kitschy.

What's this? Dreamcatchers? Except they weren't. More like intricate spiderwebs of twine, incorporating tiny glass beads that hung like morning dew among the strands. Her polite smile morphed into something more genuine, and she reached out to touch one.

"Careful," an alto voice said. "You might get caught." Blue eyes gazed up at her, dancing with humor. The artist's sculpted cheekbones would've been comfortable on a movie poster.

"They're really lovely," Evelyn said

"Thanks." They held up a work-in-progress. Their deft fingers flew through the intricate movements as though independent creatures, unaware of the person to whom they were attached.

Watching the knots form as if by magic, becoming something wonderful, she blushed, thinking how those hands might feel on her. "How much for this one?" It was over a foot across.

"Eighty-five," they said.

"Venmo okay?"

It was. They wrapped it for her. She couldn't take her eyes off those fingers. "Would you like to," she blurted before she lost her nerve, "grab a drink later?"

"Yes," they said with a slow smile. "Yes, I would."

That night, the two of them had substantially more than one drink. Talking, laughing, and kissing led to them staggering back to her apartment, where she discovered just how skilled those hands really were.

She woke foggy, dehydrated, with an uncomfortably full bladder and unable to move. Her eyes snapped open, though the sunlight hurt them. She was bound, upright, tied to the bedroom door with sturdy rope. The knots were expertly done, crisscrossing her body, keeping her immobile. The person—she'd struggled to remember their name. Something archaic. Something to do with the craft...*Weaver!*—sat calmly on her bed, watching her. When she caught their eyes, they stood, naked too—a small comfort.

"You look absolutely delicious." Spoken, crossing toward her.

"Thanks, I guess," Evelyn said. "Could you untie me though?"

"After breakfast." They bent their knees in a half-squat and assumed a look of pained concentration. For a moment, Evelyn honestly thought they were going to shit on the floor. Instead, from behind their groin, a long, sharp, dark green stinger eased into view, accompanied by a positively *anatomical* squelching noise.

"Jesus," she whispered. Her bladder let go all over her legs.

They shuffled forward in the weird stance until they were close enough to kiss her. Evelyn turned her face away. A sharp pain blossomed in her thigh, and numbness spread from it.

"No," she said, struggling against losing sensation, against the ropes.

They stroked her hair. "Shh. The venom is quick. You won't feel anything as your insides turn to liquid."

"Fuck you." It was barely audible: defiance without strength.

"I did warn you that you might get caught."

Black bars encroached on her vision, collapsing in from both sides. Before they closed all the way, Evelyn saw their cheeks stretch wide and pull back to reveal mandibles that clicked together.

As she started losing consciousness, she thought, '*Weaver*'. *They're a spider. Of course.*

MONSTROUS

2021

(Likes to eat cod; Dislikes the MAGA crowd)

Curtis leaned back against the picnic table, basking in the afternoon sun. The gulls screeched and fought over some choice morsel by the garbage cans outside the fish & chips shack. He inhaled the salt air of Cape Ann and smiled over his bellyful of fresh cod.

A quintet of small children played tag in the sand, shrieking with laughter as their game went in and out of the lapping waves. A couple college kids tossed a Frisbee. The sun glinted off the waves, and a cool breeze flowed in from the coast. It was idyllic.

A giant, white Ford F-450 pulled into the beach parking lot, engine rumbling like Armageddon. From the cab, conjoined twins, joined at the shoulder and hip, slowly extricated themselves. Both wore red MAGA hats.

Here we go, Curtis thought. But they didn't cause a scene. They ordered fish sticks and fries, and two vanilla shakes, and sat down at one of the other picnic tables. The one on the left nodded at Curtis. "Nice day, huh?"

"Yup," Curtis said. He thought it wisest to keep it to one syllable. Maybe two, since they're twins. He smiled to himself at the thought.

"Something funny?" asked the other one. There was an edge to his voice, maybe hoping for trouble.

"Hm? Nope. Just enjoying the sunshine. Makes me smile."

The brothers finished eating and ambled awkwardly down the boardwalk. From behind a Port-A-John, a woman appeared wearing a Florida Gators T-shirt and a flouncy skirt. Her skin was red with sunburn, nearly matching her MAGA hat. She met the brothers and they spoke briefly. Then, she fell in step with them, wrapping her arm around the arm of the one of the left. As they got further away, it looked very much like her arm was becoming fused to his.

Curtis shook his head. "Sun's getting to me. Better find some shade." He moseyed to a stand of trees and flopped down on a bench. He took a long pull from the insulated water bottle. It was still cold and had a few ice chunks in it from this morning. Quality product.

A 12-passenger van pulled up and parked in the lot. *Trump 2020* bumper stickers were plastered all over the back doors. They opened and the vehicle disgorged five pairs of conjoined twins with MAGA hats.

"What the absolute hell?" This was statistically impossible, he was sure. They headed toward the beach, chatting amiably amongst themselves.

Bemused, he watched them go. Twenty minutes later, an entire *bus* of conjoined twins—and triplets!—marched in the same direction. The suspense was too much. Curtis followed.

The beach curved: hot, soft sand flanked by enormous boulders on either end. Curtis traversed the shifting surface of the beach cautiously, watching his footing. It was too quiet. No one was splashing. No one played. He looked up from his sandy toes.

Stepping over the rocks, easily forty feet tall, was a monstrous human figure, bloated belly hanging to its thighs. On its head, pale white bodies, lying against deeply sunburned ones, twisted themselves to shape letters: life-sized M, A, G, and another A. It had to be a couple of hundred Trump supporters, conjoined together to make one being.

It stomped forward, crushing and old couple who wasn't fast enough to get out of the way. The next foot, comprised of faces spewing hatred, came down on an elaborate sand sculpture, obliterating it. With a hand made of fascists, it scooped up Curtis, lifting him high in the air. Torsos on its face separated to form a mouth. It spoke in twenty voices, loud and discordant, "*Now*, America is great!" and shoved him in.

Curtis tumbled through the bodies, beaten, battered, and bruised. Their hands tore at him. Their teeth bit into him. They were consuming him alive. As he was breathing his last, the monstrous form began to collapse from its own weight, the hate powering it no longer able to sustain this form. It plunged into the Atlantic, filling hundreds of lungs with salt water. For a time, it flailed in the surf, sending fifteen-foot waves crashing ashore. Finally, it was still.

By the time the authorities arrived, the crabs had begun to eat it.

INNER CITY WRITERS' RETREAT

2021

(Job: Writer/Artist; Fear of elevators)

*I*nner City Writers' Retreat. Allison rolled the words around in her mind. When you think of a writers' retreat, you think of cabins in the woods, birds chirping, streams gurgling...that kind of thing. She tried to imagine what it might be like to do a retreat smack in the middle of Detroit. If not for the source, she would've dismissed it out of hand. She got the invitation from a prominent Detroit horror writer, whose work had been made into very popular films and who was wildly prolific, churning out quality novels at an astonishing rate.

She arranged a cat sitter, made sure to cancel any and all potential commitments, and signed herself up. It wasn't exactly cheap, but nothing worthwhile ever was.

The building was tall but not ostentatiously so. The lobby was clearly once very posh but had been neglected for ages. The brass fittings were deeply tarnished, the cushions badly worn and even torn in places. The elevator button display went from B on up, skipping from 12 to 14. That latter was the highest. The number 6 was barely legible.

There were a few people milling around, mostly dressed casually. One wore a tan suit with a paisley tie. His beard was carefully tapered to a point and his mustache barely rode the edge of his upper lip, an underfed caterpillar.

There were two or three she might have recognized from dust jacket photos, but she couldn't be certain. She fought imposter syndrome the moment it insinuated itself in her brain. *I am a writer,* she thought. *I'm at a writers' retreat. I belong here.* It mostly worked.

Her room was up on the fourteenth (thirteenth, really) floor. She made her way to the elevator, suitcase dutifully rolling along behind her. She timed her arrival to the doors with another woman, intending to ride up with her. She didn't like being in elevators alone. She had an irrational fear of terrible things happening in elevators, and, perhaps absurdly, thought she was safe as long as someone else was there. They both stepped in when the doors parted.

"Fourteen please," Allison said, as the other was closer to the buttons.

She pushed the button for Allison's floor, and then pushed four. Both watched the display climb until *Ding!* The fourth floor. "Good luck this weekend," the woman said.

"You too," Allison replied. As the doors closed behind her momentary companion, her pulse pounded in her throat. The display crawled toward fourteen (*But it's really thirteen, isn't it?* She thought. *Unlucky thirteen*). Normally, she wasn't prone to superstition, but she'd make an exception here.

The display passed nine. *Only a little more,* she thought. *No problem. Nothing to be afraid of.*

The elevator stopped. The number ten had just lit up and died but eleven hadn't lit yet.

"Shit." It was a whisper. She worked to control her breathing, to not let panic set in. Her heart raced. She pushed the emergency button. Nothing happened.

"Okay," she said. "Okay. Don't freak out. I'm fine. Plenty of air in here. We're not going to fall." She opened the little door under the twin columns of buttons. The receiver was hanging there, right where it was supposed to be.

"Hello?"

"Oh, thank god," she said. "Hi. Look, the elevator stopped between the tenth and eleventh floors, and I'm stuck in there, all alone. Can you please send someone to fix it?"

There was a long pause.

"Hello? Are you there?" Allison asked.

"You said you're alone?"

Allison stared at the slightly reflective surface of the elevator doors. "Why did you ask me that?"

"Nobody else there, huh? Poor little miss, trapped all by her lonesome in the elevator."

"This is not funny," she said. Her voice shook, just a little. "I'm calling the police."

"Go ahead," the voice said. It was disgustingly confident.

Her phone had no signal. She tried to access the net but it couldn't connect. "Look, you," she spat into the phone. "I don't know who you are, or why you think you're funny, but I'm not putting up with this shit. Start the fucking elevator, *now!*"

"Okay."

The elevator lurched into motion and passed floor eleven. Allison sighed in relief and watched it climb past twelve and hit fourteen with a soft bell chime, just like it had on four. The doors didn't budge.

She picked up the receiver again. "Okay. Joke's over. Let me out please."

"Oh no. I'm afraid not. You see, you threatened to call the police. I don't think I can trust you now."

"I'm sorry about that. I panicked. I get claustrophobic. It makes me testy. I won't call the cops. I just want to get settled in my room and enjoy the weekend. All is forgiven. Please open the doors."

"You know what?" the voice said. "You almost convinced me. But…no."

The elevator dropped suddenly. She was thrown off her feet by the jolt. Somehow, she still held the receiver. "I'm falling!"

"Yep. Fourteen floors. I don't think you're gonna make it." The voice sounded positively cheerful.

"Why?" She knew she only had seconds left. "Why are you doing this?"

"Research. For a story."

The world exploded in noise and pain and she was no more.

ANOTHER SHOT AT THE TITLE
2021

(Loves wrestling, particularly "Macho Man" Randy Savage; has a cat named Annabelle)

Travis idly stroked Annabelle's fur while watching the news. The vibrating purr against his palm grounded him against the insanity on the television.

George "The Animal" Steele, one-time professional wrestler—moderately famous for portraying Tor Johnson in the movie Ed Wood—had somehow returned from the dead. He was a huge, mindless puppet, tearing through the streets of Ann Arbor, Michigan, hell-bent on mayhem and destruction.

"Well, my vicious tiger," Travis said to his cat, "I guess we know what we have to do, huh?"

Annabelle stared at him with the kind of profound apathy only attainable by housecats and CEOs.

"I knew you'd understand," Travis said, grinning. He leapt into action, flying off the couch and turning off the TV. He rooted around in the closet for the grimoire he hadn't had to use in ages. Annabelle tilted her chin slightly higher to indicate she wasn't really ready to be done being petted, but that she'd allow it this time.

Flipping the ancient, leather-bound tome to *Necromancy*, Travis located the correct spell. "Gotcha," he muttered, and set about gathering candles and table salt.

The ritual took almost an hour. After, Travis downed a whole quart of Gatorade: summoning spells take a lot out of you. Almost a thousand miles away, in Largo, Florida, the ground beneath a tree opened up. A swirl of gray/tan ash spiraled into the air and coalesced into a human figure. Moments later, Randy "Macho Man" Savage stood there, magically adorned in pink and orange Spandex and a leopard-print vest. Setting his black-and-yellow Stetson on his head, he turned northwest and started running. Before long, he was a blur. For 990 miles, people had their hair blown back by something too fast to see. In its wake, there was the impression of a gravelly voice shouting, "Ooooh yeah!"

George Steele was holding a blue metal mailbox over his head, threatening to crush a small, bespectacled man in a polyester suit. The big wrestler was pockmarked with bullet holes, and scorch-marked from Tasers from repeated police attempts to stop him. He did not bleed.

The businessman quaked in terror but blinked as the mailbox suddenly clanged to the ground. The undead former wrestler was gone.

He was, in fact, three blocks away, having been slammed into the public library building by the force of Randy Savage, who had barreled into him at the speed of sound—he had been slowing down for some time.

"You!" Steele growled. He swung a mighty uppercut, sending the Macho Man flying back fifteen feet.

Savage recovered quickly. "Me," he said, and hit Steele with a Toyota Camry.

Travis parked a few blocks away from the carnage and got out, leaving the grimoire on the front seat. He could hear the combatants from here: the thud of bodies smashing into cars and buildings and one another as the titans of yesteryear battled. Each was trying to make the other dead…again.

Travis peeked around the corner of the parking structure, ready to duck back from flying debris. It was epic. Just like the good old days, when he'd watch them on TV. The incredible athleticism. The raw strength. The skill these men had in the ring. Only now, it was fifty times more so. They were inhuman, supernatural, impossibly tough. The incidental property damage was going to cost the city millions.

Steele got Savage in a choke hold, legs wrapped around his torso. With his teeth, he grabbed Savage's hat, biting clean through the top. He spat the chunk of yellow leather on the sidewalk.

"My hat!" Savage sounded forlorn. He clenched his teeth and slammed backward with his head, catching Steele in the nose. Steele let go and Savage picked him up off the ground. He piledrove the other man into the concrete, head-first. "My *hat!*" Savage stepped on Steele's back, between the shoulder blades. Grabbing the man's wrist, he twisted up and around, wrenching the arm out of its socket. With herculean effort, Savage separated Steele's left arm completely.

He stepped back and let the other man get to his feet. For a moment, they stood, sizing each other up.

"That's my arm you've got there," Steele said. "What do you plan to do with it?"

Randy "Macho Man" Savage glanced at the arm he held. He looked the man in the eye. "This." Swinging it like a bat, he took the man's head clean off.

Putrid-smelling, yellow-green fog flowed from the spot where Steele's head had been. It pooled on the ground, heavier than air. Travis and Randy Savage watched as it slowly puddled along the curb and finally dribbled into the sewer. The body of the man who was known as 'The Animal' collapsed in on itself, dissolving into a stinking, organic soup. It, too, made its way down the drain. Savage wiped his hand on his Spandex pants.

He looked up and caught Travis's eye. "You brought me back." Travis nodded. "To defeat George Steele…again."

"That's right."

Savage nodded. "All right. I get it. Makes sense."

"Thanks—" Travis started.

Savage put up a hand, stopping him. "Just 'cause it makes sense, doesn't make it right," he said. "Don't you know, messing with dark magic has consequences?"

Travis looked at his shoes. Peripherally, he saw the big man walk toward him. He looked up.

"You brought the book, right? To send me back?" Again, Travis nodded. "Come on, then. Let's go get it."

They walked side-by-side. Travis explained that Savage had always been kind of a hero to him, and that the moment he saw that George Steele was rampaging through town, he knew exactly what he had to do. Savage said he guessed he understood, but that he kind of resented being brought back. "I mean," he said, "I was pretty happy being dead. It was quiet, peaceful. Nice change of pace from my life."

"I'm sorry," Travis said. "but, I think you saved the world."

"Nah," Savage said. "Maybe your town though."

They arrived at Travis's car. He unlocked it and retrieved the grimoire. The page on necromancy was bookmarked and he went to open it. Savage put a hand on his to stop him.

"Nuh uh," he said. "I told you there'd be consequences." He slid the big book out of Travis's hands and set it on top of the car.

"What consequences?"

Savage hit him in the gut, so hard that his fist connected with Travis's spine. He was sure his internal organs were destroyed. Wide-eyed, he gasped for breath.

"But," he managed. "you're one of the good guys."

Savage studied his face for a moment. He shrugged. "There really are no absolutes. No one is truly good or bad. It's complicated." He punched Travis again. His head bounced off the car door and stars exploded behind his eyes. His nose spouted blood. Through the one good eye he had left, he watched Savage take the grimoire and walk away, settling his hat with the missing chunk on his head at a jaunty angle. Then, black bars slowly encroached on Travis's vision and the pain faded to nothing.

CHARLOTTE'S CANDLEBOX
CATASTROPHE

2021

(Loves to run; likes 90s Alternative music; afraid of being buried alive.)

I t felt like *years* since she'd been to a show. In truth, it had been about eighteen months. When Candlebox announced their tour, and that a Detroit date was on their itinerary, Charlotte had to go.

She was fully vaccinated, but would mask up anyway, for safety. They were rapid testing at the door too, which gave her some peace of mind. She went alone. Her husband wasn't ready to reintegrate with society quite so aggressively yet, and tickets were expensive enough that *not* getting two was kind of a relief. But it was Pine Knob (nobody called it DTE—no one over thirty anyway), an outdoor venue, and she'd never run into any kind of trouble there. Most people, she'd found, were generally cool.

The opening band was someone she'd never heard of, but they played well, and the lead singer tossed out funny patter between songs. When Candlebox hit the stage, they rocked just as hard as they used to.

Forty minutes into their set, ominous clouds billowed across the sky, swallowing the light.

The band played the opening notes of "You" and the crowd exploded with enthusiasm. Charlotte sang along with hundreds of other voices to "Fuck you! I don't want it no more!" She felt like she was sixteen again, cautiously experimenting with rebellion.

Before the end of the song, thunder drowned them out, and lightning danced across the bottom of the cloud layer. Kevin Martin quickly conferred with someone on the crew and stepped back to the mic. "Sorry, folks," he said. "That's it for us. Don't want anyone on or off stage to get struck by lightning. Anyone here wants to come see us in Cleveland, we'll comp your tickets. Goodnight, Detroit!"

The rain hit Charlotte like a slap, sudden and shocking. Within seconds, it was soaking through her hair and clothing. It was warm enough outside that it felt good.

It picked up in intensity, hard like a shower nozzle spray. Visibility was reduced to the people closest to her, most of whom were scrambling toward the exit.

Charlotte was too, though she was having trouble orienting herself in the right direction. People were running willy-nilly, all over. The air tasted like panic.

Adrenaline surging, she began to run. She was a good runner. Strong. She wove through the chaos of concert goers, some who were acting like rodents when there was a cat in the room. Her feet pounded the wet grass; she was pacing herself. It had been a long walk from the car, and there was a hill.

After a moment, she settled into the groove of the run, breath and pulse rhythmic.

The crowd thinned. The grass yielded to mud, and she adjusted her stride, compensating so she didn't slip.

She'd escaped the stadium, she was certain, but she was on a downslope. She should have been climbing a hill by now. There should be cars. Gates. People. Lights.

She stopped, straining her ears, listening for …anything. There was only rain.

Charlotte shook her head to clear it, spraying water. She extricated her phone from a pocket so wet it almost refused to yield. It took several tries to unlock it with wet fingers. The screen was instantly obscured by rain. Pulling up the GPS, she asked it where the Pine Knob (Fine! DTE) parking lot was.

The bicycle spokes of it processing spun for several seconds. Then, without showing a map, or offering directions, as it usually did, it simply displayed a single word.

RUN

"What?"

RUN, CHARLOTTE!

She did. She ran full tilt, careening blindly ahead.

The ground dropped away, and she found herself sliding down a steep slope of mud. She kicked at the ground, pawed with her hands, but couldn't slow her descent. Couldn't get purchase.

At the bottom, she plunged, feet-first, into deep, sucking mud. Charlotte struggled immediately and sank more. "Great," she said, realizing she was in the throes of her childhood, television-induced nightmare scenarios. "Quicksand."

Her phone skidded to a stop nearby. She grabbed it, frantically trying to open the phone, and then the text, then Facebook apps. None worked.

The mud pulled her down another half a foot. She was in up to her ribcage.

The phone lit up with a message:

YOU RAN THE WRONG WAY

"You didn't *say* which way!"

NOT MY FAULT

The mud sucked at her shoulders.

"Call home."

NO

"Fuck you!"

Nothing.

"Help?"

NO

The mud pulled Charlotte down. She held her chin up as long as she could, gasping for sweet air in the rain. She was still holding the phone where she could see the screen.

BYE

MONICA AT ODD MANOR

2021

(Teacher/Writer; loves the strange and macabre)

Monica set down the book and looked out at the audience. She glowed from the applause and thanked them warmly, sitting back down at the table. A few hands went up and she pointed at one.

A young woman stood, dressed as a generic fantasy elf. She shuffled in place for a second, gathering her thoughts. Everyone waited politely. Finally, "Why do you write stuff that's so…grim? I mean, where does that *come* from?"

"Good question. I can't speak for everyone, obviously, but for me, personally, the grim stuff is a combination of catharsis,meaning I use fiction and poetry to help me cope with my own trauma, and a general sort of fascination with all things macabre. Speaking to the former, I can honestly say that, without horror, I'd be a considerably less stable person, emotionally. I think you'll find that a lot of horror writers are actually very nice people. The reason, at least in my opinion, is that we all have this ugliness inside us: you, me, the rest of humanity, and those of us who have a way to express it are less likely to carry it around like a parasite, eating at us all the time."

Lots of heads nodded at this. The elf thanked her and sat down.

Another few hands went up and she picked one at random. But the man next to that person stood instead. He wore khakis and a plain blue t-shirt; his auburn hair glistened, copper-like in the florescent light. "Have you ever been to Odd Manor?"

She shook her head. "Never heard of it."

He walked to the front of the room and laid a card on the table. It was black with silver embossed calligraphic print. 'Odd Manor' and an address in New Orleans. That was all. "You should go." With that, he turned and walked out.

Monica's curiosity was piqued.

After the con, life went back to normal for a few months. Teaching, writing, editing, going to the occasional Metal show. Monica was getting things together for another con, this one local, which was nice because it minimized travel. Pulling out the books she was hoping to read from (assuming she got a slot this time; they were tight this year), she came across the business card for Odd Manor.

"Hey, Vince. Look at this."

Her husband took it. "New Orleans is always cool," he said. "We should think about checking this place out."

They did. It was October, still a few weeks out from her favorite holiday. The leaves in Michigan were exploding with color and many were making their way to the ground. The air had finally cooled off from summer's brutality and mosquitoes were no longer a constant threat.

The drive south was like traveling backward in time. The trees were all green again, and the temperature steadily rose. By the time they got to New Orleans, it felt like summer all over. Still, it was lovely there, full of color and culture, gorgeous architecture and beautiful people, music and a sort of mild madness. They checked into their hotel.

The first night, they went to a blues bar and drank good whiskey. They got up around eleven the next day and drove to the address on the card. Odd Manor was well-named. It was in the French Quarter: a massive structure, four stories tall, peeling paint at least seven different colors. Gables popped out on every floor, seemingly placed at random. The door was on the second floor, at the top of an exterior spiral staircase. They climbed it and knocked.

The door opened a few inches. An eye, bloodshot, with a translucent blue iris regarded them. "Yes?"

"I got this card from a man at a convention in Michigan. He said I should come here." The eye flicked to Vince. "This is my husband," Monica told the eye.

It settled its gaze on her again. "Michigan." She nodded. "Husband." Again, she nodded. The door opened wide to reveal the other pale eye and the utterly hairless, naked person who owned them. They were sexless. No nipples or genitalia. Like a doll. "Come."

They went in.

Monica couldn't help but stare at the person's behind as she and Vince followed them. It was the same general shape of a human butt, but only a slight creasing where the crack would normally be. It tugged slightly to one side or the other as they walked. It made her wonder if they ate or drank, and, if so, how they expelled waste. She looked at Vince, asking him what he thought with her eyes. He shrugged. This was weird, but...they liked weird.

"Excuse me," Monica said. The person stopped. "May I please have your name?"

They looked back at her, over their shoulder. "That depends. What would you do with it?"

"Use it?"

"Then no. You may not. I'm using it." They continued on, leading Monica and Vince through an increasing bizarre series of rooms, down several stairs, along a horizontal escalator, and past a beaded curtain made of hundreds of tiny, carved skulls that might have been ivory. "Here we are."

The room was cavernous, decorated in shades of crimson and black. The walls hung with velvet tapestries: Elisabeth Bathory, Vlad Tepes, Henry VIII, Rasputin the Russian monk. Mad, powerful people. Murderous lunatics. Monica grinned.

There, on a plush couch the size of a small truck, sat the man from the con. Only now he was wearing a sarong that seemed to be made of liquid mercury. It slithered and shone and danced when he stood. "You made it," he said warmly, extending a hand.

She took it. Introductions were made. The man's name was Odd. Ulysses Odd. The doll-person left them. They drank absinthe and ate exotic mushrooms stuffed with quail's liver.

"Would you honor me by reading something aloud?" Odd asked. Monica protested that she hadn't brought anything. Odd dismissed her concerns. "Read this." He handed her a small, ancient, leather-bound thing.

Opening it, Monica read silently. The script inside was hand-written, elaborate loops and whorls dancing across the pages. She quickly became entranced by the author's voice. It was a love story, but about pain and loss. Heartbreak and envy. Aching need. Loneliness. "This is incredible," she whispered. "Some of the best stuff I've ever read. Who's the author?"

"Will you read aloud?" Odd said, dodging the question.

"Sure," she said. She flipped through the book until she found an entry that looked promising. She read the first few sentences cautiously, struggling a bit with some of the words. It was English, but a version so old it tasted foreign on her tongue. By the end of the first page, she'd found her stride. and the language flowed. It was pretty, this prose, almost poetic. The phrases lit up in her mind, the images danced before her eyes. She swam in the story, the blood-warm waters of the tale swamping her imagination.

Distantly, she could hear Vince's voice, feel him tugging on her arm. She shrugged him off. The story. She couldn't stop reading. She had to know the end.

The tale meandered, dove into subplots, deeply examined side characters, and forged new, unexpected paths. Monica diligently followed them, desperate to see how it all came together.

Then, her husband's hand slipped away. His voice faded to silence. The man in the mercury robes disappeared. The room they were in was washed away. There was only story, and it was everything.

She was part of it now, in the book, forever trapped in Odd Manor, a character in a twisted tale, her old life forgotten.

(Author's note: "Monica" and I belong to the Great Lakes Association of Horror Writers and are old friends. She's one of the few people I "killed" without needing a questionnaire.)

MILLER MARSH

2021

(High school biology teacher; afraid of drowning.)

Marybeth eased the big Ford van to the gravel shoulder. The side door opened before she could fully put it in park.

"*Vanessa!* In the future, kindly wait until the vehicle has completely stopped moving *before* opening the door."

The girl, nearly six feet of gangly limbs and teen awkwardness, looked at her Nikes. "Sorry, Ms. M. Just got excited is all."

Marybeth nodded. "I appreciate your enthusiasm. Please help me with the waders, okay?"

She opened the way back doors. Immediately, several heavy rubber waders tumbled to the ground, sounding like large fish flapping on the deck of a boat.

After fifteen minutes of a bunch of high school kids and one teacher stretching, pulling, squeaking and falling over, Marybeth and her class of biology students had successfully laughed their way to being ready. She'd only brought ten of them on this trip;

the rest had opted to do the research paper. Worked out well enough: she didn't have to finagle a bus and driver to bring all twenty-three.

Though it was only March and still quite cool, Marybeth's feet and legs were already sweating, trapped in the thick rubber. "Let's hit the marsh," she said, leading them toward the wetland.

Miller Marsh was a delightful find: just a few miles from the school, being in Ypsilanti Township, and virtually undisturbed by humans, despite being a five-minute drive from the suburbs.

Marybeth forged through the tall grass, legs swishing loudly. The backup chorus of noisy pants followed along. The kids tried to keep quiet, and they did well enough, for high schoolers anyway. Minimum chatter and snorts of laughter dotted their progress. The ground grew spongy, then sloshy, and soon they were knee deep in water.

Marybeth gathered them close. "This is called pondweed: this plant provides a habitat for invertebrates." They watched the leaves undulate beneath the surface. A few took pictures with their phones. Further along: "Water-celery," she said, pointing. "It oxygenates the water and reduces algae."

"Ooh," Marybeth exclaimed. "Look at this. I didn't expect to find any here. It's bladderwort." Someone snickered at the name. She ignored it. "They're cool because they're a carnivorous plant. It feeds on tiny, aquatic animals. Sort of like an underwater Venus fly trap."

"Ms. M?" Lebron asked. "What's making all that noise?" They all stood still for a moment to listen the high trilling sound that filled the marsh.

"Spring Peepers," Marybeth said. "A species of small frogs who get their name because of the sound they make every Spring. I find it soothing, actually."

Lebron shrugged. "It's all right." He ran the words together, so they were one syllable. From him, it was high praise.

"That duck's head is bright green."

"That's a Mallard, Stacey" Marybeth said. "Only the males have that iridescent green. Interestingly, they are the probable ancestor of every single breed of domestic duck."

They waded further into the cold water. It was waist deep on everyone but Vanessa and Lebron. A distant splash caught their attention. Something brown and furry slid across the surface and submerged out of sight.

"What was that?"

"Well, I can't be certain," Marybeth said, "because I only caught a glimpse, but I suspect it was a beaver."

After a flurry of sophomoric jokes and subsequent laughter, the kids regained control.

"Fascinating animal, actually," she went on. "It's the world's second largest rodent. Their teeth grow continuously, so they have to wear them down on wood. They can hold their breath for fifteen minutes, though usually only stay under for five or so. She scanned the area. "It's surprising that we don't see a dam. These guys are serious builders."

They split into groups of three and four, using their phones to take pictures of plants and insects, and one enormous bullfrog basking on a rotting log. Marybeth went off by herself—she had spotted a Great Blue Heron, a delightfully photogenic bird, and was hoping to get close enough for a decent shot.

She raised her phone and the heron burst skyward.

It was followed by roughly six feet of a brown-furred limb with claws on the end, barely missing the graceful bird. The limb sank back below the surface.

"That's," Marybeth started. She swallowed hard. "That's not a beaver." She backed slowly toward her class, not taking her eyes from the spot where she'd seen it. *But it's underwater*, she thought. *It could be anywhere. How long can it hold its breath?*

"Okay," she called over her shoulder. "We're packing it in, folks."

Her students complained all at once:

"Aw."

"C'mon."

"This was just getting good."

The kids knew that going back early meant attending the other classes they'd assumed they'd be skipping today.

"I know," Marybeth said, "but...there's something in the water—"

Sudden pressure on her left ankle, crushing the rubber wader against her skin, caused her to shriek in an entirely unprofessional way.

The teens all raised their phones to record whatever was about to happen.

Marybeth was yanked off her feet. The cold of the water shocked her as she went under. She'd barely had any time to inhale.

She was pulled.

Racing underwater, right leg flailing, fingers scrambling for purchase, she panicked. *How long can I hold my breath?*

Above, the clouds hung, absurdly tranquil, in the sky, distorted through a few feet of water.

Marybeth's lungs were hitching, aching to release the trapped air, to draw another breath. *The kids!* She thought. *If they're smart, they'll run. God, I hope they do.*

Her scientist mind prodded her, wondering what creature could possibly have hold of her. Obviously, this was predator behavior, though she couldn't rule out omnivores. She wracked her brain, trying to match reality with whatever was dragging her by the ankle, but this seemed highly improbable.

Her leg was being slowly dislocated from her hip. It was a quiet kind of agony. She tried to see the animal, but it was hard to get a proper look. She pictured an enormous head, as large as her whole torso, massive flat incisors gnawing through her leg, cracking her femur. *Death by Giant Beaver!*

She laughed at that, an explosion of bubbles, gasped, and coughed it back out. Only, there was no air to draw back in.

Only water.

Her lungs filled with it.

She fought, kicking at the thing. She tried to scream, to swear, to rail against the world.

The sky grew farther away, fading to gray, then charcoal, then black.

For a few more seconds, there was the sensation of being pulled. Then ...nothing.

GLOBAL POSITIONING
2022

(Arachnophobe)

Kayla was having a bad day. The car radio was stuck on the damn country station, the A/C was only working intermittently—leading to a sweat/freeze/sweat situation—and she was *definitely* going to be late for her meeting. The meeting that would almost certainly lead to a better position, and better pay, assuming she didn't make a terrible impression. Such as being late.

"Shit. Shit, shit, shit, shit, shit." The vents blasted cold air in her face again, and she flinched, pulling the car six inches off course. She corrected immediately but gritted her teeth anyway.

"In one mile, turn onto Ranchero Boulevard," her new phone informed her, with its jaunty voice. It pronounced the road as 'Ranch-hero' which made her snort laughter. Kayla turned down the country song—the singer's truck had just died, and his dog ran away, or something—she didn't want to miss her turn.

Ranchero Boulevard started out as a nicely paved, suburban neighborhood street, with oak trees lining the median between the lanes. After three blocks, however, it evolved into a dirt road with only occasional farmhouses and the occasional barn or silo set far back. Her phone said to take this for seventeen miles.

"That can't be right," she said aloud, but kept going, trusting the GPS.

After seventeen miles, the road was basically just ruts, hemmed in by thick trees. "In half a mile, turn left onto Arachnid Lane," her phone said. *Arachnid Lane?* she thought and shuddered. Kayla had a thing about spiders. She slowed to five miles per hour and then stopped. The sign for Arachnid Lane was hand-painted, pus-yellow on rotting wood. "Turn left now," her phone chirped.

"No," she whispered.

"Turn left, Kayla," her phone said. *It knows my name!* Its voice was decidedly less cheerful. It was, in fact, somewhat threatening. "Now."

She put the car in reverse. There wasn't enough room to turn around. Hooking her arm on the back of the seat, she looked over her shoulder. The A/C cut off at that moment and Kayla could feel the sweat immediately form on her lower back and in her armpits. Behind her, blocking her path, was a tarantula the size of a large dog. Kayla could feel her heart beating in her throat. Sweat dribbled down her ribs.

"There's nothing you can do, Kayla," her phone said. "This is the end of the line. I'm afraid you're fucked."

She stared at the impossible spider framed in the rear window of her car. She was hyper-aware of her foot pressing on the brake. Her hand was still on the shift lever. The car was still in reverse. "I don't think so," she told her rebellious phone, and floored it. The spider dodged to one side but not fast enough. Her back bumper slammed into it, bursting the thing's body like an overripe grapefruit. "Gotcha!"

Her momentum threw the car into an uncontrolled slide. She slammed into a tree.

The car spun from the impact and the front passenger quarter panel smashed into another tree on the other side of the road. The airbags deployed. She was jerked hard against the seatbelt, bruising her shoulder. Immediately, she maneuvered, trying to get the car to face the road. It was going nowhere.

"Kayla," her phone said. It sounded annoyed. "You really shouldn't have killed Benjamin." *Benjamin?* "His parents are going to be very angry. His brothers and sisters too. All six hundred of them."

"What? What the fucking *what?*" She grabbed the phone and smashed it against the steering wheel, over and over, until spiderweb cracks covered the front. The screen underneath flickered, the apps fading in and out of existence.

"Kaaaayyyyyllllllaaaa," it said, "Goooooooodbyyyyyyyyyyye."

She hit it one more time, as hard as she could, and it went black. Kayla spent several seconds bashing trees with her front and back bumpers before giving it up as a lost cause. She snagged her bag, which contained her small laptop, her water bottle, and the pepper spray she'd only ever had to show someone to get them to back off—she'd never pulled the trigger. She stepped out of the car. *Seventeen miles back to the suburbs,* she thought. *I can make it.*

She strapped the bag across her back and started running, holding the pepper spray in her hand. She made it three quarters of a mile before the spiders came. Huge, nightmarish, terrifying monsters.

She sprayed one in the face. "I was *supposed* to be going to a job interview!" she screamed at it. It flinched away, whether from the pepper spray or her voice wasn't clear. Others quickly took its place.

Kayla lashed out with fists and feet. She used her bag as a bludgeon. She sprayed so much pepper spray she started choking on the fumes herself. She fought hard, fought for her life.

She lost.

BONNIE'S BRUSH WITH DEATH

2022

(Teacher; Afraid of being unkillable.)

Six hundred fifth graders tumbled into the classroom, carrying their recess energy indoors, a space too small to contain it. *Okay*, Bonnie admitted. *There are only twenty-seven.* Just sounded like six hundred.

Gently-but-firmly, she guided the demons to their respective seats and managed to lower the ambient volume to something closer to tolerable. She was an old hand at this, knew all the tricks. Mostly, though, her kids listened to her because she respected them, treated them like people. Lots of teachers didn't.

Once the class was (basically) settled down, Bonnie called their collective attention to the white board. Pictures of historically oppressed people followed a handwritten timeline across the large space. "Who can tell me where we left off?" Six hands went up. Four were from kids who always volunteered; she chose one of the others. "Khaleel?"

All the hands dropped, except for Janine's, whose enthusiasm outweighed her ability to read the room. Khaleel spoke in a voice that strove for confidence and nearly achieved it. "We were talking about Sacagawea, and how most of our country's problems were caused by white dudes."

Bonnie pointed at her own nose and then at him. "Bingo!" Across the tops of the board, in orange dry-erase marker, she wrote out: OPPRESSORS = PATRIARCHY. She blew a large bubble of chewing gum and let it pop, slurping it back in her mouth. The class tittered. Sure, they were cool, tough, aloof fifth graders, but beneath the façade they were still little kids.

At the bell, she gave them super-easy homework and said, "See you Monday."

H ome. Saturday mornings existed exclusively for coffee (black) and loud music (currently thrash metal). Bonnie, still in her pajamas—and a terrycloth robe she once described as "orange AF" —was lying on the living room floor, letting the guitar solo wash over her. The coffee was on the floor, too, tantalizing her nose. The bass drum kicked back in, so loud it sounded like someone was pounding on her door.

Oh. Someone was.

She sat up, scrambled for the remote, shut down the TV, watched YouTube blink away into nothing. She took a long pull from the mug before staggering to the door. "Sorry. I know it's loud. I thought I was the only one around." She peeked through the peephole. A clean-cut, smiling man in a gray suit peered back. His tie was thin enough to floss with. *Mormon?*

Pulling the bathrobe closed across her threadbare T-shirt, Bonnie opened the door. "Help you?"

His thin smile grew teeth. "Yes, ma'am. I'd like to talk with you about the glory of Thanatos."

She blinked at him. "I'm sorry. Did you say…"

"Thanatos, yes. Death. Have you accepted him into your heart?"

"Um," Bonnie said. "No."

The smile fled. "Oh my. Well, why ever not? He's wonderful, you know? Brings peace to us all, in the end."

Bonnie lifted her coffee cup toward her mouth, just to have something normal to do. She was struggling to find a polite, non-threatening way to rid herself of this clearly disturbed person. The coffee was basically gone though, and the gritty dregs filled her mouth. She spat the few remaining grounds back into the mug. "Sorry. That was gross. Look, I really don't have time to talk this morning." It was her best placate-the-madman voice. "Maybe you could come back later?"

He shook his head, disappointment clear in his expression. "I'm afraid this is rather urgent."

She fired off a single, annoyed syllable. "Why?"

The man in the suit reached behind his head. From there, he drew a bronze short sword—the kind you might see in a gladiator movie. It glinted in the morning sun.

He plunged it through her heart.

Bonnie gasped. She looked down. She wasn't bleeding. It didn't even hurt.

The man removed his hand from the hilt. Gently, he tapped the pommel. "You see? Urgent."

"What—"

"You can't be killed. We're not even sure if you can die of old age. It's highly irregular. Thanatos is…concerned."

She stared at him. Looked down at herself again. *My favorite bathrobe.* "Could you…?" She gestured vaguely at the sword.

"Oh! Certainly. Sorry." He withdrew it. Along the way, it scraped against one of her ribs. The sound it made was unsettling. "So," he said, "what do you say? Are you ready to accept Death into your, um, life?"

"No, man." She laughed. "I'm gonna go dismantle the entire fucking system."

He gaped. "What system?"

Bonnie put a hand on his shoulder and looked him dead in the eye. "I'm basically a superhero, right? So, I'm going to take down the damn patriarchy. Burn it to the ground. And nobody can stop me, can they?"

S he did just that. Violently. Decisively. Once the dust settled, she gathered the sanest, most diverse, most *competent* people and put them in charge. And, for centuries, the country, and the world, were at peace. Bonnie stood at the helm, overseeing things, keeping it that way.

But she grew tired. Everyone she'd known was dead or would be soon enough. The fifth-grade class she had taught all those years ago had great-great-grandchildren, some of whom still kept in touch. She finally reached out, invited Death to meet. He showed up wearing a blue tracksuit and Asics running shoes. He handed her a pack of her favorite bubble gum. "About time," he said.

"Bite me." She popped two pieces of gum in her mouth and chewed vigorously. He started walking and, after a moment's hesitation, Bonnie followed.

Together, they walked in companionable silence toward the infinite.

(Author's note: this one was a strange and fun one to write. When someone asks to be killed but specifies that they are afraid of *not* dying, it makes you think really hard. I hope you enjoyed it too.)

11:11

2022

(Writer; loathes the patriarchy; adores her cat.)

Joanna projected an air of serenity, sitting across from the person who could change her life forever. Inside, she was a twisted bundle of raw nerve endings, crashing into one another, frantic and terrified. Finally, her agent hung up the phone with an apology.

"So," she said. "The screenplay."

"Yeah?"

"I mean, it's really good, right? Well-written, original, topical..."

"But?"

"Joanna, you know I love you." *Uh oh.* "It's just so...on-the-nose. Judgmental, you know?"

Joanna inhaled. "Okay. Yes. I'll admit that it's perhaps a somewhat harsh portrayal of certain groups. But those groups are in power. It's not punching down or anything. It's railing at the establishment, showing just how damaged our society is. It's *important!*"

Melanie put up 'surrender' hands. "You don't have to tell *me*. I know all about it. I'm a woman too, remember? The thing is, I can't sell this. Believe me, I've tried. No studio will touch it. Every single one came back with, 'we can't possibly market this to males 18-25,' which is where all the money is. Joanna, honey, I've hit dead ends everywhere I went. I just don't think the world is ready for such a scathing review of how things are."

Joanna stood. For a moment, she glared. Not at Melanie, but at the world. "Maybe the world *needs* it though."

"Yeah. Maybe it does. But the world's not going to pay for it. I'm truly sorry."

Joanna got a little drunk that night. She did a lot of scowling, some audible cursing, and shed more than a few tears. Throwing herself on the bed, still fully dressed, she glanced over at the digital clock. It was 11:11. When she was growing up, her mom had always encouraged her to make a wish at 11:11. Said it was a magical time of day. She'd made lots of wishes, and some had come true. Joanna has always been delighted when that happened, though, naturally, as an adult, understood that it had to have been coincidence.

"I wish," she said. "That all the men in power would just disappear. No! That everybody would. All of them. The whole stupid human race. If you're not ready to face your flaws, then you don't deserve to exist." *There.*

The clock shifted to 11:12.

She set down the empty glass and fell asleep.

Empty cars slowed to a stop on the street.

Cell phones fell to the floor in rooms across the world.
Televisions played to empty houses.
Dinners burned to carbon on stovetops.
Planes fell from the sky.
Ships drifted, unguided, forevermore.
Somewhere, a baby monitor was broadcasting quiet static.

T he next morning, Joanna dragged herself off the bed, still wearing the twisted, rumpled outfit from the day before. Her mouth tasted like the inside of a garbage can. She brushed her teeth, showered, and dressed in sweatpants and an old T-shirt. Something weird was nagging at her awareness but she couldn't figure out what. She attributed it to being slightly hungover and made coffee.

Finally, she figured out what was wrong. It was too quiet. Joanna went to the window and looked out. The cars were haphazardly strewn across the road. No one was walking into or out of the café. It was 8:15. Should have been streams of customers. She stared for a while, idly scratching Hercules's shoulders, who nuzzled and purred in return.

She stepped outside, still carrying her coffee cup, wearing house-shoes on her feet. She walked a few blocks, to be sure. Everyone was really gone. Her wish had come true.

Back home, she held Hercules in her lap, staring into space. Her tears dotted the cat's fur, making him twitch but he stayed there, purring against Joanna, offering kitty-comfort.

The sheer enormity of it threatened to overwhelm her. Loneliness was a sea, and she was going to drown.

She was afraid to speak. Afraid to use her own voice. The last human voice. *Maybe I should save it in case they come back.*

Finally, she settled for a whisper. She caressed Hercules's fur. "It's okay. I'm still here. You've still got me."

At 11:11 am, she tried to wish everyone back.

Twelve hours later, she tried again.

Eventually, the electricity stopped. The water no longer ran in the taps. Joanna had found a wind-up watch in a jewelry store, and she kept it running. At 11:11, twice a day, she made the same wish. It never worked.

Hercules grew old and gaunt. Her perfect cat, her companion, her only family.

When he was gone, Joanna stopped remembering to wind the watch. She forgot to eat, except to occasionally pick at scraps when her stomach screamed indignantly. She, too, grew old and gaunt.

Finally, she closed her eyes and sighed, alone in the city, alone in the world.

She never opened them again.

DAWN'S SURPRISE FIND
2022

(Likes urban foraging; fascinated by crime analysis; fear of centipedes.)

Dawn was all about the morels. Well, she was all about urban foraging, but *particularly* for morel mushrooms. They were just in season, and hiding—clever little fungi that they were—all over her hometown. There were Facebook groups, TikTok videos, and Instagram accounts, all dedicated to finding (and documenting/bragging about) the elusive morel mushroom. Part of the appeal, of course, was that they were delicious. And expensive.

She was at the very edge of her property, almost infringing on the neighbor's domain, poking around the grass, using her investigative skills to see that which wanted to remain unseen. Dawn realized she was anthropomorphizing a mushroom but couldn't help it. They really did seem like they didn't want to be found. She'd worked with the police as an evidence tech, but was training to become a crime scene analyst. She had sharper eyes than most.

There! The distinctive pitted surface of the tan cap. That's a morel all right. A small cluster of them, right in her back yard. Carefully, she cultivated them, a handful. From there, Dawn made an ever-widening circle, exploring the lawn, looking for more.

In half an hour, she'd collected almost thirty. An excellent haul. She'd add some to tonight's dinner.

Dawn didn't notice, as she was walking away, the tiny, furtive movements in the grass where she had gathered the mushrooms.

It was almost a week before Dawn was free to forage again. Life was like that, especially since becoming a mom. Her husband was out of town, and the baby was sleeping. So, when she ventured to the edge of the yard again, she was mildly stunned to find that there were morels growing all over that part of the yard now. Like, *hundreds* of them. For a moment, she just stared. Then, grinning, she fired off a text to her husband,

Kenta:

we're going to be rich! I'll explain later.

She reached to harvest some morels and stopped.

What is that? Something was crawling amongst the mushrooms. Lots of somethings. With lots of legs. *Ugh.* Centipedes. Dawn hated centipedes. Nature's nasty little garbage collectors. She looked for another clump to pick instead. But the ugly arthropods were there too. "I thought you were nocturnal," she mused aloud. She was reluctant to give up her newfound wealth of nutty, delectable fungus, so she gingerly reached to pluck the ones that didn't have centipedes crawling directly around the stem. There weren't many. She picked her way across the lawn this way, gathering one or two here and there.

She stopped. She'd almost tripped over a dead squirrel. It lay twitching, among the morels, dozens of centipedes crawling over it, feasting on its corpse. Clutching her haul to her chest, she rushed inside, panting behind the closed door. Leaving the suddenly alien landscape of her own yard behind, shutting it out. Very carefully, Dawn loaded a colander in the sink and rinsed off any traces of centipede that might still be on the morels.

Her phone went off, startling her badly. She turned off the water and checked her texts. It was from Kenta:

> Glad to hear we'll be rich. Please explain at some point. 😌 🩶

She smiled. She was overreacting. Nature was weird. That's all it was.

She checked on her child. Still sleeping, snoring slightly.

Dawn couldn't get the image of the poor squirrel out of head. She didn't want anyone else in her family to come across it accidentally, so she got the shovel out of the garage. In the back, morels were exploding across the lawn. She could barely see the grass for all the beige, conical tops. It was like they had all grown in the last fifteen minutes. *Impossible.*

She picked her way among them, until she got to the squirrel. It was completely skeletonized already. Dawn stared. She knew this was unnatural. She turned back. Sweat dribbled down her ribs. On her right ankle, something writhed. "Ah!" She kicked it off. They were on the left foot now. Climbing. Into her pantleg. Dawn stomped on the centipedes, crushing dozens. More and more climbed her legs. Tiny, stinging mandibles pierced her skin. The immediate itch felt like madness.

Dawn laid about with the shovel, squashing them. The lawn was a carpet of segmented bodies with ten thousand legs. It came for her.

The venom spread through her bloodstream, finding her brain. She dropped to her knees and was quickly covered completely, a human-shaped mound of crawling vermin. Thankfully, she started to go numb. Her mind shut down. She was saved from having to feel it. Being eaten.

She had time for one thought: *Damn it. My family's gonna find my skeleton. They don't need that kind of trauma.* Then she was gone.

(Author's note: This person's husband hired me to "kill" his wife. Immediately afterward, he hired me to kill him, too, in a related story, the first time I'd been asked to do so. That one follows.)

WHILE KENTA WAS IN OHIO
2022

(Works with chainmail; does ballet; spent a lot of time in Japan; fears being alone.)

Kenta kissed his wife Dawn for the last time on Saturday morning. He loaded the commissioned chainmail bikini (cosplayers with disposable income were great) into its fancy-ish padded cardboard box and put it in his car. The client had paid extra for delivery and, rather than shipping it, he'd decided to drive it to Columbus. Might as well make a weekend of it. *It's a pretty cool town, especially for Ohio.*

He rolled in around one pm. The farmer's market at North Market was over, but the restaurants were still serving food inside. He ordered from the Satori Ramen Bar. It wasn't half-bad, for a restaurant in the States.

He met with his customer after, trading cash for steel. It had taken months to make the piece, and he charged accordingly. When they parted ways, Kenta spent a few hours in the Franklin Park Botanical Gardens. It was peaceful. Among the thousand shades of color and nearly overwhelming scents, his phone chirped.

Dawn. She said they were going to be rich. *Okay, sure.* Cool. He asked her to provide details of this windfall when she had time and stopped to admire a cluster of tulips.

Once he tired of nature's splendor, for now anyway, he paced the sidewalks for a bit, just getting a feel for downtown Columbus. Nothing was really drawing him in, but it was nice to be somewhere other than home. A poster caught his eye, slightly torn, on a lamppost. He took a picture of it with his phone and hustled back to his car.

About nine miles out of town, there was a delightfully quirky... thing. An art installation, totally immersive, science fiction/fantasy themed. It was bizarre. Just the sort of thing he was looking for. He wandered around in there until his stomach reminded him that the time for dinner had long passed.

After a quick bite, he checked into a hotel that was acceptably not-sleazy, but still cheap enough. He fired off a goodnight text to Dawn, but she didn't respond. *Probably asleep.* It was kind of late.

The next morning, Kenta checked out, tossed his overnight bag in the car, and headed home. He stopped to hit a restroom off the highway and shot his wife a text to let her know he was probably ninety minutes away. He got the 'message sent' notification. Nothing else. He stared at the screen. It didn't change. The first pricklings of unease crawled up the backs of his knees.

It took a good deal of restraint not to speed until he crossed the Michigan border. Once he did, he pushed it to eighty.

The car was barely in park when he got out, racing across the driveway to the door. He burst in. "Dawn?"

The baby was crying. Almost screaming. *Alone. Full diaper.* What the hell? He searched the house. No Dawn. He went out back—

The entire backyard was beige. It was completely full of what looked like—morel mushrooms? Toward the property line, they were piled into a thick mound, where before there had only been flat grass.

Holding the sniffling infant, he thumped his way toward the shape. There was something alarmingly familiar about it.

When he got there, he dropped to his knees. A skeleton. Wearing the same clothes Dawn had had on when he left.

At first, he was too numb to notice anything else. When he became aware that he was being bitten, it was too late. They were already crawling all over him. Centipedes. Hundreds. Maybe thousands. He held the baby high above his head, shaking his arms to dislodge the things before they could climb higher. He knew he should get up. Run. But his legs felt half-buried in the dirt. He was a man capable of leaping into the air, but now he couldn't even stand.

The venom hit him. He lost the strength to hold arms up anymore, so he pulled the baby in close, to his chest, and wrapped as much of himself around as possible, giving whatever protection he could. For as long as he could.

Shrieking filled his ears and he vaguely wondered whose it was. Then he was gone.

THE WEEDING

2022

(Loves to garden; loves candy; isn't good at communicating with his partner.)

Barney grasped the weed at its base, pinching right at ground level. A single robin sang in the tree above him, and someone was mowing their lawn a block or so over. The dirt was still damp from yesterday's rain. The rich scent of the soil filled his sinuses. He eased the plant—Barney didn't know what kind, just that it belonged to the greater 'weed' classification—upward, roots and all. *Satisfying!* Like ripping off your enemy's head and pulling the spine out with it.

That was the last of them. He'd collected them, fallen green soldiers, piled high and dusted with drying dirt. Barney's garden was now immaculate. He'd imposed order on chaos. *If only everything else was this easy.* If only he could 'weed' the parts of his relationship that weren't bearing fruit, as it were. He would have a lovely garden, growing nothing but happiness and contentment. Unfortunately, people were not like garden plots. You can't simply pluck out the things about them you don't like.

For a moment, he thought he heard horse's hooves, though muted. Almost like the coconuts in the Monty Python movie about King Arthur. He smiled at the thought. He'd always liked that film.

Inside, Barney washed his hands and forearms thoroughly and splashed his sweaty face. He poured himself a large glass of cold water and used it to chase a handful of Skittles. He'd always delighted in the way they crunched in his teeth, and the explosion of sugary goodness on his tongue.

In the dining room, hunched over her laptop, hard at work even on a Saturday, was his love, his partner, his nemesis.

When they'd first started dating, she'd seemed so *perfect*. Quick-witted, smart, sexy. He fell hard for her. Now though, he couldn't help but see her...flaws. She had all these *ideas* about how things were supposed to go, supposed to be. Some of them polar opposites of his own. Why was she so complicated? All these layers, these characteristics, these *weeds?*

She glanced up. He recoiled slightly, like he'd been caught spying. She gave him a tight smile that seemed to say, "I don't know who you are anymore."

He ate another handful of candy. It stabilized him a bit. "I need to pick up some more of these. We're almost out." She nodded. "It's pretty nice out. I might walk." Again, she nodded. "Of course, I could drive. It'd be faster."

"You should walk."

"Okay."

The sun was low in the sky and the air still cool. Barney let his mind wander; his feet knew the way to CVS, just on the edge of their suburb. His ears caught the clack of hooves again, louder now, though still far. Sounded more horse like, less coconutty.

Yeah, but really: what is the air speed velocity of an unladen swallow? He chuckled to himself.

Maybe he could talk to her, he thought. Maybe try to nudge her in the right direction. Get her to see his point of view, instead of her stubbornly insisting on having her own. *Ugh.* Why couldn't he have fallen for someone more *pliable?* He immediately felt guilty for thinking something so uncharitable, but it was definitely how he felt, he had to admit.

The distinct *clack* of hooves was getting close now. Barney looked around. Why was someone riding a horse here, in the suburbs? He'd never liked the animals. Too big. Unpredictable. Intimidating.

He was at a crossroads. To his right, a two-story colonial, recently painted a pale, inoffensive green. The attached garage was still the same badly chipped yellow both had been before they painted the house. Maybe the people who lived there would get around to it before the end of Summer.

Barney stopped where he was. He could hear it breathing now, the horse. The way it snorted on the exhale. He could hear the jangle of tack signifying a rider. Barney's feet were absolutely rooted to the spot. He counted the hoofbeats on the asphalt. Sweat dripped down his ribs on both sides.

Barney could *smell* the animal: hay and musk and urine.

There. A massive beast. Easily eight feet at the shoulder. Eyes black like a shark's. The rider, wearing battered armor, was muscular but obese, face so badly scarred it was barely recognizable as human. *Maybe it's not!* The hand that held the reins was wide as a dinner plate.

The rider glared at Barney with undisguised, nearly palpable disgust. The horse stepped closer, nearly crushing Barney's toes with a hoof. The rider palmed Barney's head like a basketball, lifting him off the ground. Barney's vertebrae cracked like he was on the chiropractor's table. It felt surprisingly good.

The rider's voice was the grinding of gears, a sliver of glass in the sole of one's foot. "I deem you...unnecessary."

Barney started to protest.

With a quick jerk, the rider snapped Barney's neck. With a savage twist, the monstrous being tore the man's head clean off. The body, limp, collapsed to the ground, spine still dangling from the base of Barney's skull.

The rider smiled at his horse. "I love it when I get the spine too. So satisfying." Shoving the head in a saddlebag, the rider spurred on the horse. The day was young, and there was much weeding yet to be done.

(Author's note: the person who hired me to do this one was the partner who was feeling estranged from "Barney" and I believe this was pure catharsis for her.)

RAIN FALL

2022

(Musician; teacher; afraid of heights.)

Chaz ducked his head and hunched his shoulders against the driving rain. He hadn't brought an umbrella because the forecast called for 'partly cloudy with only a twenty percent chance of rain.' *Stupid Michigan weather.*

Downtown Ypsilanti was devoid of its usual pedestrian traffic, though Michigan Ave was still teeming with cars, buses, and trucks—they plowed along the wet road like enormous salmon swimming upstream.

Dodging a slowly dissolving KFC bag on the sidewalk, Chaz ducked into the shelter of the scaffolding. They'd been working on this building's façade for months now, and the steel structure with wooden planks had become part of the city's landscape. He paused, taking a moment to breathe dry air. The fat drops pounding overhead sounded like the percussion section of a garage band with more enthusiasm than skill.

A series of bangs and clangs joined the cacophony, driving Chaz toward the nearest doorway. He flattened himself against the wall, just as an adjustable wrench hit the pavement where he'd been standing. "Hey!" he called upward. "Be careful!"

Scuffling sounds came from quite high, followed by a small, frightened voice. "Help."

Jesus. A kid.

Chaz looked around for someone. A parent. Police. He was alone. He shouted up: "Yeah. Okay. Hold on. I'm coming up. You're gonna be okay."

He started climbing, the metal cold and slick. Every time he looked up for a handhold, rain stung his eyes.

She was at the top, three floors up, shivering, eyes huge with fear. Poor kid was soaked.

"How'd you get up here?"

"I don't know."

The planks they were on were slick with wetness. With great care, Chaz eased himself toward the edge. Though it only swayed slightly in the wind, Chaz imagined the whole structure could collapse at any moment.

"Okay," Chaz said. "Okay. We're going to climb down together, right?" She nodded. "Good. Let's go. You got this. It's gonna be fine." He maneuvered himself over the edge, holding on with one hand and reaching out with the other.

A blast of wind caught him off guard, nearly dislodging him; the rain stung his cheek and neck. "*Fuck!*"

"That's a bad word."

"I know. Sorry. I got scared."

"It's okay. I understand." She smiled at him.

He blinked water away and smiled back. "Ready?"

With great trepidation, she maneuvered herself between Chaz and the ladder portion of the scaffolding. Together, they inched downward.

"What's your name?"

"Chaz. What's yours?"

"Cassandra. Cassie, though, for real. I'm in second grade."

"Nice to meet you, Cassie. Are your parents—" A huge gust of wind cut him off. With his left arm, he clung to her. The wind tried to take her. The fingers of his right hand slipped. They were losing their grip on the wet steel.

She tilted her head back to look at him. He could tell she also knew they were in trouble.

The wind gusted harder. Chaz lost his grip. "Hang on!" he yelled.

She did.

On the way down, which seemed to take much longer than possible, Chaz noted how pretty everything looked, how clean and shiny.

When he hit the sidewalk, it felt like everything inside him broke all at once. He'd had no idea this kind of pain was possible.

Cassie had been holding onto his shoulders. Her small body was curled against his chest. She pushed herself up, palms on his ribs —Chaz winced—and studied his face. "Chaz? I'm gonna go get someone. It's my turn to help you. Stay here, okay?'

He almost laughed. He couldn't nod, or speak, or move at all. *Paralyzed,* he thought. *Well, doesn't that suck?*

Cassie took one last look, maybe waiting to see if he'd respond, and ran off. She seemed unharmed. *Good.*

He lay there. The rain beat down on relentlessly, pounding his face. He couldn't turn away. It fell in his open mouth, and he swallowed some.

It came harder. Chaz coughed involuntarily, choking a bit. The back of his throat was filling up with water.

Maybe fifteen feet away, a car slowed down, brakes squealing horribly. It paused there, but then drove away. *You should really get those pads replaced,* Chaz thought.

His throat constricted, trying to keep water out. He made a gargling, strangling sound and made a conscious effort to hold his breath. His body was no longer his to control however.

After a moment, his throat convulsed open. It wasn't that much water that got in his lungs. Chaz could remember hearing, as a kid, that you could drown in an inch of water. *I'll be damned,* he thought, as his body spasmed, trying—but unable—to cough it up. *I guess you can.*

The rain kept falling. He no longer felt it.

NORWAY SPRUCE

2022

(Makes furniture out of branches; his little sister travels the world.)

"What is it?"

The FedEx driver shrugged. "Heavy. That's all I know." He wheeled the large box through the doorway, unhooked it from the handcart, and took Donovan's signature, wishing him a good afternoon.

Alone with the package, Donovan walked around it. It came up to the bottom of his ribcage and was easily three feet wide. The shipping label said it originated in *Geirangerfjord*, Norway. Near it, in Sharpie, in aggressive caps, was the note: CHECK IT OUT, BRO!

His sister, of course.

It took some time to get through all the packing tape and open the top of the box. Inside was a sea of biodegradable packing peanuts. Hiding within those was a huge chunk of wood. Donovan cut away the rest of the cardboard box, spilling peanuts everywhere. He brushed aside the ones on top to reveal a sticky note containing a quick, cryptic message: *Norway Spruce. Killed by lightning, 2007. Rare Find!* That was it. Donovan sighed. He loved his little sister, but she could be a bit much sometimes. Still, it was a beautiful piece of wood. Despite being cut fifteen years ago, it smelled richly of the forest.

He swept up the peanuts and recycled the cardboard. Pulling a chair across the room, he sat, contemplating his gift. What would it be? Table? Plant stand? He'd made plenty of each. The thing was enormous and brimming with potential.

He spread a tarp out, grunting with effort as he lifted one side, and then the other to get the canvas all the way underneath the wood. Laying out his tools, he got to work, though he had no clear idea what he was making. *Sometimes, you just let your hands do their thing and see what happens.*

Hours later, sweating and desperately thirsty, Donovan eased himself away from the project. He stretched his back, popping several vertebrae. He shook out stiff hands that threatened to cramp. Wood shavings surrounded him. The chunk of trunk before him was far from complete, but there was something there. A hint. A shadow. A fleeting impression of what would be.

Donovan drank two full pint glasses of cold water and spent fifteen minutes in a hot shower. He ate a bowl of vegetable stir fry over noodles and slept for nine hours.

The next day at work, he struggled to focus. In his mind's eye, he could see something taking shape in the spruce. Could see his tools chipping away, revealing what was hiding inside. *What is it?* He still didn't know.

Finally, he was done for the day. He quickly ate dinner and returned to the wood. When he realized he couldn't see what he was doing anymore, he turned on the lights. Evening had snuck up on him. While he was paused, he drank some water but then got right back to work.

The next time he looked up, it was one am. "Ugh. I have to stop." Showered. Scrubbed the moss off his teeth. Slept.

Donovan didn't go into work the next day. Said he was taking a personal day. After breakfast, he immediately picked up his tools and started carving. He worked all day, stopping only for food and bathroom breaks.

It wasn't a table. Nor a plant stand. It wasn't furniture of any kind. It was a figure. Bipedal. Large head. Sinewy arms. It was so close to being finished. He ate a quick snack, turned the lights on against the creeping dusk, and got back to work.

At 3:14 am, Donovan stood up from where he'd been kneeling among the shavings. The tools hung limply from his fingers. He was exhausted, spent. *There it is.*

A sprite. A fairy. A goblin. He didn't have the right word for it. It was gorgeous work, better than he thought himself capable of. But it was ugly too, brutish. Sharp cheekbones, cat's eyes, thin lips over smiling, movie-star teeth. Ears rising to points. Six long, delicate fingers on each hand. Muscular legs ending in hooves, split in two toes, like a deer's. It was sexless.

It was also like nothing he'd ever done, and way beyond his skill.

Awed, he gently stroked its cheek. The wood was smooth and oddly warm. The carving leaned into his hand, blinked and smiled at him. Donovan jerked back, stunned. It spoke, voice musical, language unintelligible.

Donovan fought through his shock. "I don't understand. What are you saying?"

The creature looked up and to the right, then nodded. "I... am...sor-ry."

Donovan sat back on his haunches. It was speaking English with a thick accent. "Sorry for what?"

The small, wooden creature, in the exact manner he had done, stroked Donovan's cheek. "For...this." It drove a single, spindly finger into Donovan's throat, piercing the carotid artery. It held its creator close, letting the blood flow over itself, bathing in it. "I...need it...to...live. To be...complete."

Donovan's sinuses filled with the copper stink of his own blood. He lost feeling in his arms and legs. He collapsed on top of the fairy being he had brought to life. The thing he had unwittingly unleashed on the world. His last thought was, *I should have just made another table.*

CLOSING SHIFT
2022

(Manager: pizza restaurant; favorite color is lavender; fears mice and oblivion)

The front door was locked, the ovens shut down, and the last driver had clocked out and gone home. Samantha closed her eyes for a moment and listened to the barely audible hum of the neon sign.

Saturday nights are the worst, she thought. Except for the tips. Her share of that was $32—not at all shabby. That's like a movie —*with* popcorn and a slushee.

She ran the daily reports and counted the till. Every penny accounted for. Good. Recounts were a pain. Samantha set up a cash drawer for tomorrow's opening shift and dropped the rest in the safe. Pulling on her coat, she remote-started her car to warm it up. She flipped off all but one light switch—the one that always stayed on—turned off the "open" sign, a bit belatedly, she had to admit, and took a step toward the door.

Movement caught her eye, fast and furtive, low to the floor.

Samantha started badly. Her heart raced. In the dimness, she could just make out the tiny form by the walk-in cooler. *Mouse. Ugh.* She made a mental note to call the exterminator and headed for the door once more, giving the rodent a wide berth.

It darted in front of her, cutting her off. "Eep," she said. *Great. What am I, a damsel in distress?* She was grateful no one was around to hear that embarrassing noise.

The mouse was directly in her path, quivering but holding its ground, utterly un-mouselike in its behavior.

Something's on its head.

Pushing through her mild phobia of mice, Samantha slowly squatted and leaned toward the creature. Its whiskers shook so badly, one fell out. She got right down by the mouse. It gazed up at her.

It's a hat.

It was. A lavender bowler hat, perfectly to scale—mouse-sized. It sat up on its haunches and inclined its head to the left. It was a human gesture: *this way.* The mouse retrieved its fallen whisker and scampered across the pizza joint, under the basement door.

A bit freaked out—but a *lot* curious—she followed, opening the door and hitting the light switch over the stairs. Monsieur Chapeau—she had named him—was already at the bottom, tail twitching, head gesturing: *this way. This way already!*

She descended. It was all flat cardboard pizza boxes, Coca-Cola-brand boxes of syrups—connected to the fountain upstairs by yards of rubber tubing—and large cans of CO_2 down here. Plus a couple cases of napkins and straws.

M. Chapeau led her past the furnace to a corner of the basement she'd never had cause to explore. It was a six-by-six-foot space with nothing but three cardboard file boxes and a plywood board leaning against the far wall. The boxes were stacked in a pyramid and labeled 'Daily receipts' and dated 2008, 2009, and 2010 on top.

The mouse in the hat gave her a meaningful look and disappeared behind the piece of plywood.

"Okay, Monsieur. I'll bite."

She lifted the board from the wall, revealing a crudely carved tunnel. It was only three feet high and disappeared into the darkness. M. Chapeau was just at the edge of where the light penetrated. He was up on his haunches again. With his tiny forepaw, he doffed his lavender hat, and executed a bow, his fallen whisker held like a cane. He returned his hat to his head, turned away, and scuttled into the dark.

She had to crawl, phone's light held before her. After a moment, the tunnel widened, and she stood. Brushing off her hands and knees, she continued to follow the mouse, walking upright now. He always stayed just at the edge of her light and led her farther and farther along.

She passed a few branches and side-tunnels and marveled at how this had existed underneath her town this whole time. The mouse took several turns, and Samantha kept thinking, *I'll remember how to get back…*It wasn't long before that became impossible. It was like a rabbit warren, if the rabbits who'd made it had been about fourteen feet long. *Great,* she thought, as images of giant, carnivorous rabbits played on the movie screen of her imagination. *Murder bunnies.*

The tunnel had been steadily, yet subtly tilting downward for some time. She was definitely lost. For quite a while now, she'd been berating herself for following a mouse into some underground labyrinth. It was just so…weird, and she was curious. Gradually, she became aware that the walls were glowing. Some sort of lichen coated every surface except the floor. She turned off the light on her phone. Battery was at 57% but service was at a solid zero. She fired off a quick text to double-check:

> MOM. LOST UNDERGROUND. FOLLOWED MOUSE WITH HAT. WILL EXPLAIN LATER.

After a few seconds, her phone flagged it as unsent.

"All right then," she said. "Lead on, Mr. Hat." She had downgraded him from French to English, because she was annoyed.

The mouse led on. Turn after turn, and always slightly downward, through bioluminescent walls with no end in sight. She was tired. Her feet hurt. She stopped and sank to the floor. Mr. Hat turned and regarded her.

"I want to go back," she said. "I want to be home."

The mouse climbed up her shirt. She recoiled slightly but let it happen. He sat on her shoulder and his whiskers tickled her cheek. In a very small voice, he said, "This is your home now, Samantha."

She swept him off with a hand, got to her feet, and ran.

Samantha was a runner. She'd done 5Ks. She was young and strong and had plenty of stamina. She ran on and on. But no matter which way she turned, which passage she took, the path never changed. Same walls. Same downward slope. Same mouse around every third, fourth, or fifth turn.

She'd been walking—and running—for hours. Yet she wasn't hungry. Or thirsty. Her feet hurt, but it felt like they always had, and always would.

KEN MACGREGOR

Samantha walked. She sat. She laid down on the floor. She screamed profane things at the ceiling. Tried to catch the damn mouse and crush it. Nothing changed.

It was just her and Mr. Hat, the hateful creature who had trapped her here. Her last coherent thought before her mind began to unravel, was, *Shit. I left the car running.*

A BUG IN THE PROGRAM
2023

(Podcaster; gamer; has a somewhat love/hate relationship with the dog; afraid of bugs)

For the final two hours of The Weekly Tedium, Ellis practically hummed with the need to leave. He willed the clock to accelerate, but every time he checked, instead of the forty minutes he was sure had passed, it was four. *Come on!*

The evening had been painstakingly planned. For over a month, they'd been putting this podcast together, and he was stuck here, doing this mindless thing, over and over and over and over, and it was never going to end.

To distract himself, he went over it again in his mind: one GM, five players, approximately six hundred dice, the Mighty Tomes of the Rules as They Apply to the Game, a giant bag of delicious, greasy burgers from Bobcat's, and—of utmost importance—the microphones dangling from the cords gaff-taped to the ceiling to capture it all. He smiled. No…he *grinned*.

Nine hours (or, possibly, ninety minutes) later, his shift was finally over. Ellis enthusiastically punched the clock, told everyone in earshot to have a good weekend, and breezed outta there.

At home, he showered, changed, kissed Anna, scowled at the dog, and scooted over to Mike's house. Mike was the GM by default. He had more room, no kids or animals to get underfoot, and a husband who was more than happy to have a night out with his non-geek friends. Nate, was, in fact, leaving just as Ellis arrived. He smiled with perfect teeth. "Have fun murdering pretend people, Ellis."

"Always do." Ellis offered a fist-bump and Nate hit it before sliding out the door. "What's up, my fellow podcastians?" He thumped into his seat and arranged the character sheet, pencil and the favorite polyhedral dice in front of him.

Forty-five minutes later, the game was in full swing, and the mics were picking up everything. Intrigue. Puzzle-solving. Action. Critical hits! Perception checks. Healing potions. Treasure. Magic items. Experience points. The damn bard hitting on *everyone*. Again. Also slurping, chomping, belching, farting, laughing, groaning, shouts of joy, and cries of dismay.

God, it was great.

It was almost midnight by the time they wrapped it up. Ellis made sure the recording was saved to Wavepad. "I'll start editing tomorrow. Hopefully have it uploaded sometime on Sunday. Cool?"

Mike shrugged. "Whenever's fine. We don't have a hard deadline."

"Sooner the better though, right? We do this every week, we're going to attract followers. Other gamers, if nothing else."

"Yeah, man. Sure thing."

Ellis put his gear in his bag. "You all right, Mike?"

"Uh huh. Yeah. No. I'm good. Drive safe, man." He was lying, Ellis was sure. Looked like a kid, holding an empty cone while their ice cream slowly melted on the sidewalk.

"All right." He tossed the bag over his shoulder. "Hit me up, you want to shoot the shit or anything, okay?" Mike said he would. There wasn't much else to say, so Ellis went home.

In his own house, he shouldered past the Great Dane to get through the door. He always did. "Why do you have to be so big?" Super Sam wagged his tail and tried to lick Ellis on the face. He always did this too. Ellis ducked out of the way. "Gross. You're gross. Anna, your dog is gross."

From the other room, she chastised him. "He is an angel and perfect in every way. How was the thing?"

"Fun! I think we got some good stuff tonight."

"Cool. There might be a little pop left, if you want it."

"RC?"

"Dr. Pepper."

"Oh, the horror! Guess I can settle. For now. Why does no one carry RC Cola anymore?"

"Because it's no longer 1987?"

"Harsh, Anna. Unnecessarily harsh." He cracked an inferior beverage and drank it anyway. "Something's going on with Mike."

"What?" Super Sam laid his giant dog head on her lap and she lavished affection on him.

Ellis pointedly ignored the dog and the love he was getting. "He was off tonight. Normally, he's Storyteller Extraordinaire, you know? But he was dialing it in. I mean, it was still cool, and we had a good time, but I could tell his heart wasn't in it."

"Probably he just has something going on in his life outside of Friday Night Geekfest and it's affecting him."

"You're making fun."

"I am."

Ellis scooped up the Dr. Pepper with a flourish. He nodded curtly in her direction. "Madam." With chin in the air, he huffed out of the room. At her laugh, he poked back around the corner. "I love you."

"Yeah? Cool. I love you too." She maneuvered around the dog to go kiss him. It was one of the better kisses he'd had, and he took his time enjoying it.

"Damn." Leaning back in his chair, Ellis frowned at the screen. The entire audio from the night before was polluted with an unidentifiable click/scratch sound. It was so clear he was surprised he didn't hear it during the game. "Must be one of the mics." He ran the software to clean and refine the audio, but that sound was still there. He tried to isolate it, but it hid among the dialogue waves.

For three hours, he sifted and combed, prodded and poked, tested and tweaked, to no avail.

Ellis broke for lunch, washing it down with Dr. Disappointment. He told Anna about the scratching sound, and she listened with him for a moment. "Yeah. That's annoying. Can you get rid of it?"

"Not so far. I'll keep trying. This sucks. Mike and I tested these mics too. Maybe it's the wires. The connections? Ugh."

She scratched between his shoulder blades. "Wanna go for a walk? It's nice out? You-know-who has to go anyway."

He shook his head. "No. Thank you though. You and the monster go ahead."

"He is *not* a monster. He's—"

"A perfect angel. I know, I know. Go ahead. I want to see if I can make some progress here."

After another ninety minutes of frustration, Ellis gave up. He texted Mike to see if he could come look at the recording gear. Mike replied that he wasn't home but that the spare key was in the usual place and sure, why not, go ahead.

Anna wished him luck. He avoided another sloppy dog-kiss and drove over to Mike's. The gaming stuff was put away. The table now sported a glass vase with a variety of orange and red flowers, accented with fernlike fronds and baby's breath. There was an embroidered mat underneath that with horses galloping the perimeter. That'd be from Nate's mom. She had this thing about horses. Whole house had horse stuff, and they couldn't get rid of it because she'd be devastated.

The microphones still dangled from the ceiling; inoffensively tiny, black Lavaliers barely noticeable if you were not looking for them. Ellis checked each one, then the wires for any damage, the connection points of each. Everything was shipshape.

Crossing into the study, he nudged the mouse on the desk. The PC screen came to life as he sat down. Ellis entered the password and opened the audio file. He snapped the headphones into place. "Okay. Let's see if it's corrupted at the source."

It didn't take long for him to realize that this version was completely fine. No scratch/click noise at all. Just the lovely sound of a bunch of friends having a blast playing D&D. Smiling at the memories that played along with the audio, Ellis chuckled. *That's Carl's stomach growling, signaling it was time to eat.* Clearly, something had gotten corrupted in the transfer. He reached up to take off the headphones and stopped. Dimly, he heard a click. A scratch.

Ellis pressed the headphones tighter against his ears. *Click-scratch. Scratch-click.* "What *is* that?" Nothing on the screen to indicate anything unusual. He leaned forward and turned up the volume. Click Scratch. Click.

His left ear exploded in pain.

Shrieking, Ellis threw the headphones from his head. He fell on the floor, tossing himself side-to-side, trying to dislodge whatever was in his ear. It was moving. *Going in!*

He found his feet, lurching to the bathroom. Turning his head, trying to see. He tilted the mirrored cabinet door open and looked in the other mirror. There! Shiny black something slipped inside his ear canal. "Ah! Fuck!" He slammed backward, denting the drywall by the door.

Ellis caromed off the walls in the hallway. He found the kitchen mostly by accident. The wet bar. He snagged a bottle of vodka and yanked out the cap with his teeth. He poured some in his ear, and it burned like fire.

Inside his head, the insect writhed and squirmed and burrowed ever deeper.

Ellis staggered up, slipping in the booze all over the floor. His shoes squeaked on the way to the door. He pulled it open. Mike and Nate blocked it with their bodies.

"You. There's. I."

Mike nodded. "I know."

Nate put a gentle hand on Ellis's shoulder. "For what it's worth, I'm sorry. We didn't want to."

The itching in his skull felt like madness. Ellis smacked his ear with a cupped palm. It failed to help. He opened his mouth. To accuse. To scream. To vomit. To…something. But he didn't do any of those. He said, "Anna," because she was what he needed. Everything was wrong and he needed his wife. He'd even take the damn dog too if he could have her here.

"Shh," Mike said. "She'll be okay. She's young. She'll find someone else."

"What? Am I? Is this?" Thinking was becoming difficult. The click/scratch noise was everywhere now. Blood ran out of both nostrils, staining his favorite T-shirt.

Nate looked genuinely concerned. "Not much longer, Ellis."

Ellis lost the ability to stand. He stared at their feet. *Nice shoes.*

Click! Scratch! Click!

"I really am sorry, man," Mike said. "Like, *really* sorry. I didn't have a choice."

Ellis tried to ask him for clarification. He thought, *I sure would like a clarinet on that. No. A charity. A …thing.*

Scratch. Click.

A click. That's what I need. A scratch and a click. His smile was full of blood. *I am a fourth-level clarification.* His eyes went wide. *That's the word!*

Ellis's heart kept beating for another four minutes, though it felt like forty, and he died.

THE FARMHOUSE JOB
2023

(Mows lawns; afraid of pigs and the unnatural)

Pulling up in front of the farmhouse, Melody can tell this is going to be one hell of a job. The grass is over the knee and there's easily an acre-and-a-half of it, if not closer to two.

Her client steps off the front porch with an embarrassed smile. She strides down the concrete walkway, the only clear space in the massively overgrown lawn. She puts out a hand. "Sophia. Nice to meet you. I'm sorry about the state of my yard. Ever since Nick passed"—she waves away any potential condolences before Melody has a chance to speak—"It's been a long time. Anyway, we've been having Clyde do it: he's the boy from the Sanders' farm. Clyde Sanders. But he up and went off the college, surprising the heck out damn near everybody, and now we haven't had anyone to mow the lawn. You come highly recommended, Ms…"

Melody tells her, but insists she just use her first name. "Believe it or not, I've seen a lawn higher than this one. My mower can handle it. Probably take an hour-and-a-half."

"Fine, fine. You can stay for lunch after. I'll make us ham and cheddar sandwiches. The cheese is from the dairy three miles northwest of here. The ham we make ourselves."

So that's what smells so bad. Pigs. She suppresses a shudder. Melody hates pigs. She doesn't want to make a bad first impression, however. "Sounds great. Thanks."

Sophia goes inside, calling out to someone out of sight. Melody puts down the ramps, unhooks the riding mower—she has named it "Demi Mower" after the actress because Melody's hilarious—and backs it off the trailer. She pops on the headphones, opens Spotify, and listens to Led Zeppelin pounding out "The Immigrant Song" as she cuts through the grass like an avenging Valkyrie. She'd started in the corner farthest from the house, setting the blades to five inches. Before long, the smell of grass overrides that of pigs.

On the seventh song, she mows around the corner and stops. The motor idles beneath her. She pulls the blades up for safety. There is the pig pen. The *sty,* she supposes it's called. It's closer to the house than Melody would have put it. Not that she'd ever have pigs. Ugh. Disgusting animals. She can see six pigs. Young, she supposes. The size of German Shepherds.

There is a kid in the pen. A girl, maybe ten, eleven years old. Skinny, but wiry with muscle. Hair in one tight ponytail high on one side. She's filthy in jeans and a tank top that may have started out white in some long-forgotten age. She stands absolutely still as the animals snuffle and snort around her.

Melody starts to wave, but some instinct stops her. *It's her face,* she realizes. It is blank, utterly without emotion.

Thankfully, the lawn ends well shy of the sty's fence. Melody doesn't have to get closer than she is now. She puts it back in gear and continues mowing, leaving a crisp, clean, green carpet in her wake.

She makes a neat turn to double back and lets the throttle drop to zero. The girl is now on her side of the fence, staring at Melody with that blank face. *How did she move that fast?*

Melody keeps the girl in her sightlines as she finishes the row. She turns her head at the last possible second as she brings Demi around. She needs to look to make sure she doesn't run into the house. When she turns back, she gives a little involuntary shriek.

The girl is right in front of her.

She hits the brakes and stops less than a foot from the girl's toes. "Jesus, kid. Thought you were a goner." She tries for a light, jokey tone—we're all sure surprised *that* happened, huh? —but she can't keep the quaver of fear out of her voice.

The girl leans forward, bending at the waist, lower half still rod-straight from feet to hips. Her sinewy arms dangle, as if forgotten, banging against Demi's engine. Her upper body stretches toward Melody, head forward, never breaking eye contact. The stink of pig shit assaults Melody's nostrils. She pushes herself back as far on the seat as she can.

The girl's blank stare is less than a foot away. Her arms thump limply on the sides of the mower.

"Rebecca Jane!"

At Sophia's shout, the girl snaps upright, taut like a rubber band. She turns her dead shark eyes to the house, summons a plastic approximation of a smile, and says, "Yes, Mother?"

"Stop bothering people. Miss Melody is mowing the lawn. 'Less you wanna do it?"

Rebecca Jane shakes her head, once in each direction. She looks back at Melody. The smile turns off like someone hit a switch. She scuttles away, back to the pigs, running on all fours like a wolf. Bright green blades of grass stick to the soles of her feet, stark against the filth that coats them. The girl covers the distance impossibly fast.

"Sorry about that, Melody," Sophia says, as if everything is just fine, thank you very much. "She's just curious is all. We don't get a lot of company." Melody feels her face trying to manufacture a calm, professional expression, but she's certain she still looks as panicky as she feels. "Now, hop to it. Lawn ain't gonna mow itself." Sophia's laugh is a single barked *HA!* She closes the door behind her.

Melody lowers the blades, engages the throttle, and keeps one eye on Rebecca Jane as she finishes the lawn. All the while she's thinking, *Almost done. I can leave in ten minutes. Why am I not leaving now? Finish the job. Just finish the job.* The girl in the pigpen doesn't move. At all.

When she has Demi Mower back on the trailer, secured once again, Melody works up her nerve and approaches the house. She knocks twice and Sophia opens it immediately. She hands Melody her fee, plus a $20 tip.

"Won't you come in? I was just about to make those sandwiches."

Melody stammers apologies and excuses. Another job back in town. Have to stop by the store. So sorry. She backs down the steps, sweat dripping down her ribs, and trots to the car. She almost makes it.

Rebecca Jane grabs Melody's wrist with one hand. It's spattered in pig feces and iron-strong. With the other hand, she cuffs Melody in the temple. Melody sees stars and goes limp. She's aware of being dragged but is too dazed to make herself fight back.

Rebecca Jane heaves her up and throws her over the fence into the pig enclosure. When she does, Melody's shoulder is dislocated. The pain brings her back to life. She kicks the girl in the shin, throws a handful of pig shit at her face. Rebecca Jane seems unfazed. "What the *FUCK?*" Melody screams the last word.

The girl hunkers next to Melody, staring with her blank eyes, head tilted farther to one side than possible for a human neck.

Melody whips out her keys with her good hand. She thumbs off the safety and treats Rebecca Jane to a faceful of pepper spray.

For a moment, nothing happens. The girl sits there, pinning Melody's legs with her hands, staring back at her. Then, Rebecca Jane's jaw falls off. It thunks in the dirt. A sinuous tongue protrudes from the hole in her face, the tip grazing Melody's cheek. It's hot and slimy, and she recoils. Following the tongue-thing, a fleshy tube squelches from the hole. It opens at the end to reveal row upon row of lamprey teeth, sharp and glistening with saliva.

Melody whimpers and tries to scoot back using her one functioning arm. The hands just above her knees clamp down harder, threatening to break them. The lamprey mouth moves in, inches from Melody's throat. She can feel her pulse throbbing there. Its hot breath smells like bacon. She pukes all over herself.

The fleshy tube latches on to her skin, and the teeth puncture. She can *feel* her lifeblood being sucked from her carotid artery. She punches the girl again and again, but it doesn't seem to bother her. She's screaming every foul thing she knows at the monster who's killing her.

"Rebecca Jane!"

The girl disengages, slurping the feeding tube back inside her head. She looks at her mother.

"Get the money first. And take off her clothes. That's a polyester blend, I'm pretty sure, and I don't want the pigs eating it." She goes back inside.

Rebecca Jane removes the cash from Melody's pockets and reaches for the bottom of her shirt. Melody fights her with everything she has, pounding her one good fist against the girl's chest and stomach. Rebecca Jane cuffs her once more, harder this time, and Melody goes limp. Her head is swimming and saliva fills her mouth. She pukes again and thinks, *there. Now you have to touch that, bitch.*

The girl carefully sets Melody's things outside the sty. Her horrible flesh tube reemerges and she goes back to feeding on blood.

As Melody slowly loses consciousness, she notices movement. The pigs, edging closer, waiting for their turn.

TRAGEDY IN TOY STORY LAND

2023

(Registered Nurse; obsessed with Disney World; afraid of heights and planes)

Justine was half asleep on the hospital's breakroom cot when the song playing on the small, portable radio ended. The DJ burst in, all excited: "This is it, folks: the moment you've been waiting for. Your big chance. One lucky caller gets an all-expense paid trip to Disney World! Just one, I'm afraid. That's all the promoter offered. So, if you're flying solo, give us a call now!"

Suddenly wide-awake, Justine dialed the number the DJ had rattled off. Busy. She hung up and tried again. Ringing. She scooted her back to the wall and tapped her foot on the bed.

"Hello! WCVR. You're the winner!"

"What?" Justine's voice caught and she repeated it. "*What? Really?*"

"Yep. What's your name?" She told him. "Great. Thanks, Justine. Hang tight for a sec, and we'll get your information. Congratulations!"

"Oh my god, thanks!"

The DJ made the announcement on air, and Justine heard herself say her own name. He played another song and came back on the phone to get everything he needed from Justine. "The trip is Friday to Sunday, August 11th to the 13th. You're gonna want to stock up on sunblock."

"August elev…that's in three weeks."

"Yep. Is that a problem?"

"No. I can make it work. I mean…*Disney World*. I'll find someone to cover my shifts. Thank you, really."

Justine got her shifts covered, but only for those days. She had to work the Thursday and following Monday. She would have to fly.

Justine hated airplanes. Hated *heights*, really, but especially being up high, in a machine that someone else was operating, going insanely fast, with absolutely nothing in her control. That was just asking for trouble.

Stop it, she told herself. *You're going to Disney World for free.* Everything would be fine. People flew on planes every day. She focused on the destination instead. She'd been fantasizing about going to Disney World since she was a kid. This was going to be epic.

She was about 2/3 of the way through the TSA line that double-backed on itself six times. Justine was wearing slip-on shoes over footie-socks and carrying an empty water bottle. Finally, when it was her turn, she passed through without any delay. When she got to the gate, she still had more than an hour to kill before her flight, so she dug the latest Stephen King novel from her bag. This was one of his more polarizing ones, with people either loving or hating it, and she was trying to go in with an open mind.

She got so engrossed in the book that she missed the call for her seat. She quickly joined the line of people heading along the jet bridge. Justine stowed her bag overhead, keeping out only the novel and her water bottle. She introduced herself to the woman sitting in the window seat.

"Clarina," the woman said. "I know. It's a weird name. My parents wanted to make sure no other kids at school would share a name with me. I was like, 'Fine, I guess, but did you have to make me sound like I was a musical instrument?'"

They both laughed. The plane nudged into movement, rolling backward on the tarmac. They stopped and the captain's voice came over the speakers to announce the weather in Orlando, when they'd likely arrive, and that they were now preparing for takeoff.

Justine put the book in the pocket in front of her. She turned off the screen above that; she had no interest in watching anything. She glanced past Clarina to the people scurrying like ants outside the window.

The airplane picked up speed on the runway. Justine gripped the armrests, knuckles draining of color. She clenched her jaw. The chorus of a Taylor Swift song played in her head on repeat. She closed her eyes so she wouldn't have to see the plane explode in a giant fireball.

A warm, soft hand enveloped her own right hand. Justine opened her eyes, trying unsuccessfully to keep the panic from appearing.

"I've got you," Clarina said softly. "It's gonna be okay. Almost there."

Justine nodded her thanks, not trusting her voice to come out as anything but a scream.

After what felt like hours, the plane leveled off. Justine peeled her fingers from the armrests. She inverted the right one to squeeze Clarina's hand. She found her voice. "Thank you. That helped. A lot."

"Anytime, honey. In return, you can answer a question for me."

"Shoot."

"Why in the name of Almighty God are you willingly going to *Florida*? In August, especially."

Justine laughed. "Disney World. I won a free trip."

"*Did you?* That's lovely. And way better than my reason: my aunt passed away—now stop: I didn't much know her at all—She died and left me a house. I have to go figure out what in the world to do with it. 'Cause I sure ain't moving to a state with alligators and politicians who are roughly the same level of nasty."

"And Florida Man."

"Exactly right." Clarina gestured at Justine's book. "Any good?"

"Yeah. So far. Only a few chapters in. He's one of my favorite authors.:

"Mm. I don't care for the stuff he writes, generally, to be honest. But I saw *Stand by Me* and *Shawshank Redemption* and I will freely admit that the man knows how to tell a story."

"He really does. I have to admit that I'm a big horror fan, and he's one of the best."

"To each their own. I happen to enjoy liver and onions, but I know that's not everyone's cup of tea, and that's okay too. Diversity is what makes people interesting."

The conversation steered companionably away from Florida and Stephen King, and onto more mundane topics. Clarina was a social worker—"A good field, but run by incompetent people"— she was "somewhere north of forty, and that's all I'm admitting to," and her second grandbaby was "just born, like two weeks ago!"

They were an hour or so into the flight. Snacks had come and been eaten. Small plastic cups of ice sat in the depression on each tray. They jumped, rattling the ice, as the plane shuddered violently around them. Justine whimpered involuntarily.

"Sorry, folks," the caption said. "We're experiencing some rough air, as you've probably noticed. Should only last a little while. Current temperature in Orlando is 98 degrees. We should be arriving a few minutes ahead of schedule. The flight attendants are buckling in for safety now, but will come around to clear any trash you may have shortly."

Justine rode out the turbulence with a white-knuckled grip. She stared dead-ahead at the blank screen on the seatback in front of her.

"Hey. *Hey.*" Justine looked at Clarina. "Today is not the day I die, do you hear me?" Justine nodded. "Good. So, this means this is not the day you die either. Got that?"

"Yeah," she said through clenched teeth. "I got it." Seconds later, the plane passed through whatever was causing the turbulence and flew smoothly again. Justine wiped away tears. The rest of the flight was great. Even the landing—which, once again, had her gripping the armrests, wondering if her fingerprints were permanently embedded there—was nice and gentle.

Clarina walked her through the terminal to baggage, where a man in linen pants and a short-sleeve shirt with a tie held a sign with Justine's name on it. "Ooh, look at you, getting a limo and everything. Girl, you rock this weekend!" She opened her arms and Justine hugged her.

"Good luck with the house and everything."

"Thanks, honey. Take care of yourself. And watch out for Florida Man!"

They hugged again. Justine introduced herself to the driver. She rode in the back of an air-conditioned, quite comfortable sedan to a hotel that was both of those as well. It wasn't one of the themed hotels, but it would do just fine.

J ustine grabbed a quick dinner at the hotel restaurant (included!) and spent the rest of the evening planning her itinerary for the next day. She was 100% going to the Hollywood Studios park: Toy Story Land had been calling to her since it was first built. *Might even ride the Slinky Dog,* she thought. She'd already faced her fear of heights once and survived. A coaster should be doable. A small one anyway.

In the morning, before she could lose her nerve, Justine was standing in line. *So many lines. We're always waiting in lines, to get the next thing.* Just behind her, a mother blearily smiled at her over a Starbucks cup as identical twins bounced like pistons on either side of her. "No kids?" she asked.

"Just me."

"Lucky."

The lined crawled glacially forward. Finally, Justine, Starbucks Momma, and the Piston Twins got on the Slinky Dog ride. When everyone was safely secured, the coaster clocked gently forward along the tracks, climbing a hill that looked small until

Justine reached the top. The cars stopped there, and Justine gripped the steel bar.

A noise like a giant mosquito moved closer as the Slinky Dog started to go downhill. Someone was piloting a drone, positioning it so that it was recording the coaster from underneath it, right in front of it, hovering above the tracks, right in its path. Probably a parent whose kid was on it, looking for the most dramatic angle.

They picked up speed. The wind rushed in Justine's face. The twins laughed as everyone's stomachs flipped a little. The drone was still there, maybe 50 feet ahead. The couple in the first car waved at it frantically, shooing it out of the way.

The drone lurched to one side, then the other, as if it couldn't decide. Justine lost sight of it.

Crunch!

A jolt. Slinky Dog's nose tilted left and looked down at the crowd below. He leaned slowly over, like he was drunk. For a moment, it seemed like maybe the cars would hang there, suspended forever.

Then, Slinky Dog and his passengers were plummeting toward the ground, some fifty feet away.

Everyone was screaming. Lukewarm cinnamon cappuccino splashed the back of Justine's neck.

In her mind, she could hear the captain's voice saying they were experiencing some rough air. *It's called 'turbulence', asshole.* She had a pang of regret about the patients she'd never get to follow up on, the ones she was supposed to see Monday.

The noise as Slinky Dog hit the ground was the loudest thing she'd ever heard. Plastic, blood, and vomit spewed outward. Metal screamed louder than the crowd.

The pain was instant and explosive.

Then there was nothing.

THE UGLY DUCKLING STORY

2023

(Reporter for a local paper; raises chickens; outdoorsy)

"I'm sorry…a *what?*" Maggie pulled the phone away from her face and glared at it, as though she could see Darcy's expression through the glass.

"It's a legit ugly duckling story, Maggie. You gotta do it. You're uniquely qualified."

"Because I have chickens."

"Because no one else is available."

"I hate you. I want you to know that."

"I know. I'll text you the deets."

"Nobody says that anymore." Darcy had already disconnected. Moments later, Maggie got a text:

Carl and Priscilla Tooms, #10 Cornwall Lane

and a zip code way out in the township.

Maggie's phone had an app for voice recording, and a camera of course. Still, she brought a notebook. *Some things are better done the old ways.* Maggie scribbled at the top of the page: 'Tooms—oversized chicken' and the date. "World's ugliest chicken, my ass," she muttered, tossing a Go-Bag in the front seat. In it were snacks, a water bottle, portable battery charger for her phone, basic first aid kit, aerosol hand sanitizer, and a pack of wipes. The latter were more leftover pandemic habit than anything. She plugged her phone into the car because GPS ate the battery life, punched in their address, and followed the gentle voice that only occasionally mangled street names.

"Arrived."

Carl and Priscilla's house was a modest two-story, painted within the last year or two, unremarkable save for the turquoise front door. The chicken coop, to one side and a bit back, was done in the same color. The effect was, Maggie had to admit, aesthetically pleasing.

The Tooms themselves, in jeans and T-shirts, suntanned arms, faces, and necks, matching green John Deere caps on their heads, seemed like the nicest people on the face of the Earth. They were all welcoming smiles and asking Maggie if she wanted coffee or something to eat, before she even identified herself as a reporter.

"Thank you," she said. "Coffee sounds lovely. But do you think I could see the bird first? The one that's been causing the hullabaloo?"

"Oh now," Carl said. "I wouldn't call it a 'hullabaloo'. It's not all that. More of a 'mild hubbub'."

Priscilla tapped his arm. "Possibly a 'to do'?"

Maggie let the notepad hang at the end of her arm and put her pen hand on her hip. "You're poking fun."

"Gently, dear."

Carl ambled toward the chicken coop. "C'mon. I'll show you Petunia."

"That's what we named her," Priscilla said.

Petunia, it turned out, really *did* fit the 'ugly duckling' stereotype: she was roughly four times the size of the other chicks, and—rather than the soft, yellow fluff of the others—was coated in coarse, charcoal-gray feathers. She had three front-facing toes and one shorter in back, like the rest, but above the back one, a bony protrusion jutted out. *A spur?*

Petunia ate from a pile of feed, alone. The other birds, even the adult hens, gave her a wide berth.

"Nobody seems to like her much," Maggie said. She took a few pictures.

"Nope," Carl said. "Had to isolate Clarabelle—the dominant hen—she tried to kill Petunia there."

Maggie interviewed them over coffee. She asked about the bird, of course, but also got background on them, the farm, the other animals there (mostly goats, for milk). Petunia was only a week old. They found the egg away from the individual hen's nests, so neither knew who the mother was. "We found it in the straw," Priscilla said. "Bigger than normal, but not like a goose egg or anything." They put it in the incubator and the chick inside hatched within hours of the others.

Maggie scribbled notes. "So, there's no way to tell which hen laid Petunia's egg, or even if it was any of them. She might not even be a chicken."

Carl slyly rested a finger against the side of his nose. "Could be a swan even."

"Like the story."

"Uh-huh."

"The whole thing's pretty strange, I'll admit. However, it's a stretch to believe that a swan, or some other bird, snuck into the chicken coop, laid a single egg, and disappeared into the night, like some kind of avian ninja."

Carl gave her side-eye. "Now who's poking fun?"

Maggie admitted she was and apologized. "I *do* think there's a story here though. I'd like to come back in a week, see what kinds of changes there might be, keep tabs on Petunia, if that's okay."

"Sure." Priscilla cleared away the mugs, rinsing them in the sink. "Give us a call before you head over, and we'll make sure they're a fresh pot of coffee on waiting for you."

"Perfect. Thanks again." Maggie put their (landline!) number into her phone, told them hers, thanked them again, and drove home.

Maggie drove out to Cornwall Lane the following Saturday and Priscilla met her at the door, hot cup of coffee held out. "Hi, Maggie. Welcome back."

After a few minutes of small talk—"Carl's out picking up feed right now." —Caroline led her to the chicken coop. Once again, the hens and other chicks were milling about the enclosure. Most of the chicks were noticeably bigger now and developing tiny feathers. The bright yellow was fading to brown or white as they grew to more closely resemble the adults.

Petunia, on the other hand, was nearly as big as some of the hens already. Her feathers were beginning to turn a glossy black in spots. Her beak had a downward curve to it that hadn't been noticeable before. It more resembled a raptor's beak than anything fowl.

Maggie snapped several pics. "Priscilla...I don't think she's a chicken. I don't have any idea what kind of bird she might be, but it's definitely a far cry from chicken."

"Yeah. We know. We've been researching it, trying to figure out her breed. No luck so far. Maybe when she's grown."

Maggie did a quick image search on her phone: lots of possibilities, but none looked exactly like Petunia. "How does she behave?"

"She eats *a lot*. Three or four times as much as the others. Otherwise..." She shrugged. "Pretty normal, I guess. The weirdest thing is that the others still won't have anything to do with her. They keep their distance, almost like we let a fox in the coop with them, instead of a bird. Not that we would do that, of course. But that's how they act: like she's a predator."

"Maybe she is?"

"Hope not. Hate to come out here one day and have Petunia be the last bird standing." Priscilla chuckled at her own joke.

"Have you thought about moving her?"

"Oh, sure we have. But, so far anyway, this is working out. Chickens are social creatures. Doesn't do them good to be isolated."

"But...she's almost certainly not a chicken."

"I know. But I'll treat her like one until I know what she is."

"That's fair."

On Tuesday, Carl called Maggie. He sounded out-of-breath. "You might want to come on out here."

"What's up?"

"Let's just say I'm guessing it's newsworthy."

She grabbed her Go-Bag and drove to the Tooms' farm. Carl and Priscilla waited at the end of the gravel drive. No one was holding coffee this time. When Maggie walked up to them, they both gestured toward the chicken coop without a word. The three of them walked in silence.

As they got close, Maggie caught a whiff of a thick, coppery stink. She froze mid-step when she saw what had happened.

Petunia was in the coop, nearly doubled in size from just three days ago. Her feathers were drenched in blood. The corpses of hens and chicks lay mutilated everywhere. She was currently eating the innards of a large, white hen.

Carl spoke quietly, his voice devoid of emotion. "That's Clarissa. She's our best layer. Was. She was our best, I mean."

They stood, the three of them, side-by-side, staring at the carnage. "Pretty sure," Priscilla said, "that Petunia is definitely not a chicken."

Maggie snorted laughter. "Sorry. God. Sorry. Nothing about this is funny. I think I'm in shock a little bit, to tell you the truth."

"Yeah," Carl said. "Yeah. I feel that."

"I'm so sorry about your hens and chicks, you two. This is awful."

"Thanks," they said together.

Maggie walked around the chicken coop, taking pictures. "This may end up being a much bigger story than you were expecting. This may be the kind of story that draws camera crews and gawkers. Helicopters over your farm and thrill-seeking conspiracy theorists knocking at your door. It could disrupt your lives. That kind of thing." She turned back to Petunia to take more pics. "Did she…Did Petunia get bigger in the last few minutes?"

The bird was still gorging herself on chicken guts. It was a different hen; Clarissa was nothing now but feet and a beak. Petunia *was* growing, and visibly. She was almost turkey-sized now. When she came up for air, Maggie could see tiny teeth, sharp and serrated, lining the beak. She zoomed in with her phone's camera. The tiny spurs on the backs of her feet were now a couple of inches long, tapering to wicked-looking, downward-curving points.

One of the goats bleated, and Petunia's head shot up, rotating in that direction. "Uh oh," Priscilla said. Petunia stretched her wings, extending them out so they were more than three feet across. After a few running steps, she launched herself in the air.

Instinctively, Maggie ducked and covered her head, almost dropping her phone.

Petunia was caught in the netting that covered the coop's enclosure. She screeched in what must have been frustration. The sound was like a hawk's, only deeper. It gave Maggie chills. "Oh. She can't get out. That's a relief—"

The oversized bird had flipped herself over and was tearing at the netting with her talons. She was shredding it with her spurs like it was cotton candy. When she'd torn a big enough hole, she pushed her way through it.

The goat saw Petunia coming and tried to run, but it was tethered. The bird landed on its back, immediately tearing chunks out and eating them. The goat screamed as it was being killed.

She fed. She grew.

"Get inside." Maggie pitched her voice just loud enough to be heard. "Call the police. Tell them, I don't know, that there's a mountain lion on your property or something."

Priscilla touched Maggie's arm. "What are you going to do?"

"I'm leaving. I'm not equipped to handle a carnivorous bird the size of a pony. I'll call you. The police will come. They'll capture Petunia, or put her down. Either way. Gah, I can't believe I'm still calling this monster 'Petunia.' Go. Get in the house. Now, please."

They did. Maggie got behind the wheel. She waited until Carl closed the door of the house, and timed closing the car door with it.

Petunia looked back and forth between the house and the car, whole head covered in fresh goat's blood.

Maggie was scared. She wanted to be as far away as possible from here. She started the engine and slowly pulled down the drive. Looking in the mirrors, she had lost track of the giant bird. "Where are you?"

Her whole windshield was suddenly covered in glossy black feathers. The weight of the bird sent the whole front of the car crashing downward. Both front tires burst with explosive pops. Maggie shrieked and, reflexively, hit the horn.

Petunia's hawklike screech rang in Maggie's ears. Her knees shook and she had a death grip on the wheel. The bird's huge talons scratched at the glass, trying to get through.

"Get off my car, you fucking nightmare!" She frantically searched for a weapon. *The Go-Bag.* While Petunia continued her nails-on-the-chalkboard assault on the windshield, Maggie unwrapped a granola bar. In her other hand, she positioned the hand sanitizer spray nozzle out, finger on the trigger. She opened the door, just a crack, with one finger.

Petunia's head whipped around to stare in at her from that side of the car. As soon as the bird's face showed up, Maggie shouldered the door open hard, into her face. Maggie stumbled outside. Petunia was already recovering and standing up to her full height. She looked Maggie in the eye.

"Here," Maggie said, loudly, and more confidently than she felt, holding out the granola bar. Petunia tilted her head and inched closer, investigating. When she got in range, Maggie sprayed the sanitizer right in Petunia's eyes. She dropped everything, turned and ran for the house.

She made it seven feet before she was hit from behind. The weight pushed her flat, banging her face against the gravel. The stones pressed painfully against her cheek.

Both of the spurs pierced her lower back at once, deep enough to do major damage to internal organs. It was excruciating.

She turned her head and came face-to-face with Petunia. The stink of blood and alcohol-based sanitizer filled her nose. Lightning fast, the bird took her eye.

Maggie screamed. She thrashed, trying to dislodge the monster on her back. With her remaining eye, she could see her own blood spilling onto the ground. Also, there was Carl, running from the house, wielding a shovel like a baseball bat.

Idiot, she thought. *Poor, brave, dead idiot.* She felt the bird rip out a chunk of meat from her shoulder. There was momentary relief as the weight lifted, but then Carl was bleeding out next to her. She wheezed from collapsed lungs. *Hell of a scoop though,* she thought.

NO RETURNS
2023

(Loves yard sales; collects action figures)

D oug, yawning, shuffled into the kitchen, to find Ted
Bundy sitting on the table.

He was still only 18 inches tall, but had no business being there.
Doug had thrown him out the day before. He should be at the
bottom of the garbage can, covered in apple peels and coffee
grounds. But here he was, pristine and vaguely threatening, just
by existing in that space.

I t started the day before with Doug brandishing the
handmade garage sale map. "Ready?" He'd asked Sara.

"As I'll ever be." She slipped a hand through the crook of his
proffered elbow.

He drove. She navigated. Oh, sure, they could have plugged
everything into her phone, or his, but Doug had been going to
garage sales for ages—part of the fun was the treasure hunt feel

of the whole thing. GPS felt like cheating. Though, he kept the option in reserve if needed: being a stickler for tradition was fine, right up until it meant missing a sale.

When they set out, it was the crack of 7:45 on Saturday. The closest one started at 8. Most of them closed up by 5 or 6, and Doug had mapped it so they should be able to hit them all. Some sales would continue on Sunday, but Sunday's for suckers: all the good stuff is long gone.

First house was, not to put too fine a point on it, mostly crap. Though Sara managed to find a book she'd been wanting to read, and Doug snagged a Skeletor figure—slightly scuffed but original. He talked the woman there into selling both things for $2.

The second garage sale was better. There was a box of DVDs for a quarter each. Doug picked up $3 worth of classic horror movies. Sara agonized over a shawl: "Gorgeous, but $12? I don't know…" The man wouldn't budge on the price. Said it belonged to his late wife. It stayed on the rack.

1:45 and it was getting quite hot. They had been to several garage sales with varying degrees of success. Sara directed him to a tree-lined boulevard. The intense aroma of lilacs hung in the air. There were *two* sales on this block, though only one had been advertised. They parked by the other and worked their way back to the one on the list. There, he found a table full of knickknacks and toys, including a double figure set, still in the box, from "The Six Million Dollar Man." It was Steve Austin and Bigfoot, who had been played by Andre the Giant in the show. Price tag said $5 and Doug bought it. He didn't even think of haggling.

"Oh man." The guy selling was maybe pushing 60. "I remember that episode. You?" Doug nodded. "This was my brother's. He was kind of a Bigfoot fanatic. Even went looking for him once.

Didn't find him. But he did come back with just about the worst case of poison sumac in human history. Getting this for a grandchild?"

Doug shook his head. "It's for me. I collect them."

"Toys?"

"Action figures, specifically."

"Takes all kinds, I guess."

"I guess it does." Doug thanked him and walked Sara across the street. They loaded the new acquisitions in the car and went to the surprise sale.

This one featured three different sets of wedding china, prompting Doug to wonder—multiple marriages? Generations? Previous garage sale purchases that sat around in this person's house for years and is now being sold that way again?

Another table, behind all the flatware, consisted of a hodgepodge of bric-a-brac all jumbled together. Cymbal-wielding, grinning monkey, wind-up, chattering teeth, stuffed St. Bernard, model '57 Plymouth Fury, red, and an action figure Doug had never seen before.

Caucasian male. Good-looking, in a kind of everyman way. Jeans, button-down shirt, and a bomber jacket. It was 18 inches tall, and wore an arrogant, sneering expression that seemed incongruous on a child's toy.

Sara sidled up next to him. "Who's that: Captain Smugface?"

Doug chuckled. "I don't know. Never seen him before. Feels like I should recognize him though."

"That's a dollar." They looked up. "No returns." She was *old*. Like, centenarian old. Dandelion fluffs of hair clung to her scalp above a face so craggy with wrinkles it looked more Shar-Pei than human. Her perfectly straight, gleaming white dentures clashed horribly with that face. She wore a threadbare bathrobe hanging slightly open to reveal skin that resembled parchment.

It was hard to believe she was standing unassisted as she shook visibly, probably just from being alive this long. "I'll take it." Doug handed her a single.

She yanked the bill from his hand. "No returns."

"You said that."

"Mm."

On the way home, Sara examined the strangely familiar action figure, turning it this way and that, when some lunatic cut them off at a roundabout, nearly hitting their car.

Doug laid on the horn. "I have the right-of-way!" The toy grew quite warm in Sara's hand and she dropped it. Doug glanced at her. "What? What's wrong?"

"Nothing. Can you believe that guy? Learn how to yield, right?"

"Right!"

He pulled into their driveway not long after, and they unloaded the garage sale finds. Sara reached out and poked the action figure with a finger—cool plastic once again, if it had ever been otherwise, and not just her imagination—and picked it up. She set it next to Skeletor and Steve Austin/Bigfoot, all on the dining room table. She fixed a glass of lemonade for herself and one for her husband.

Doug put his arm around her waist. "Let's find out who Captain Smugface really is." He snapped a picture of it and prompted his phone to do an image search. He got an immediate hit. "Jesus Christ."

Sara looked at the screen. For a while, nobody said a word. The screen image showed the same nasty smirk as the toy. The name below it was Ted Bundy.

"Why would anyone even *make* that?"

"We should bring it back."

"We can't. She said 'no returns'."

"Throw it away then, please? It was only a dollar, and I don't want it in the house."

"Yeah. Okay. Good call." Doug pitched it headfirst into the kitchen trash can. He pulled the bag shut and immediately brought it outside to the curbside can, making sure the lid was nice and tight. He brushed his hands together, wiping away the fact that he'd touched the thing in the first place. *Serial killer toys. Sheesh.*

When he got back inside, Sara told him she'd looked it up: apparently, there was a bit of a cult demand for the things. "Who knew?"

"Certainly not me. People are so...odd."

"Sara?" It came out as a croak, barely audible. He cleared his throat and called her again.

She came to stand beside him. They stared in silence at the impossible sight on the kitchen table. "Shit."

"Yeah."

"How...?"

"I have no idea." He pulled a pair of latex dish gloves over his hands before touching the figure. "I'm bringing it back though. Right now."

He drove to the boulevard where they'd picked it up the day before. The wedding china was gone: sold or put away. The ancient woman was carefully folding the legs of the last display table. She watched him approach, Ted Bundy action figure in one gloved hand. "No returns. I told you, twice."

Doug dropped the figure at her feet. "Keep the money. Keep that too." He turned and left without waiting for a response. Taking off the gloves, he drove home.

When he walked in, Sara's expression stopped him cold. She stepped to the side. The 18" Ted Bundy was standing on the dining room table again.

"What do we do?" A whisper.

Doug shook his head. With effort, he unclenched his jaw. He slowly became aware of the latex gloves dangling from his hand. He pulled them back on. "Stay here."

He snatched the damn toy and strode across the house. He pulled the claw hammer from its drawer and took both outside to the driveway.

The sun blazed, almost as hot as yesterday. He placed Ted facedown on the concrete.

The front door opened behind him. "Doug? Maybe you shouldn't…"

Doug brought the hammer down on the back of its head.

There was a moment of white-hot, explosive pain. Blood poured past his ears and ran in rivulets off Doug's face. He blinked it out of his eyes. *What?*

Next to him, but sounding muffled, as though heard through a thousand pounds of gauze, he heard Sara scream once and then sob.

The action figure had flipped over somehow. It looked up at him as he bled on it. It wasn't crushed. It was fine.

Doug opened his mouth. He struggled to make words.

"Sh. Don't talk." She was doing her best to staunch the flow of blood from his head. "I've called an ambulance."

Finally, Doug managed to speak. "N-No returns." He fell to one side and his eyes rolled back in his head. His lungs stopped, followed by his heart.

The Ted Bundy figure was gone.

HYPODONTIA
2023

(Social worker; loves carrot cake; was born with one fewer tooth than normal)

E lectra kept her expression carefully, pleasantly neutral, as she always did with a new client (or with unpredictable clients). This young man, maybe early 20s, had clearly been wearing the same clothes for days. Dirt was caked on the cuffs of his jeans. Purplish bags hung under each eye. Whenever he spoke, he covered his mouth with a hand.

"Things…aren't the best right now."

Electra nodded. "Do you want to talk about that?"

"Not really. But I guess I have to, don't I? If I want help, right? That's the system. That's how it works. This ain't exactly my first rodeo."

"Well, the system exists to help people who need it, who are struggling. In order to do that efficiently, it works best if we understand exactly how you need help."

Behind his hand, he muttered something unintelligible. Then, "I got kicked out. Last week. My boyfriend and I had a huge fight, over something stupid, to be honest. Anyway, he took my keys away from me and shoved me out the door. I had $37 in my pocket. Been using it to eat, but it's gone now."

"I'm sorry. That sounds awful."

"It ain't great."

Electra jotted a few lines on the legal pad. "Are things with your boyfriend reconcilable?"

"I don't know that word."

"Can you make up again? Do you want to go back, live with him?"

He considered this. Electra waited. "No. I don't think so. I mean, Clay? He can hold a grudge like nobody else. I think we're probably done. Honestly, I can do better anyway."

"Okay. Let's focus on what's next then. Do you currently have a job?"

"No."

"Anywhere you can stay? Family? Friends?"

"No. Not really."

"Well, I can connect you with a shelter. You can stay there until you find something more permanent. It's a nice one, actually: they've got beds, clothing, showers, and they'll help you find work. Might be the best option for now."

His shoulders drooped a bit, but he nodded. "Okay. If that's what you think is best."

"I do." She gave him a warm smile. "I know this is hard.

Nobody wants to be in this position. But we'll do everything we can to help you, okay?"

"Yeah."

Electra stood up and held out her hand for him to shake. When he did, a jolt went through her arm, and she could smell ozone. "Ow! Goodness. That was some serious static electricity." She laughed, rubbing her palm.

"No, it wasn't. That was me. My way of saying 'thank you'. I'm a healer, you see." For the first time, he spoke without covering his mouth. Electra tried to keep the revulsion from showing on her face. He was missing most of his teeth, and the few left were rotting. His breath stank like fish left in the sun too long.

She forced a smile. "Well, thank you then. That's a lovely thought." She led him downstairs to the processing department. "Let's get the ball rolling, shall we?" Leaving him with the people who would assign him to a shelter, Electra wished him luck and went back to her own desk. Almost without realizing she was doing it, she vigorously rubbed sanitizer into her hands.

A few days later, Electra was going over pending cases. She felt an odd sensation in her gums where her missing tooth should have been but never grew. *Hypodontia*, they called it. You couldn't see the gap, because it was farther back, but she was acutely aware of other people's teeth because of it. Both the perfect, straight, shiny teeth most people sported, and those who were missing some. She felt a secret, shameful kinship with the latter, whose mouths were less-than-perfect. That young man's mouth was a cautionary tale: *there but for a quirk of fate, go I.*

She probed the area with her tongue. It felt different. No longer smooth. It itched a bit, that spot. It was…bumpy. *Is that a tooth?*

O ne week later, Electra could *see* the tooth coming up, filling the gap. It was pushing its way through the gum, crowning like a newborn. It hurt. Her dentist said it was certainly unusual but not unheard of. "The human body is capable of amazing things."

Three days later, it was all the way grown in, perfectly even with the teeth on either side, like it had been there all along. She noticed, too, at the front of her mouth, directly between the incisors, there was a tiny, white protrusion. Like a little fang, edging its way downward. There was an ache back by the molars, as if more teeth might be growing there as well. Her canines seemed a little longer than usual.

Electra's whole mouth was constant discomfort with frequent explosions of pain. She could barely sleep. Eating anything other than yogurt and soft cheese was impossible. *Thank goodness carrot cake is soft enough to tolerate.*

She returned to the dentist. When she looked in Electra's mouth, she literally took an involuntary step back. "This isn't possible." She said multiple extractions were in order. That they should begin immediately. Electra panicked and left.

At work, she dug through the records, finding which shelter the young man had been assigned. Driving over, she asked for him, even knowing that what was happening was impossible, one hand over her mouth.

When he strolled out, he looked like a different person altogether: clean, well-rested, and smiling with perfect teeth. "Oh hi!"

"Make it stop." It came out *schtahp.*

"I'm sorry." He cupped Electra's cheek with one hand. A massive shock passed into her face, and she jerked back with a whimper. "I can't. Best I can do is to make it go faster, so you don't suffer for as long." He turned on a heel and walked away.

Electra could *feel* the new teeth pushing through, crowding out the other ones. She could *hear* the porcelain grinding. Tears of pain, frustration, and rage flowed down her face, past her overfull mouth. Back in the car, she violently flipped down the sun visor and opened the mirror. Twin bars of lights came on to either side of her reflection, illuminating the travesty of her mouth.

She stared.

Her lips were stretched thin, pushed back to accommodate the growth of all the new teeth. While she watched, the skin over her cheekbone split open and a tooth emerged. They edged out of her nostrils, her ears. She fumbled for the key with fingers that suddenly had molars sprouting from the sides. Her arms and legs were bleeding from dozens of wounds as new teeth pushed through the skin. White shapes appeared in her hair as her scalp split to allow the teeth through.

Feeling trapped in her own body, Electra struggled to work the latch on the car door. Finally, she got it open and staggered to her feet. She was blind; her eyes had grown teeth. Her thoughts were hazy, and she realized teeth must be growing in her brain.

She stood, unsteady, already more teeth than woman.

Someone screamed.

Electra turned in their direction. She tried to say, *It's okay. I just have to go see the dentist. Multiple extractions needed.*

She teetered on the edge of balance. Then she fell.

On impact with the concrete, she exploded in a cascade of teeth. Ten thousand molars, cuspids, incisors, bicuspids, and whatever the hell else the rest were called. They clattered and clicked and bounced.

When they were still, the only sound was the gentle *ding* of the car's open-door alert.

THE BROWN
2023

(Obsessed with the color brown; likes "sad boy" music; could "live in a museum"; afraid of being buried alive)

The Modern Art Museum opened three years ago. You've been meaning to go since day one, but never seem to find the time.

Today, that changes. No way are you going to miss the color exhibit.

On social media, the museum has teased glimpses of the different rooms: just quick, blurry flashes, with hardly any discernible details. Yellow, Blue, Red, Green, Purple, Gold, and Brown.

You stare at the picture of the Brown room, zooming in with your phone, trying to make out the things in there. Details are too vague, but the shades run the gamut from khaki to auburn to the color of a rich, dark soil. You find the spectrum enticing, and you buy a ticket online.

The next day, you queue up with college students, families with strollers, couples holding hands. Your tour guide leads you, en masse, beginning with Blue. The ceiling is painted like a cloudless sky. Displays feature denim clothing, including the oldest pair of jeans ever found. A large topaz sphere dominates the room, surrounded by sapphires, tourmalines, turquoise, chalcedony, aquamarine, and something called 'jemerejevite' you've never heard of. It's a lovely, pale blue crystal. One entire wall is taken up with a photograph of an enormous, piercing blue eye. It goes on and on, everything, everywhere blue.

You break away from the group, striking out on your own. You skulk through the Yellow Room. Above, the sun fills the entire ceiling, making it seem hotter than it really is. There are statues of lemons, real sunflowers and daisies, a taxidermized Labrador with a neon yellow Frisbee in its mouth. Beautifully cut yellow garnets, jaspers, tourmalines, and citrines catch the light in a dazzling display.

Pink features an absolutely lovely sunset on the top of one wall and above. Several iterations of Barbie's Dreamhouse are collected here, along with dozens of brands and flavors of bubblegum, also rose quartz, pink diamonds and opals, and a colossal picture of a human tongue.

The Purple Room has a life-sized statue of Prince in his signature 1980s outfit. There are lots of other things here, but you figure that one statue probably could have sufficed for defining Purple.

Finally, you arrive at Brown. It is glorious.

Behind a pane of glass, there's a mouth-watering display of every kind of chocolate known to humankind: it ranges from the palest milk chocolate to one so dark it's almost black. Mannequins are sporting outfits of every conceivable shade of brown one could dye fabric, from khaki onward. There's a massive tub of potting soil in the center of the room that smells like memories of early spring: your mother in the garden; you can almost hear the birds trilling, looking for a mate. You plunge your hands in it, past the slightly dry top layer, into the cool loam below. A sanitizing wipes dispenser is next to the tub, because, clearly, you're not the only one who succumbs to this urge. You clean your fingers and move on.

The walls are lined with pictures of animals: kangaroo, groundhog, mole, beaver, dog, cat, mouse, warthog, koala, and a few species you cannot name, though you recognize a few from nature documentaries and such. The floor is painted to look like mud; the ceiling to resemble thick, urban smog.

On the opposite wall from where you came in, a light pulses beyond some sort of opaque, brown curtain. It draws you. As you approach, you discover that the curtain is a brown liquid, suspended somehow in an archway. Is it a waterfall? You reach out, touching it with your fingertips. The liquid parts for you but does not splash. As you advance, your hand is swallowed by brown.

What's on the other side? you wonder. The need to know gnaws at you, but you hesitate. This is new, outside your scope, potentially dangerous.

You can now hear the tour group. They're approaching the Brown Room. You don't want to share this experience with a crowd. It's why you left them in the first place. Your whole hand is still there, engulfed in the suspended liquid. You shrug a little. *It's a museum exhibit. How dangerous can it be?*

You step through.

After you pass the thin stream in the archway, moving forward becomes slightly more challenging. Each step is like slogging through brown Jell-O in slow motion. The floor beneath your feet is soft, spongy. The Infinite Brown surrounds you. From somewhere—hidden speakers perhaps—the song "Criminal" by Thomas Reid plays softly, filling your ears with melancholy. In the distance, gentle waves lap at an unseen shore. You are pulled to the sound. You want to feel the water spill over your toes. Taking off your shoes and socks in anticipation, you abandon them and trudge ahead.

Each step toward the lake—for you are now convinced that sound can only be a lake, though your rational mind, for just a moment, wonders how there could be a lake inside a building downtown—brings you farther from the mundane as you embrace the Brown.

The atmosphere around you thickens. Forward momentum is more difficult. Still, the sound of the water impels you forward. Your bare feet sink a little more into the soft floor with every laborious step.

Somewhere (grade school maybe?), you remember hearing about a small town in Massachusetts where a water tower full of molasses burst. The people there could see the wave of goo coming, flowing slowly toward their houses and shops, thousands of gallons poised to crush the buildings in its path. Many ran. Some, likely nonplussed, bemused, stood and watched. The molasses pooled around their feet, and it was like cement. By the time they realized they should have run, they were trapped. It pulled them down, slowly covering them while the houses around them were crushed beneath its weight. The poor residents of that town drowned in sweet, syrupy semi-liquid death. It was like a modern parody of the tragedy of Pompeii.

It's like that here, now, for you, in the Brown.

Your feet are stuck. You cannot move. The air around you thickens, slowly solidifying, pressing in on your skin.

The sound of the lake taunts you, so close yet unreachable.

You think to yourself that maybe a trip to the museum was not, in fact, the best idea after all. *And yet,* you think, *at least I'm surrounded by my favorite color.* It's a tiny comfort and doesn't really help alleviate the rising panic.

You can't move your arms now. Your torso's locked into place above your immobile legs. Only your head is free; only your neck has any mobility. You cock an ear toward the lapping waters of the lake, straining in that direction.

Slosh, slosh, slosh.

The sound stops. Your ears are full of Brown.

You take one last, big breath and hold it, postponing the inevitable as long as possible.

The Brown oozes up to cover your face, occluding your nostrils. You can no longer let the breath out. It is trapped in your lungs, pulsing violently to be released.

Your eyes bulge; you panic.

The Brown closes over your head.

That last breath is trapped in your lungs, just as you are trapped in the gelatinous Brown. You struggle to somehow thrash free.

You try—and fail—to scream.

You mercifully black (brown?) out. Then you die.

THE SHADOW
2023

(Dislikes loud noise, especially lawnmowers early in the morning; fears unexplained ghosts in old photographs)

7:23 am

The low-flying prop plane in his Hitchcockian dreamscape gradually morphs into the reality of a lawnmower outside Steve's bedroom window.

His mouth tastes like the crater of an extinct volcano and his brain is full of packing peanuts. He winces at the clock. "Stupid Flanders." The neighbor had earned this nickname (never spoken to his face) by being an over-the-top goody-two-shoes who would be easy to hate if he wasn't so damn nice all the time. "Doesn't he know it's the weekend. People're sleeping."

He buries his head under the pillow, but it only mutes the noise a little. Sleep quickly becomes a lost cause. Steve tosses the pillow aside and sits up with some effort. He glares at the window, projecting annoyance, hoping some of it reaches

Flanders and his hi-diddly-mower. He blearies his way down the hall, the pressure on his bladder suddenly urgent.

Coffee. News. Breakfast. Shave. Shower. Human again.

9:43 am

A package arrives, a large beige padded envelope with no return address. Steve lifts and turns it, trying to guess what's inside. It's got some heft, solid, maybe 18 inches long and 12 high, inch-and-a-half thick. *Coffee table book?* He tries to remember if he ordered anything.

"Huh." It's a photo album. Old. The prints are black-and-white, almost sepia-toned. Clearly a family album, as many of the faces recur throughout. You can see the progression of the kids aging every couple pages. On the inside back cover, shockingly yellow by contrast, a sticky note with the handwritten message: *Interesting, right?! – Bill.*

Bill shares Steve's fascination with certain esoteric phenomena. Now that he knows who'd sent it, he goes back to the beginning, examining the photos more closely. One thing is immediately striking: no one is smiling. Not even the children. They look… stoic. Determined maybe. Like being photographed was an ordeal they were forced to endure.

Their clothes are simple, probably handmade, but well-kept. Subtle patches adorn a knee here, an elbow there. Everyone's hair is carefully combed, and the women wear lipstick on their thinly pressed mouths.

Each picture had been taken in the same room, from the same angle. The background details evolve over time: a new chair, a painting of the coast, a kerosene lamp. The whole scene seems to be lit from an off-camera window, providing differing shadows and textures depending on time of day, and likely time of year.

That shadow has eyes.

Once seen, he can't imagine how he'd missed it before. It isn't just eyes either. The shape is clearly humanoid. *There's an arm!* Fingers curling around the back of the chair.

"Shit." Steve whispers. His heart races. "'Interesting' is the understatement of the year, Bill." He shuts the album, half-expecting it to flip back open violently, like a horror movie jump scare. It sits there instead, immobile, smelling faintly organic, like a long-dead houseplant gathering dust. The dark brown leather cover is riddled with a network of fine cracks, soft and supple like a well-worn jacket.

Steve dumps his cold coffee in the sink and pours a fresh cup. His mind's eye replays the shadow's face, peering out from behind the shoulder of the man he'd named 'Father', sitting in an upholstered wooden chair. Was it looking at the camera? *Was it looking at me?*

12:14 pm

The computer screen is over-bright and hard to look at. Steve's eyes can't focus, and he's already forgotten most of the email he's just read. Rubbing his temples, he leans back. *Not going to get anything done today.* He flops together an uninspired sandwich and washes it down with an equally unmemorable glass of ice water.

He is staring off into space when he realizes that he's tapping a tiny drum solo with his fingers on the cover of the album. He stops and stares down at it. *Maybe I imagined it.*

Steve lifts the cover a fraction of an inch and lets it fall. *I'm being ridiculous. They're only pictures.*

He opens it.

There. In the very first photograph, unnoticed the first time through. A man-shaped shadow, in the corner, far back, easily missed if you didn't know to look. It's on the floor, behind the youngest child: a toddler in an oversized nightshirt. Its knees are drawn up to its chest, head tilted toward the camera, sepia eyes looking out. *At me.*

Steve searches the rest of the pictures on that first page but can't find any other evidence of the shadowman. He turns to the next. Third picture in, shoulders cheated toward the camera now, one leg stretched out, definitely gazing past the family, directly into the camera. The figure seems poised on the verge of movement. Steve can't shake the feeling that, if he takes his eyes off it, it will move, get up, come at him. Keeping it in his periphery, he scans the other photos on this two-page spread but doesn't see the shadow anywhere else. A trickle of sweat falls from his armpit, down his ribs.

He turns the page.

On the right, bottom-inside pic. The shadow's on its haunches, straining forward, a predator about to pounce. It's close to the front now. It *looms.*

Steve's lower belly is tight. The hair on his forearms prickles upward. *I should stop here,* he thinks. His hand rebels and turns the page.

There! It's upright now, striding forward. The family, frozen in time, tries not to look at it, but Steve can tell they know. They glance at it side-eye, fear evident in their body language. A girl clutches her stuffed rabbit to her chest.

Jesus! Get out of there! Steve knows this is irrational. They can't escape. It's just pictures, probably a hundred years old. Maybe more. But this poor family is trapped in there with this thing. What's going to happen?

He has to know. He turns another page.

It's coming. Reaching out. The shadowman takes up most of the frame. One hand reaching, spindly fingers grasping. Steve wipes away the sweat collecting in his eyebrows. For several seconds, he stares, trying to see if it moves, convinced it will, praying it does not.

Finally, he overcomes his paralysis and turns the page.

1927

Midafternoon. Father has everyone arranged. The photographer is holding up a hand, letting them know it's almost time for the semiannual portrait. No one is talking about the new person, huddled in the corner, knees drawn to his chest. It's barely there, this shadow of a man, a lost, haunted look about it.

Maddy tugs on his sleeve and he frowns down at her. "Daddy," she whispers. "The shadow man's name is Steve. I don't know how I know it, but I do."

The photographer snaps his fingers. It's almost time.

"Hush now," Father says.

As the picture is taken, the shadow Steve looks directly at the camera, sepia eyes sad and pleading, gazing out at himself across time.

ENCOUNTER WITH AN OLD FLAME
2023

(Plays drums and guitar; loves guacamole; afraid of being trapped by past errors)

B radley sighed. The opening 'band' was two kids, twenty if they were lucky, each with a laptop, reciting angsty poetry over an '80s synth beat. The crowd, inexplicably, seemed into it. *I am very old,* Bradley thought. He scooped up a mound of guacamole with a chip and scarfed it down; it was surprisingly good for sports bar fare.

His band was headlining. The stage was already set up for them. His kit loomed in the semidarkness behind the Synth Beat Boys (not their actual name but might as well be). The large cymbal caught the stage light and gleamed. Bradley mentally reviewed the setlist for the third or fourth time. Nothing too new. Comfort zone material. His big solo built in, a few songs before the end of the night, where the rest of the band takes a break to pee or get a beer, or both. They're all outside right now, taking advantage of the unusually warm November evening. Bradley scrapes the last vestiges of guac out of the bowl, planning to join them.

A woman sits beside him. She looks vaguely familiar in that way some people do. She's 30-40, silver speckling rich brown hair. Makeup is subtle. Hints of crow's feet and laugh lines accentuate rather than detract from her prettiness. A heavy cut stone dangles from a thin gold chain around her neck.

"Opal," he says.

She glances down and back up at him. "That's right. You've got an eye." She extends a hand. "Sissy. How'd you know?"

"Bradley." He shakes. "I used to sell them. Stones, I mean. Crystals, tarot cards, you know."

She smiles and rolls her eyes a little, sharing a joke, rather than judging. "New age-y stuff?"

"Yep. Back in the day. Another life."

She raises her drink: looks like scotch on the rocks. He taps the glass with his own, a pint of whatever beer they were giving the talent for free that night. "We all have a past," she says. "I prefer to look ahead. You're with the band."

He gapes at her. "How could you possibly know that?"

Sissy laughs. Something about that laugh strikes him as so familiar. "You've got drumsticks in you back pocket."

"Aw geez. Thought you were maybe reading my mind."

On stage, the poetry comes to an abrupt halt. Both young men bow their heads in sync. "Thank you," they say together. They close their laptops and exit to a smattering of applause and finger-snaps.

Sissy claps politely and smiles. "They were adorable."

"Heh. Yeah. Good way to put it." He drains his beer. "You sticking around? We're not nearly as exciting as the poetry, but…"

She lays a hand on his. A static charge startles him and he flinches. Something about her expression nags at his subconscious. He's about to ask, *Do I know you from somewhere?* when his bandmates bustle in. It's time for sound checks. "I'll stick around," Sissy says. She dips a finger into his bowl, scraping up the last of the guacamole and sucking it off.

Bradley watches this, somewhat bemused. It is an overtly sexual gesture. "All right then. Good." He gets up to head to the stage. "See you after."

They perform about two-thirds original songs and the rest covers. One of which, "Whip It," by Devo, is a huge crowd pleaser. Bradley glances at the table where he'd been sitting every so often and is rewarded with a small wave from her each time.

Something creeps up to the edge of his memory: a tiny, distant klaxon, warning him. *About what, though?* He has no context for his unease.

His solo comes around. Bradley goes full-bore on it. Sweat flies from his hair as he lays into the drums. He plays as fast as he can, hitting his favorite combinations, improvising *a lot*, spins one stick up high while playing with the other, making the cymbals crash like copper thunder. He is definitely showing off, but also having the time of his life. From the audience, a flash of light catches the opal pendant; it appears to swirl like a whirlpool pulling at Bradley. He freezes for half a second, sticks poised in the air, feet hovering above the high-hat and bass pedals. The sudden silence is startling. *Opal. Sissy. Melissa. Of course!*

He resumes playing, rolling through the rest of the kit one last time, hitting the cymbals heavily, almost cacophonous. It's the signal for the rest of the band to return to the stage. They finish that song and one more and call for a short break. Pete stands close to Bradley. "You good?" Bradley nods. He's not though. May never be good again.

———————

M elissa had been a mistake. A colossal error in judgment on his part. She'd started out as a customer in his new age shop: fun, flirty, maybe a little dangerous. And, twenty years ago, Bradley was powerfully attracted to her. She's *still* attractive, though much older, with salt in her hair instead of the dyed pink she'd had back then. Now she wears a classy, flattering, A-line dress instead of her former look of miniskirts and torn fishnets, see-through tops and lacy bras beneath. The change is so drastic, Bradley didn't recognize her. The opal triggered it though. She'd been obsessed with that particular stone, because—not in spite of—its reputation for being 'evil'. They had met outside of the shop for drinks, mind-bending drugs, and eventually sex. He blushes now, remembering some of the more…adventurous moments.

Sissy. No. Melissa is staring at him, smirking as if she can tell what he's thinking about. Bradley shudders. He avoids her during the break, choosing to sit at the bar with his bandmates. They reclaim the stage, rounding out the evening with another 35-minute set. Bradley plays guitar and sings on the one ballad they perform, aggressively avoiding eye contact with Melissa the whole time.

They wrap up and thank the crowd. The applause is, as always, gratifying. It's past one and Bradley is tired. He nurses one last beer as he takes apart his drum kit, putting it away. There's a comfort to post-show cleanup. He almost has everything broken down and ready to load in the car when Melissa lays a hand on his forearm. She squeezes. "You were always strong," she says. "Strong hands. Talented fingers."

Bradley feels heat rise in his cheeks. "Thanks. I guess."

"You remember me. I saw the moment when you did. Your expression…" she does a chef's kiss gesture. "Priceless."

He takes a big breath. "Yeah, well. That was a long time ago. We were practically kids."

She leans into him, lips nearly touching his. Her breath smells of cinnamon and scotch. "I'm betting you could still rock my world."

"I-I'm seeing someone."

"I don't care."

She helps him pack the rest of his kit, working right next to him, thigh touching his. He can feel the heat emanating from her skin. She'd always run hot, he remembers, borderline feverish. They load his car, and she gets in the passenger seat uninvited. She gives him directions to her place. Bradley's a tiny bit buzzed, high off performing, and, if he's being honest with himself, excited to be doing this. Risk had always been a turn on. He rarely engages in it now. Makes his heart race.

Inside is more booze, a few lines of coke—which Bradley hasn't touched in years—a lot of kissing, and a rapid transition to her bedroom. Melissa sweeps off the comforter with a grand gesture. Beneath it is a bare mattress covered in plastic sheeting.

"What—"

She kisses him hard to shut him up. "You'll see." She undresses him slowly, stroking and kissing skin as it is revealed. Once Bradley is naked, she steps back, shrugging out of her dress. She's not wearing anything underneath.

The plastic is cold and clingy, uncomfortable, but Bradley is focused on the heat of her, the musky animal scent of sweat and sex. He positions himself to enter her but she says, "Wait." Reaching to the bedside table, she picks up a thin, shining razor blade.

"Whoa. Hang on." Bradley pulls away, but she catches him with her lower legs around his hips and drags him back.

"Sh. Don't be afraid. It's for me. I want you inside me now." She arches her pelvis upward, rubbing against him, rekindling his flagging arousal.

Bradley, despite his misgivings, can't resist. He slides slowly into her and watches, fascinated and a little freaked out as she draws the blade across her left breast, a couple inches above the nipple. Blood seeps from the cut as a moan escapes her throat.

They find the rhythm of their bodies like no time has passed since they did this. On every fourth or fifth stroke, she cuts herself again. Blood runs across her chest and abdomen, pooling on the plastic beneath her. It is weird and disturbing but—Bradley has to admit—it's also hot as hell.

Her excitement is mounting. He can tell she's close. It brings him over the edge too, and he thrusts harder and faster. She rides the waves of pleasure with him. He tenses as his climax hits, holds his breath and grits his teeth.

At that exact moment, Melissa slashes upward with the blade, slicing his carotid artery. Blood gushes out, splashing over her. "Yes!" she cries out.

Bradley falls off her to the side, clutching his throat with both hands, trying to staunch the flow. Blackness begins to encroach on his vision.

"Sh. Sh. I know," She's stroking his hair. "Thank you, Bradley. I feel more alive than I have in years."

Bradley feels cold and distant. He thinks, too late, *I knew I should've just gone home.* He can feel her fingers in his hair still, an absurdly tender gesture from his murderer. There is a sudden, intense smell of copper filling his sinuses. Then that fades, along with everything else and there is nothing.

TREVOR'S SUPER-SECRET PROJECT

2023

(Afraid of centipedes; loves baking/cooking)

"Tada!" Bill lifted the lid of the bakery box. The class gathered around to peer in. There, in neat rows, separated by ruffled tissue paper, sat 48 sugar cookies decorated as Santa Claus, snowpeople, and Xmas trees. Everyone, including Mr. Cooper, made appreciative noises.

Trevor, with his affable smile of perfect white teeth, batted playfully at Bill's arm. "You *made* these?"

Bill grinned. He couldn't help it; he was proud. "Yeah. I love to cook. Especially baking. Even have a business selling stuff like this. These, though, are on the house. 'Cause, you know: 'Tis the Season and all that."

Everyone got two cookies each. To a one, they would've gladly eaten five more. After class, Trevor approached Bill in the hall. "It's cool that you have this baking thing. Not enough people pursue their passions, you know?" He nodded, appearing to agree with his own point. "I got a thing: arthropods. Fascinated by them. I've been breeding them. It's wild."

"Huh." Bill ran a hand through his curly hair. "That's cool."

"Wanna see 'em?"

"The …arthropods?"

"Yep."

"Um. Sure. I guess."

"Cool." Trevor texted Bill his address. "Tonight good?"

"No. I have to work. Tomorrow's good though. Sevenish? I'll grab a pizza or something."

"Seven's good. Let me get the pizza though: you brought dessert today. Only fair."

Bill laughed. "Deal. Catch you later."

On the way home, under a stereotypically gray and gloomy Michigan sky, Bill admired the house-and-lawn decorations. Some lights were already on, though dusk was still a couple hours away, flashing green and red. Solid white icicles dangled from the eaves. A ten-foot inflatable snow-family complete with magical top hats and carrot noses hugged against the wind.

No actual snow yet—thanks to climate change—and it was still in the 50s, but Bill was definitely feeling the Christmas spirit.

Arthropods, he thought. *Strange thing to obsess over.* Bill didn't remember much about them. His last biology class was some time ago. He knew the term encompassed a lot of species: everything from spiders to lobsters. Invertebrates with an exoskeleton; something about their legs. Probably.

Trevor was cool though: smart, charismatic. Probably wouldn't be a terrible thing to cultivate a friendship with a guy like that. Not that Bill wasn't cool. *But can you be* too *cool? No, you cannot.*

B ill arrived seconds after the pizza delivery woman did. They stood on the porch together somewhat awkwardly until she finally rang the bell. Trevor opened the door, paid for the food with a generous tip, and ushered Bill inside. The obligatory tour was quick as the one-story house was quite small. There were two doors Trevor ignored: one in the hall, and one off the kitchen.

"I inherited the house from my folks. They're not dead or anything. Just moved to Florida. Feels a lot bigger now that it's just me."

Bill nods. "Only child?"

"Yeah."

"Same."

They ate off paper plates and washed it down with Pamplemousse LaCroix straight from the can. An elaborate saltwater aquarium dominated one corner. Bill peered into it. "Shrimp?"

"Yeah. Told you I'm obsessed with arthropods. These little guys require a very specific environment. Water has to be just the right temp; saline level, and oxygenation have to be spot on. Very easy to kill if you're not careful. Lot of things are like that." He shrugged.

"Makes you cherish them even more, probably."

Trevor looked at him for a long time without saying anything.

Bill felt himself blushing. "You know?" Trevor said. "That's very insightful. You're absolutely right."

The only things left of the pizza were crumbs and bits of coagulating cheese in the box. "Come on," Trevor said. "I wanna show you something." He led Bill down the hall to one of the closed doors. "This used to be my room. I took over my parent's bedroom when I got the house." He opened the door with a flourish.

The first thing Bill noticed was the red light bulb in the ceiling fixture; its warmth was palpable. The second was the steel racks along each wall, bolted at the top to keep from tipping. The racks were supporting glass cases, maybe twenty in all. In them were spiders, scorpions, beetles, termites, ants, wasps, and katydids. Multiple varieties of each type. Bill recognized quite a few of them. Whatever he couldn't identify was conveniently labeled. "This is amazing!"

"Hey, thanks." Trevor was grinning. "Someday, I'll show you the super-secret project. Not today though. Need to get to know you better first."

Bill wasn't sure if he was joking, or maybe flirting, or what. So, he hedged his bets and said, "Sure. Something to look forward to."

"Exactly."

For an hour or so, they toured Trevor's former bedroom, with its former occupant going into great detail about some of his favorites: "This is the Deathstalker Scorpion. It can be aggressive, and its venom is painful. It can actually kill a child or an adult with a heart condition. Mostly, it eats crickets though."

"Wow."

Finally, the tour ended. At the front door, Trevor shook Bill's hand. "You going out of town over break?"

"Naw. You?"

"Nope. I'll be here. You want to come back over maybe?"

"Yeah. I'd like that."

"Cool."

B ill had family obligations on Christmas Eve and the day of, and he was invited to no fewer than three New Year's Eve parties. However, he had no plans for the 26th through the 30th, so he arranged to come see Trevor's 'super-secret project' on December 27th.

It was nearly 60 degrees out at 2:30 in the afternoon when Bill rang the doorbell. Trevor answered the door in shorts and a T-shirt, holding a Labatt's Blue Light in one hand. He gestured toward Bill with it. "Want one?"

"Little early for me. Thanks, though."

"All right. Come on in." He opened the door wider; Bill stepped past him, and he closed it. "Crazy weather, amirite? Summertime in December."

"Yeah. What are you gonna do?"

Trevor set the beer bottle on the counter. He pulled a keyring out of his pocket and met Bill's eyes. "Ready?"

Bill shrugged. "I guess. Still no idea what we're doing but I'm curious for sure."

Trevor clapped him on the back. "Good! Curiosity is what drives science." He unlocked the door by the fridge. It was a deadbolt. When he pulled it open, heavy weatherstripping scraped across the floor in an arc. "Let's go."

Beyond the door were the stairs to the basement. Trevor flipped the wall switch and an unseen bulb bathed the area below in red light. Once they were both on the stairs, Trevor closed the door with the audible click of an automatic lock. It was a keyhole on this side too, instead of a manual lock. "Can't have anything escaping," Trevor laughed.

"Anything?"

Trevor just smiled. It looked almost sinister in the red light. "Let's go. Excitement awaits." He trotted down to the bottom.

Bill glanced back at the closed (locked) door, his curiosity piqued still, but a vague unease was settling on his shoulders. *Trevor's clearly not afraid,* he thought. *I'm being paranoid.* He descended.

Bill looked around. It was an ordinary basement: concrete floor sloping down toward a drain in the middle, hot water heater, furnace, and a couple of storage rooms whose walls looked like they were built from pallets. The thick wooden joists above were all decorated with what looked like the fringe from a 1970s-style suede jacket. Only this stuff was about a foot long and maybe an inch thick. Something else was weird about it, but Bill couldn't put his finger on it. He was puzzling it out when he realized the fringe was moving. He stretched up on his toes for a closer look and jerked back. "Are those…"

"Centipedes, yep." The pride in Trevor's voice was clear. "Crossbred over generations, selectively encouraging certain traits and suppressing others. Aren't they amazing? By far my favorite arthropods."

"I hate centipedes." Bill regretted saying it immediately. The look of hurt and anger on Trevor's face was startling. It was the sort of naked emotion you'd expect from a five-year-old, and seeing it on an adult was shocking. He put up his hands. "I'm sorry. That was unkind. I have a phobia."

Trevor was suddenly all smiles. "No offense taken. I think most fears come from a place of misunderstanding. Centipedes are actually fascinating! I think once you know more about them, you'll feel more comfortable. For example, you see how they're suspended upside down like that? They're holding on with their ultimate legs—that's the pair farthest back on their bodies. The front pair is called the forcipules—those are gripping prey, and for injecting venom for those species which carry it. Other species use the forcipules as sensory organs. Isn't that cool?"

Bill swallowed. A bitter almond scent tickled his sinuses. *Cyanide? Is there poison in the air?* Couldn't be, he rationalized. Trevor would die too. *Unless he's built up an immunity,* his brain supplied, unhelpfully.

"You want to hear the best part? I've *trained* them. They obey me. Crazy, right? True though—I bred it into them, working over generations, gaining their trust, gently nudging them to see me almost as a god. Pretty heady stuff, I know."

"Trevor?" Bill's voice was nearly a whisper.

"Yeah?"

"Why am I here?"

"Come on, man. You're a smart guy. I bet you can figure it out."

"Am I prey? Am I food?"

Trevor put his finger to the tip of his nose. "Ding, ding! We have a winner, folks!"

Bill lunged forward and punched Trevor in the face with everything he had. At the last second, Trevor rolled with it. Otherwise, he would have been on the floor. He took Bill's second punch on his forearm, and retaliated with a knee to Bill's gut, knocking the wind out of him.

"Whoo! Hell yeah." He clapped for a few seconds. "Good effort, man." The centipedes, hundreds of them writhed in agitation on the joists. Trevor's gleeful expression evaporated. "Not good enough though. *Sic 'em!*"

The centipedes dropped as one, swarming over Bill. He scrambled to his feet, running to the stairs. He made it up three steps before the pain overwhelmed him. He fell hard, breaking a tooth. Bill lashed out, swatting, crushing, beating at the tiny bodies all over him. He screamed in rage and pain. The bites came insanely fast.

Trevor was still lecturing, that son of a bitch. "That weird almond smell? That's hydrogen cyanide. They exude it from their skin. It helps to subdue their prey. Works on contact. It's quite effective, really."

Bill slowed down, physically and mentally. His thoughts were thick and sticky like toffee. With sudden clarity, a phrase rose to the surface: *I'm dying.* It was immediately followed by: *I knew he was too good to be true. Cool guys suck.*

His whole world was clicking, crawling, biting, chewing noises, which he noted with a detached sort of horror, only vaguely aware it was happening to him. Eventually, the sounds dissipated, and the world faded to black.

OPENING DAY AT THE SPACE MUSEUM

2023

(Nurse's Aide; dislikes people who move slowly; afraid of being kidnapped)

When Angelica first merged onto the highway, traffic had still been moving. Not fast, but not like this. She'd only gotten a couple miles toward home when the view before her became a tapestry of brake lights, stretching as far ahead as she could see.

Ugh. All she wanted was to get home, take a shower, and disappear into a good book.

The cars slowed to a stop. Across the median, going the other way, commuters sped effortlessly along, like they had not a care in the world. Angelica snarled at them.

Directly ahead, an older-model Ford Escort belched noxious exhaust, some of which seemed to be filling Angelica's own car. She wrinkled her nose, wondering if the other driver could read the distasteful expression on her face in their rearview mirror.

To her right, a tractor trailer. It was big enough that Angelica could only see the wheel and the bottom part of the driver's side door, which was painted Granny Smith green. The word 'logistics' appeared in all caps above what she assumed was a serial number. Its engine idled with a loud rumble.

On her side of the car, a minivan, maybe a Chrysler. She didn't recognize the make. In the passenger seat, a skinny-faced teen with an upturned nose gazed into the abyss of her iPhone.

Directly behind Angelica, the lowering sun glared off the windshield of a champagne-colored Dodge something-or-other from the mid-1980s. It had that distinctive bump in the hood that seemed to be all the rage back then. She could just make out the driver's face. He looked bored out of his mind.

On the radio, Bob Seger was singing about how nowhere compared to Katmandu. Angelica's stomach harmonized with him for a moment. She fed it a Snickers to tide her over until she could get home and have a proper meal.

The Escort's reverse lights flashed on briefly as the driver put it in park. The brake lights went out a second later and the engine cut off, thankfully ending the fumes.

The big truck killed their engine too. Tracey rolled down her window, sticking her head out as far as she could. The river of vehicles stretched ahead into eternity. She turned off her own car and sighed.

What if it was an accident? There could be people badly hurt. She hadn't heard sirens, but maybe they were too far away. She suddenly felt guilty for being annoyed at her own inconvenience.

"What the hell?" It was the teen next to her, whose window was also open. She was staring past Angelica's car, past the truck. Angelica turned her head, trying to follow the girl's gaze. With the sun dipping toward the horizon, slowly turning the sky pink and orange, she almost missed them. Then one moved and she could suddenly make out several. Maybe 30 or 40, spread out along the side of the highway.

They were...*people-shaped* was the term her brain supplied. Too tall, and skeletal-thin, to be actual human beings, but the idea was there. Bipedal, elongated arms hanging limp at their sides, legs with strangely high knees rising and falling like pistons, propelling them forward as the beings lurched toward the traffic jam.

A blaring horn and the scream of hot rubber on asphalt made Angelica whip around. She was just in time to hear the THUD of impact, to see the being, at least 15 feet tall, flip over the Cadillac Escalade, limbs floundering as it fell into a ditch between east- and westbound lanes.

The SUV pulled off to the side, hazards on, headlight assembly smashed, grill cracked in several places. The driver, a 40-ish professional in shirtsleeves, caught Angelica's eye. He looked panicky, confused.

The creature got up. It swiveled its featureless head as if seeking something. It stopped when its 'face' pointed at shirtsleeves guy. The man put up his hands, palms open. "Hey," he began. The being lunged forward. Its long, spindly arms scooped the guy up as if he weighed no more than a rag doll and loped into the woods with him.

The teen climbed out of the minivan. "Nope. Fuck this. I'm out." She started running. Her father ran behind her, both abandoning the car. He yelled at her to "go faster!" Both were snagged midstride by the tall things.

Angelica's heart pounded. The beings *(monsters!)* were taking everyone who fled their cars. The truck driver, a burly woman with short, spiky hair and a Rosie the Riveter tattoo, beat one of them with a huge wrench. She smacked it again and again on the head, to no apparent effect. It carried her into the distance, the thump, thump, thump of the wrench slowly fading in the distance.

Angelica held the steering wheel with both hands. *You don't see me,* she thought, over and over, mentally projecting a force field of invisibility around her whole car. She held the button to raise her window back up; to her ears, the tiny whirring sound was much too loud.

I'm not here. Just an empty car. You don't see me.

A tall monster with empty hands turned its 'face' toward Angelica. It was horribly backlit by the horizon: orange sunset bleeding into red.

Silently, she mouthed the words, "You don't see me." Her sweat made her clothes cling to her skin. She could taste chocolate-covered bile in the back of her throat. *Please,* she thought. *Just go away.*

Behind her, a horn went off. She jumped, but the creature was no longer facing her. In her sideview mirror, she watched the driver of the Dodge muscle car step out. "Hey, motherfucker!" he screamed at the tall being. "Over here!" Angelica realized he was looking at her. He winked. *Oh my god. He's saving me.*

Then he was gone, snatched up by another one of the damned things.

Her monster swiveled its attention back to her. It leaned in close, tilting its head. Listening? Sensing somehow? It reached impossibly long arms out, caressing Angelica's car, feeling along the hood, the windshield. She could make out intricate whorls, almost human-fingerprint-like, on its fingertips. The tall being reached around the side of the car, finding the door handle, somehow intuiting its function.

Angelica locked the doors.

Its fingers splayed out, flattening against the glass, inches from her face. They spread, almost liquid, to the edges of the door, forcing their way past the weatherproofing and into the car. The metal protested as it was pulled with a great deal of force.

Angelica started to cry. Pulling her phone out, she texted her kids:

I love you.

She scrolled through pictures of them, blinking away tears as they fell.

With an awful wrenching sound, the door to her car exploded outward, flung carelessly aside by an impossible creature.

Angelica undid her seatbelt, understanding that it was going to take her regardless, and not wanting it to hurt any more than necessary. Her phone pinged.

Hey Mom. What's up?

She was lifted. It began running. The speed was immediate and wind whistled in Angelica's ears. She fought to hold the phone steady and tapped out

Nothing. Everything's fine. Be good.

She lost her grip on it before she could hit send. "*Nooooo!*" The phone bounced off the creature's leg and tumbled out of sight. In mere seconds, she was hundreds of yards away from her phone—her last connection to her family. An absurd thought crossed her mind: *Well, at least I'm not stuck in traffic anymore.* She laughed at that and the creature pointed what should've been its face down at her. "What?" she said. "It's funny."

Without reacting, it continued to stride along, eating up miles. Hundreds more of the bipeds, each carrying a single human, ran as well, heading in the same direction. *Where are we going?* She got her answer soon enough. The tall beings began to close together, funneling toward a single point. That point was an immense structure, oblong-shaped, milky-white in color, larger than a shopping mall. Military trucks, Humvees, and helicopters surrounded it but—so far anyway—seemed to just be observing.

They continued to observe as hundreds—maybe thousands—of human beings were carried through an opening in the structure (*Spaceship. That's what it is.*) Angelica sighed as she and her being (*alien*) crossed the threshold. They lined up along the interior walls, shoulder-to-shoulder. The aliens, once in place, were utterly motionless.

The person to her left, an older man looked asleep, or maybe unconscious. To her right, a young woman looked back at Angelica with wide, frightened eyes. Angelica had seen that panicked look at the hospital plenty of times. She reflexively went into professional calming mode. She spoke softly. "Hey there. My name's Angelica. What's yours?"

"Frankie. Frances, really, but only my grandma calls me that. What's going to happen to us?"

"Nice to meet you, Frankie. To be honest, I'm not sure. I suspect we might be going for a ride though."

"To, like, another planet?"

"Could be. Be wild if so, huh?"

"I guess." Frankie looked around at all the people being held by statue-like alien beings. "Would've been nice to be asked."

Angelica nodded. "Yeah. Guess we'll have to make the best of a bad situation."

"You sound like my dad."

"Sorry."

"It's okay. I like my dad." She stared at Angelica. Her eyes had lost most of that deer-in-the-headlights stare.

"Well, thanks then."

The door slid soundlessly shut, cutting off the view of the night full of apparently impotent military vehicles and personnel. Inside, a faint aqua glow illuminated Frankie's face. There was an unsettling sense of motion for a moment and then it was still again.

"I think," Frankie said, "we might be on our way."

"Yeah, but...to where?" Eventually, they would find out. But, right about then, exhaustion took over and Angelica slept, still held in the unbreakable grip of her abductor. When she came to, she was momentarily disoriented with no idea of where she was or how she got there. It came back quickly when she opened her eyes.

Frankie was snoring softly. On the other side, the old man still had his eyes closed but was grinning now. *Oh. That's rigor.* The man was dead. He must have been for quite some time for rigor mortis to set in. Angelica shuddered a little to think she'd been sleeping a few feet from a corpse. She had seen death, of course, and plenty of it. You didn't work in health care without being exposed to it. This was upsetting though. So impersonal. Did he have a family? Were they worried about him? She swallowed hard. Her own family must be frantic by now.

Quite a ways off, someone coughed violently for several seconds. *Good,* Angelica thought. *Maybe we'll give the aliens COVID. Of course, they may not even have lungs or anything remotely like our own circulatory systems.* She shrugged.

For a long while, nothing changed. Then Angelica experienced the sudden sense of movement again, and it was jarring. Frankie woke up and asked what was happening.

"If I had to guess, I'd say we're landing."

Frankie looked past her and her eyes got huge. She whispered, "Why's he smiling like that?

"He's dead. That's rigor mortis."

"Oh god."

The aliens reanimated all at once. They slapped cool, transparent globs over the human's mouths and noses. At first, Angelica fought it, but she couldn't get it off. It tasted like sweet, clean air and she understood that they were protecting her (and everyone else) from their planet's atmosphere—or lack thereof. They even put one on the dead guy's face; maybe they didn't realize he was dead. Maybe they had no concept of death. Who knew?

The same space in the wall opened, allowing in soft purple light. The tall aliens filed off the ship, each carrying just one person. Angelica goggled at the strange architecture: no windows or doors anywhere. It looked seamless, like someone had poured out each building from a mold. They were uniform in style and nearly in shape and size, with a few variations. All were the same milky-white as the ship.

They were carried to a tremendous dome and brought inside, three abreast. Since they were close enough, Angelica reached out and held Frankie's hand. She had started to reassure the other woman. "It's going to be—" when they were pulled apart. Angelica was borne to a section of blank wall. The being lifted her so she was level with its own head, turned her around so her back was flat against the wall.

Its hand elongated again, spreading across her torso, pushing Angelica tight to the wall. "What are you doing?" she asked. Its other hand lifted her left arm above her head and pressed it flat. One fingertip touched her wrist, putting pressure between the radius and ulna.

White hot pain flashed as it created a spike from itself and drove it through her wrist into the wall. She cried out, her voice somewhat muffled by the gelatinous mask. The creature repeated this procedure with her other arm and then each leg.

Angelica was pinned there, *Like a damn butterfly.* She could see Frankie stuck too, not far away. There was somebody over there in scrubs too, and she felt a pang of kinship. Hundreds of people. On display like insects at the museum. Curiosities.

An exhibit, she thought. Her wrists and ankles were on fire with pain. Her blood pooled beneath her. She tried to calculate what would kill her first: the shock or blood loss. *At least I won't starve to death.*

Several of the tall beings stopped in front of Angelica, presumably to watch her die.

INFESTED

2023

(Respiratory therapist; likes pizza and the color orange; afraid of spiders)

Gloria lifted the business end of the stethoscope and placed it on a different section of the patient's back. "Deep breath, please. Let it out." Finally, she pulled it out of her ears, letting it drop to its place around her neck. "I'm hearing some probable restricted air flow. I doubt it's anything serious, but I'd like to get some X-rays just so I can take a look." She consulted the digital clipboard. "How long have you been experiencing discomfort?"

Calrence cleared his throat. "Maybe four or five days? Not exactly sure when it started. I just kinda noticed it, ya know? Maybe a week? I don't know."

"Can you rate your pain on a scale of one to ten?"

"Three, maybe. It's weird though. Feels like I can't quite get enough air. I get winded after a few steps up stairs. And my lungs are ...itchy?" He shrugged. "I don't have the right word."

"Okay. I'd like you to go down to radiology now, if that's okay. Rather than waiting. Just so we can rule out some things and try to find you some relief. Sound good?"

"Yeah, Doc. Sounds good. Thanks." Clarence pulled on his flannel, button-down shirt. It was plaid, yellow and orange.

"I like your shirt. Orange is my favorite."

He grinned. "Mine too. Not enough people appreciate the color orange."

"They do not."

Radiology was backed up. Gloria didn't get the results for almost an hour. She had taken a quick lunch and had seen two other patients. Clarence was back in the exam room. She looked over the X-ray results while he hung his flannel up on the same hook as last time. There were shadows on the edges of his lungs, possible lesions or scar tissue. They didn't look like tumors anyway. *Small favors.* However, the sheer number of them was cause for concern: she counted at least 15.

"So, the X-ray revealed some unusual anomalies. Probably just scar tissue. You have a history of asthma, right?" Clarence nodded. "Just in case, though, I think it'd be prudent to order a CAT scan. I'd like to have a more detailed picture of what's going on, okay?"

"Sure, Doc." He blinked a couple times, staring at the wall.

"Hey," she said softly. He looked at her. "I'm sure it's fine." He nodded. "Okay. I'll set up the CAT scan for as soon as possible. If you want, I can prescribe a rescue inhaler..."

"I have one. Albuterol."

"Perfect." Gloria walked him out of the room, pointing the way to the exit. They said goodbye and she watched him shuffle down the hallway. He seemed much older than his 38 years.

When she had seen her last patient of the day, Gloria scrubbed her hands, wrists, and forearms, grabbed her jacket and purse, and started heading to her car. She stopped halfway across the lobby. "Clarence? What are you still doing here? Do you need me to call an Uber or something?"

He looked up, seeming dazed. "Yeah. Okay." He stood on shaky legs. His face paled dramatically and there was a greenish tinge to his skin. He doubled over, coughing hard. Hands on his knees, he stopped and shook his head. Standing fully up, he reached into his mouth with a finger and thumb. His eyes grew wide. From inside his mouth, Clarence pulled a live, wriggling spider and gazed at it.

"What?"

Gloria stared, trying to keep the fear and revulsion from her face, yet knowing she was failing. Clarence dropped the spider on the floor. "Kill it," Gloria hissed. But it ran, zigzagging across the carpet, disappearing under a chair.

"That was inside me." Clarence shook his head. "In my lungs."

"Impossible." Gloria was whispering, distracted. That horrible thing was loose in the building. It could be *anywhere*. Days from now, she might open a drawer and it'd crawl across her hand. It could drop on her from the ceiling. Her heart raced.

"Oh no." Clarence paled even further. He hugged his arms around his chest like he was trying to keep himself from coming apart.

Gloria took three involuntary steps back. She held up her palms. "Clarence? Don't—"

He gave a mighty, convulsive cough. Spittle hit Gloria in the face. *Damn it.* She was unmasked. Clarence dropped to his knees, hands on the floor. He looked like he was going to vomit. Instead, he gave a groan. The kind of noise you make when you just found out everyone you love is dead.

A second later, spiders poured out of his mouth. Dozens. Hundreds. Maybe thousands. They hit the floor and spread, a second carpet.

Gloria ran. She bolted out the door, sprinting to her car. She unlocked it and spent a frantic minute searching herself for unwanted arachnid passengers. Finding none, she quickly got behind the wheel and locked the doors. "Shit!" She backed out, nearly hitting a passing car. Their horn was loud and judgmental.

Once she was home, Gloria reheated a couple slices of pizza and took a long, nearly scalding shower. She turned on the TV and scrolled options for a while, unable to decide what to watch. She texted her supervisor: Not feeling so hot. Need some time off. Please cover my patients. Thanks. *And maybe call an exterminator,* she added mentally. Poor Clarence. She was wracked with sudden guilt. Was he okay? How could he be? Did he survive the ordeal? *Jesus. Did I just allow a man to die because I was scared?*

No. He was in a building full of medical professionals. Someone would've helped him. *Yeah. Keep telling yourself that.* The other thing bothering Gloria was the X-ray. There was only the barest hint that something was wrong with Clarence's lungs. Yet, a few hours later, he was coughing up a crazy amount of spiders. Though, really, *any* amount of spiders in your lungs is a crazy amount.

From the brief, horrified look she'd had, Gloria thought that the nasty little things were all the same species of spider, though she was hardly an expert. It made sense: it'd be a lot more disturbing if a random assortment of creatures had spewed forth from a human mouth. This way, at least, they were likely from the same egg sac...

She set down the glass of water she had been lifting to drink. *An egg sac.* The bulbous shadows on the X-ray. How did they get inside his lungs in the first place? What if he had somehow breathed it in when they were so small as to be nearly microscopic? Some creatures lay eggs in warm, moist environments. Could this be an evolutionary adaptation? A new kind of spider whose eggs thrive in human hosts, growing to maturity rapidly and spawning withing days? *Nature is amazing.* Always changing, finding new and interesting ways to thrive. Anything was possible.

Gloria cleared her throat. She gave a single, close-mouthed cough and shuddered. She finished the water and set the glass in the sink. It took much longer than usual to fall asleep that night.

Gloria woke up coughing. Inside her chest, a maddening itching, tickling sensation that made her want to scratch through her skin, her ribcage, and into her lungs. She pictured herself digging into the cilia with her nails, quieting the damn itch. She shook out her fingers, trying to dispel the thought. *My god,* she thought. *If this is what Clarence felt, how did he stay so calm?* This was immediately followed by: *Fuck. Are there spiders in my lungs?* She mentally replayed the examination—he'd been feeling discomfort for four or five days, he'd said. So, it couldn't be from his coughing in her face. *Okay. Cool. This is something else.* A cold. An infection. Something treatable. *This is my field.* She would figure it out.

She took deep, slow breaths to center herself. Her phone chimed: work texting back, letting her know that time off was no problem. They had to fumigate anyway. 'Weird spider infestation. Feel better.'

Gloria closed the text app and opened Google, intending to search 'itchy lungs'. The top headline read: "SPIDER PLAGUE?!" with an attached video. Her fingers shook as she pushed play. A newscaster appeared, serious expression hovering over his white shirt and gray, striped tie. "All over the greater Michigan and Ohio area, reports are coming in of this bizarre, and—frankly—unsettling phenomenon. People are apparently …coughing up spiders. That's right. This is not a hoax." They cut to a montage of several people, one video after another, of the exact same scene she watched play out with Clarence.

She coughed, hard. Immediately, she checked to see if anything (*spiders!*) had come out. Nothing. *Oh, thank g*—

Another massive coughing fit followed. Gloria's chest heaved. Her ribs ached. Something wriggled in her trachea. "No. Nonononono." She coughed up two spiders at once. Immediately, she threw up on them. For several seconds, she watched them struggle in the fluid congealing on the floor. "Drown, you fuckers."

Coughing took over again. It hurt. It felt like it would never end. She hugged herself around her ribs, tears falling freely from her eyes. She gagged for a moment and spiders poured from her mouth. She could feel them stepping on her tongue.

Gloria knew she was in trouble. Her lungs had clearly sustained damage. She fought hard for each breath. Both sides of her chest felt like a spear had been driven through it. Twin spears. *That's a pneumothorax, I bet.* Her thoughts were sluggish, heart rate— which had been racing—was slowing down to a dangerously slow pace. *Not getting enough oxygen,* she noted with clinical detachment. *I might be dying.*

She slid to the floor, lying down. The acrid stink of her own puke only bothering her in the abstract, though it was inches from her nose. She was on her side, slowly losing the strength to hold up her head. The spiders that had (*wriggled and jiggled and tickled*) been inside her milled about her place, crawling on floors, walls, windows, and furniture. A few scurried close, in front of Gloria's face. One raised its forelegs. Then another did. Then all of them, a tiny, eight-legged army poised to strike.

"G-go to Hell," she managed.

Then the biting began. Her heart, already barely hanging on, gave out.

NOT THE BEST DREAM

2023

(Enjoys romance novels; dislikes frogs)

Haley set down her copy of *Love Doesn't Count*, the somewhat racy story of Vanessa Cliffs and her doomed (or is it?) romance with Count Francis. She threw herself onto her back on the thick, quilted picnic blanket. The sun warmed her face as she closed her eyes and imagined the Count's strong arms lifting her up for a deep, passionate kiss. She'd show him he didn't need that tramp, Vanessa. She could be his perfect match.

A loud, close "quack" interrupted her fantasy. Haley turned her head toward the sound and cracked open one eye. "Quack." A mallard, male, with the distinctive iridescent green head feathers, was right there, just at the edge of her blanket.

"Nyaaah," Haley said, doing her very best Bugs Bunny impression. "What's up, duck?" He quacked once more with something that sounded like urgency, looked over his shoulder, and quacked again. "You want me to follow you?" The duck actually nodded. *Whoa.*

"Quack!"

"Okay, okay." She got to her feet. "Let's go." Haley was now convinced she had fallen asleep in the afternoon sun and was having a very realistic, if bizarre, dream. She followed behind his shiny green head toward the pond. The duck occasionally checked back to make sure she was still there. She was. She wouldn't miss this for the world.

Haley watched the little guy's butt-wiggle all the way down to the water's edge. He turned to her and quacked emphatically. "What's up? I don't see anything." But then she did. *Ugh.* Frogs. Big ones, too. Glistening like they were dipped in mucus. *Nasty.* "Okay, so—this had better be important, Mr. Duck, because I *really* dislike frogs."

The mallard looked annoyed, which was a neat trick with a face barely capable of movement. With his gleaming green head, he indicated that she should look to the right, a little further along the shore of the pond. There, at the base of a sprawling elm, was a door. Like one of those fairy doors she sometimes saw in the neighborhood, only this one was big: came up to mid-thigh. Next to it, a grotesquely huge frog, the size of a pug, reached out a hand and opened the door with a flourish and a little bow.

Haley made a face. "This is some Lewis Carroll bullshit right here," she grumbled. Still, she got on her hands and knees and crawled through the door. She gave the giant frog side-eye until it backed up enough for her comfort before passing it.

Naturally, the other side wasn't simply the inside of a tree. On the plus side, Haley didn't fall into a pit or anything. The door led to a dimly lit space with ceilings at least 30-feet high. The door behind her was no longer visible to her, lost in shadow maybe. Thick velvet curtains hung in rows, accordioned closed. In the gaps between them, Haley could make out gleaming hardwood flooring lit by colored spotlights. *I'm backstage.* A five-and-a-half-foot opossum stepped out from behind a painted flat. "Good heavens! Why are you still here? That was your cue.

You're *on!*" The stage-managing marsupial wore paint-spattered jeans and a grey sweatshirt; she exuded an almost overwhelming musk. She ushered Haley onstage, skinny paws frantically propelling her forward, despite Haley's protests.

Haley skidded to a halt stage left, half-blinded by the bright lights. She looked out over a sea of chairs occupied by shadows obscured by dancing spots in her vision. *I don't know my lines,* she thought. An immense tortoise, roughly the size and shape of a Volkswagen, was eyeing her expectantly. "Um," she faltered. "Sorry I'm late. I got lost."

A surge of somewhat discordant, clicking laughter rose from the audience.

Haley was inspired. "I guess I took a wrong turn at the subconscious!"

Crickets.

Literally. The house lights came up, flooding the auditorium with harsh white light. Each chair was occupied by a human-sized cricket. Roughly 600 insects in total. Haley stood very still. The massive tortoise craned its neck, stretching it farther than she would've thought possible. It tilted its head to regard her with one eye. "Run," it said. She hesitated. "RUN!"

Haley did. She shot into the wings, caroming off the stinking opossum, who hissed in surprised outrage and promptly fell over, playing dead. She ran past the green room where she caught a glimpse of half-dressed humans and anthropomorphic animals playing cards and smoking cigarettes. They looked up at her but didn't seem particularly surprised or interested.

The corridor went on forever, but finally ended in a security door under a glowing red exit sign. Behind her, she could hear the clicking of several hundred oversized insect legs scrabbling on the cement floor in full pursuit. She reached the door, slamming into the bar to open it, hands partly obscuring the words, 'Do not open: alarm will sound.' A wailing siren whooped to life. The door didn't budge. *Locked.* Haley turned around.

The crickets were coming. On the floor, walls, and ceiling: a writhing mass of giant-fucking-bugs.

They grabbed onto her with tiny pincers at the ends of their legs. Haley flinched, expecting pain, thinking she'd be torn apart, eaten. But they were gentle, lifting her up, crowd surfing her back down the hall, onto the stage, where they carefully set her on her feet. She watched them shuffle to their seats. The tortoise was gone. In its place stood a dashingly handsome human man draped in tailored satins and silks. Count Francis, exactly as she'd pictured him.

"My dearest Vanessa—"

"Haley."

He blinked. "Right. Apologies. My dearest Haley, how I have longed for this moment." He crossed to her, wrapping Haley in his arms. She could feel the hardness of his carapace beneath his fine clothes.

Carapace?! Haley shoved him away. The audience gave a collective gasp. Haley took a step back. "You're a bug too, aren't you?"

Count Francis shrugged and looked sheepish. His finery fell to the stage floor, where it melted into colorful mist. He stood momentarily naked, and Haley appreciated the view for the half-second she could. His skin dissolved into liquid, which sloughed off to reveal a gleaming black, six-foot ant. Its mandibles opened and closed as if it were chewing something. The third set of legs unfolded from its thorax where it had been hiding them. The ant spoke with the same voice it had used in its human guise. "Haley, no one can love you like I can." It reached for her with its four upper limbs. "Once you go ant, you never go back."

The audience tittered.

Haley stomped a foot petulantly. "I hate bugs. I hate this dream. I want to wake up!"

Count Giant Ant stroked Haley's cheek with one foreleg. "Honestly, my dear, I think you're better off here." The audience clapped, hooted, and hollered. There was a distinct whistle from one of them.

"I am *not*. I demand to wake up. The dream ends *now!*"

The ant raised its limbs in a passable approximation of a shrug. "Suit yourself."

Haley opened her eyes. She was back on her quilted blanket, copy of *Love Doesn't Count* beside her. The sun was noticeably lower in the sky. *Wow. Good nap. Weird dream though.* Everything was back to normal.

Except, of course, for the greenish-brown toad the size of a house cat sitting less than a foot from her face. "Ah!" she cried.

"Ah!" said the toad. "You startled me."

"I startled *you?*" Haley was incredulous. "What are you doing here?" I thought I was awake."

"Oh, you are," the huge toad assured her. "You're hallucinating badly right now, but you're not dreaming anymore. Hi. I'm Bertram. I'm a cane toad. I'm dangerously toxic, but I guess you've probably figured that out already."

"Why are you talking?"

"I'm not, really. This is all in your head. I am, however, quite real. I'm physically here. Some dumbass smuggled me up here from Guatemala. When he found out I was poisonous and potentially fatal, he released me into the wild. Irresponsible, if you ask me. Anyway, you dozed off and I snuggled up to your face for warmth—"

"Gross."

"Wow. That's hurtful."

"Sorry. Go on."

"Forgiven. All right. So, I snuggled up to you. You moved in your sleep, and I got scared. I mean …humans are predators, you know, and you're just enormous compared to me. I released the poison in my back sacs and I'm afraid it got into your sinuses. Honestly, I feel pretty guilty about the whole thing."

"…Poison."

"Yes. I'm really sorry. It's quite toxic to mammals. Causes hallucinations and …death."

"I'm going to die?"

Betram the toad nodded sadly. "Afraid so. Well on your way to death, actually. The toxin acts against your nervous system and your heart. Most of the damage is already done. At this point, it's just a waiting game. Not a question of 'if', but 'when'."

"You're a hallucination?" Haley was hopefully grasping.

"No," the toad said with an exasperated sigh. "I explained that. I'm real. My *voice* isn't. You're definitely imagining that part."

"How do I know all this stuff about cane toads?"

"How should I know? You probably read it somewhere. School maybe? The internet? The human brain retains a lot of stuff you never think about consciously. I'm guessing, obviously. I'm just a toad. I can't even read. This is all you, kid."

Haley could feel tears welling up in her eyes. "There are so many things I want to do still. I'm not ready to die."

"Nobody ever is, I bet." The toad cocked his head to the side. "Oh. There it is. Your heart's stopping. Been nice chatting with you, Haley."

"You killed me."

"I mean, not on purpose."

"I'm just…" Haley struggled to finish the thought. "…just gonna close my eyes for a second."

"Sure."

Haley let her eyelids drop. She listened to the birdsong in the park. A gentle breeze stirred her hair. She let out a breath she didn't realize she'd been holding. She didn't draw another.

THE FINISH LINE
2024

(Runs a bike shop and co-runs a nonprofit; loves a local ribs truck; afraid of growing old)

At the five-mile mark, Hal's right knee started to hurt. He coasted to a stop, took a long pull of the water bottle, and checked to make sure his seat hadn't slipped down a bit. His toes, when his feet were off the pedals, still barely made contact with the pavement, so that wasn't it.

He mentally reviewed any recent injuries and couldn't recall hurting his knee. "Huh." He still had to bike five miles home, though the original plan was to do eighteen total. Ten would have to do.

By the time Hal dismounted and put his bike away, his knee was hot and throbbing. He limped inside, had a quick snack of leftover ribs, downed several ibuprofen, and iced his knee. He sat on a towel to keep from getting sweat all over the couch, until his knee was numb from the cold. After his shower—lukewarm to help drop his body temperature back down to normal—Hal winced as he stepped over the wall of the tub. "Son of a..."

Simone called out from the other room. "What's wrong?"

Hal deflected the question. "Meh. Just gettin' old, apparently." He could hear his wife laugh. Hal smiled. She had the best laugh.

A t the bike shop, one of the regulars was getting the handlebar grips replaced on her 18-speed Titan Pathfinder. She studied Hal as he struggled to get the new ones in place. "You all right, man?"

"Yeah," Hal said, grunting with effort. "Wrists are a little stiff, that's all." When he finally had them all the way on, Hal rang her up and held the door as she walked the bike out. Alone once again, he looked down at the body that seemed to be betraying him. He called his doctor and made an appointment.

H is regular doctor didn't have any openings, so Hal saw Dr. Schaeffer ("Call me 'Bill'"). The doc poked and prodded Hal's right knee, made him flex his leg in various ways, and examined both of Hal's wrists. "I'm seeing some slight inflammation here, and your range of motion seems a bit restricted. I'd like to get X-rays to rule out damage. Honestly, though, I think it's just arthritis."

Hal smiled at him. "I don't think it's arthritis, Bill. I'm still a young man, and I stay fit."

Dr. Schaeffer put up his palms. "Hey, I'm just guessing here. X-rays will rule that out, if it's not present."

"Yeah, okay."

The X-ray showed conclusive evidence of moderate-to-severe arthritis in the right knee, and moderate arthritis in both wrists. Hal looked from the screen to Dr. Schaeffer and back a few times. "Well," he said quietly, "…shit."

The next time he took the bike out, Hal wore a knee brace. It helped. However, at about the three-mile mark, he started feeling fatigued. *Maybe I'm coming down with something.* He briefly wondered if he'd been exposed to Covid. It was less of a threat now, but it was still out there.

He cut his ride short again and pedaled home, taking it easy the whole way. The rapid test said he was negative. *Small favors.* Hal laid back on the couch, telling himself he was just going to rest his eyes for a moment.

Simone woke him up two hours later. He had to blink several times and squint to read the clock across the room. Even then, he could barely make it out, it was so blurry. After a big glass of water and a quick shower, Hal stared at his reflection. He turned his head one way and then the other. "Nah," he said. "I'm imagining things." When he sat down later, across from her, Simone blinked at him.

"Are you …going gray?"

He put his fork back down. "You see it too?" She nodded. "It's fine, right? I mean, it was inevitable, I guess."

"Right."

An unspoken worry sat heavily above the dinner table.

T he next morning, more than just the clock numbers was blurry. The whole world looked slightly out of focus to Hal. He had to stretch his muscles just to be able to move without discomfort that bordered on pain. *This is new,* he thought, *and I don't much care for it.*

He called a local optometrist who had an opening at 3:15. Hal noticed that he had to turn up the volume on his phone to hear the receptionist. *Great. Losing my hearing too.*

His hands trembled slightly as he slid the phone in his pocket. He studied them. New spots, several shades darker than his normal skin tone, dotted the backs of each hand. He could remember seeing the same thing on his grandfather's hands. His "I'm getting old" quip popped into his head, so vivid a memory he could hear his own voice. He whispered to himself, "I was joking. It was a joke." It no longer felt like one.

T he eye doctor found 'indeterminate macular degeneration,' and asked Hal a lot of questions about head injuries ("No"), diabetes ("No"), and possible eye infections ("Not that I'm aware of"). "This normally occurs in people of advanced age, though it's not unheard-of in younger people."

"Is it curable?"

"Unfortunately, no. However, there are several things we can do to slow the advance and keep most of your front-facing vision from getting worse for quite some time." She went on to recommend vitamins C and E, copper, and zinc. She discussed a number of drugs Hal could take as well. "In the meantime, I'd avoid driving if at all possible."

"I generally ride my bike."

"Perfect. Better for you and the environment."

"Exactly my thinking."

"Still," the ophthalmologist said, "I'd be careful there, too: macular degeneration can eventually lead to a complete obscuring of your frontal vision, but it can make moving faster than a walk potentially hazardous even before that."

Hal sighed. "Biking—bikes—it's all a huge part of my life. You don't even know."

She reached out a hand as if to comfort him; halfway there, she hesitated and let her arm drop. She looked down at it for a moment like it was an alien thing. "I'm very sorry. I wish I had better news."

"Not your fault. I'm just getting rather a lot of bad news lately."

S imone was staring at him.
"What?"

"It's just…" She shook her head. "You know what? Nothing. Never mind."

"Well, now you have to tell me. You can't leave me hanging like that. What's up? I can take it." He smiled at his wife.

"Okay. Um. Is…is your nose getting bigger?" He blinked at her. "It's not," she quickly said. "I imagined it. Forget I said anything."

Hal pushed his chair back and left the table. A moment later, Simone appeared next to him in the bathroom mirror. "It *is* bigger," he said. "I've got some mean ol' crow's feet too." He met her reflection's eyes. "What's happening to me?"

I t was Dr. Schaeffer again. When he first came into the room, he took his time studying Hal's face. Hal's hair was mostly gray and thinning noticeably. His eyebrows were practically nonexistent.

Hal smiled at him. "That bad?"

"I—" The doctor shook his head. "Excuse me. That was profoundly unprofessional. I am nonplussed, sir. You appear to have aged fifteen years or so in a few days."

"Yeah. I had noticed that."

"Quite so. I'd like to do a blood draw. This looks like Werner's Syndrome, though that's incredibly rare—even more so at your age. Usually, it sets in around the early twenties. It's possible though."

"'Vernor's syndrome'? Do you get it from drinking ginger ale?"

Dr. Schaeffer chuckled. "Named for Otto Werner, with a 'w'. He was German. It's also known as "Adult Progeria," premature aging."

"No shit?"

"Well, I'd need a blood test to know conclusively, but yes, that'd be my guess."

Hal agreed to the blood draw. While the doc was filling vials, he asked, "What if that's not it?"

Dr. Schaeffer capped the final vial of blood and set it beside the others. "Then we figure out what it actually is and work out how to treat you. In the meantime, please be careful. You may have complications such as weak bones from possible osteoporosis, or diabetes; there could be blockage in your blood vessels." He paused, seeing the growing alarm on Hal's face. "I'm not saying any of this is currently the case, or that it's inevitable. I merely wish to convey that there *could be* complications, and that taking it easy would be the wisest course of action."

Hal sat with all this new information. The medical terms swirled in his mind, a chaotic soup of words. He latched onto one phrase. "Accelerated aging? Does that mean I'm going to die a lot sooner?"

The doctor assumed a neutral expression and said reassuring things about waiting for the results, etc. But, for a half-second there, Hal could see the truth, naked in the man's eyes. *I'm going to grow old and die,* he thought. *Like, soon.*

Simone held Hal against her. They were both out of tears for now, empty and exhausted. Hal had to turn off the music that had been playing: he was having trouble hearing Simone's voice over the ambient noise. *Actually going deaf now.* "Hey," he said, voice rough. "I want you to donate my road bike to The Ride Way."

"What are you talking about?"

"When I die. Give it to the kids. Or sell it and donate the money. Either way."

"I mean, I get it. I just assumed you'd want to be buried with that thing."

"Are you kidding? It'd never fit in the coffin."

Their laughter bordered on hysteria, but it felt damn good.

H al was gaining and losing. Gaining new body aches, liver spots, and skin tags (*Gross*) in all kinds of interesting places. Losing his sight, hearing, and ability to focus on things and to stay awake. Over the course of just a few months, he had effectively aged forty years.

The blood test way back when—was it three months? Was it decades ago?—had come back positive for Werner's (Vernor's!) Syndrome. Hal had put all his affairs in order as soon as he heard. Now, he sat with Simone. Her fingers, still young and strong, holding his frail, nearly skeletal hand, stroking his swollen knuckles and parchment skin.

"The worst part," he croaked, again surprised at his own voice, "is that I can't *do* anything. Can't ride. Can barely walk. God, I hate this."

"Sh. I know. I know."

She had cut up the rib meat from Sworden's into tiny chunks for him. He chewed slowly, savoring the tangy barbecue flavor on his tongue, and washing it down with one of the better local microbrew stouts. He'd discovered them recently. *Good beer. Have to get more.*

"I'm just gonna rest my eyes for a minute."

"Of course."

Hal leaned against her, and she stroked his hair. He sighed and started to drift off to sleep. He could still feel her fingers on his scalp, but he was also dreaming he was racing his bike, passing other cyclists, wind in his face, adrenaline surging through his young, strong body. His knees pumped like pistons. He grinned as he saw the finish line coming. He passed the last other bike. He was going to win.

A small smile played across his face. He took in a big breath and let it out in a long sigh.

He never drew another.

UPGRADE

2024

(Runs an open source LINUX operating system; loves pork tacos; afraid of ghosts)

S helly was biting into the best carnitas taco—from a food truck, no less!—she'd ever tasted when the alert went off on her phone: *Something's wrong with the OS.* She sighed and started the car, quickly wolfing down the rest of her glorious dinner.

She sat at the keyboard just staring at the screen for a while. The whole center was a repeating line, forming a column.

```
SIGKILL
SIGKILL
SIGKILL
SIGKILL
```

…All the way down. "Okay. That's new."

She went in, poked around a bit. *Okay.* A parent process had died and failed to take its children with it. *All right,* she thought.

That happens sometimes. Shelly rebooted the system. The screen went blank, then:

SIGDONTDOTHAT

Shelly blinked. *That's not one of the signals.* At least it wasn't one she'd ever seen. "Guess it's time for a hard reset," she mused aloud.

SIGIWOULDNTDOTHAT

Shelly sat back hard in the chair. *It can* hear *me?*

Okay. There was a mic. Camera too. Somehow, someone was pranking her, she was sure of it. Who among her hacker friends was capable of it? More to the point, who among them would *do* it? This sort of thing is a little more scary than funny. Shelly wasn't coming up with anyone who even could be the guilty party. "Also, why?"

SIGAREYOUASKINGME

"I was thinking out loud, but—I mean—if you can answer…"

SIGIAMAGHOSTPROCESS

"No such thing as a ghost process."

SIGTHEREISNOW

"Okay. Look. I got an automated alert. I did a system check and found a zombie process. Whoever this is, you're not funny, coming up with another supernatural entity term. In fact, you're not funny at all. I don't appreciate this. I'm going to do a hard reset and run some hardcore antiviral software and wipe you off the face of the planet." Shelly was breathing hard by the end of the speech. Her adrenaline was up. Her dander too.

SIGYOUBETTERNOT

"Watch me." Shelly literally pulled the plug. The screen winked out, went dark. She waited a full minute before plugging it back in. She ran the antivirus and waited for the system to come fully back online. For a few minutes, everything seemed like it was back to normal. Then:

SIGTHATWASABIGMISTAKE

Shelly swallowed. "Shit."

SIGIWILLMAKEYOUPAYFORTHAT

"Motherfu—" Shelly grabbed the power cord for the second time. It sparked and shocked her. She jerked back, shaking out that hand. "Ow!"

SIGDONTTOUCHME

Shelly sat on the floor. She didn't have much choice. Her legs refused to hold her up any longer. She gaped at the words on the screen.

The hard reset. The antivirus. These things should have locked out whoever was hacking into her system. What was happening simply wasn't possible. *Let's not forget the weaponized outlet.* She begrudgingly had to accept that this was no hacker.

So, what is it?

Shelly wracked her brain. Sherlock Holmes says that, once you've eliminated the impossible, whatever's left, however improbable, must be the truth. "So, what's left? Who are you?"

SIGIAMNOONE

"Then *what* are you?"

The previous message faded. Several seconds passed. Finally:

SIGTHEGHOSTINTHEMACHINE

An uncontrollable shiver ran through Shelly, from the base of her skull to her knees. *Ghost.*

She'd heard the term 'ghost in the machine,' of course: something about the mind being separate from the body. *Also, it's a manga or something.* She made a face. *No. That's* Ghost in the Shell.

This, however, seemed to be a more literal sort of thing. An actual ghost in an actual machine. *My haunted server,* she thought. *Sounds like a terrible paranormal, science fiction romance.* Shelly knew she was fixating on trivialities to avoid dealing with a reality that had turned suddenly somewhat alarming.

She was also still on the floor. Without taking her eyes off the monitor, Shelly got to her feet. She cleared her throat. Did it again for good measure. "So, um, how'd you get in there?"

SIGLASTUPGRADE

"Seriously?"

SIGYESSERIOUSLY

"Great. That's great. A *ghost* came with the upgrade. Of course it did."

SIGDIDYOUREADTHEFINEPRINT

Shelly glared at the letters. "No. One. Ever. Reads. The. Fine. Print!"

The licensing agreement Shelly had accepted unread (except for the first few, and last few lines, because at least she had made an effort) popped up on the screen. It auto-enlarged for ease of readability. Some of the text highlighted itself, about halfway down. Sure enough, right there in the middle, in black-and-white, in plain English, was the phrase, "This upgrade comes with a supernatural entity, either benevolent or malevolent—there is a roughly fifty percent chance of either."

"No one reads the fine print." Her voice was barely a whisper.

Wait. She reread it. "…either benevolent or malevolent…" It had shocked her with the plug. It had told her not to touch it. Definitely malevolent behavior. *Shit.*

"So, um. What do you want, O ghost in the machine?"

SIGYOURLIFE

She swallowed. "Um." She blinked several times. "I'm sorry, but I'm going to need some clarification here. Do you mean you intend to replace me, take over my life, build some sort of simulacrum version of me? Part of some widespread *Invasion of the Pod People*—or whatever that movie's called—where all of humanity is subverted in some soul-crushing way, or…"

SIGNOIWANTYOUDEAD

"What the fuck?" Shelly backed away until she hit the wall and stayed there. "What the fucking fuck?" She step-slid toward the door. Before she could reach it, the deadbolt slammed home. Shelly grabbed the knob to turn it back to open, but it wouldn't budge. She used both hands, awkwardly grasping it, but couldn't get it to turn with all her strength. Slowly, she turned to face the screen.

SIGTHEREISNOESCAPE

"Just. Hang on a second. Give me a second." Shelly skulked over to the wall where the circuit breakers hid behind a thin metal door. "Just let me process this for a minute, okay?"

SIGISTHATAJOKE

Shelly stopped, hand hanging midair, almost there. She stared at the monitor. "What? I don't get it?"

SIGPROCESS
SIGHUMANPROCESSOR
SIGISTHATAJOKE

Shelly leaned against the wall with one arm and give a big, fake laugh. "Ha Ha Ha, right, right. Processor." She whipped open the panel and flipped the master switch, plunging her home into darkness. "*HA!* Got you!"

As her eyes began to adjust, she started to make out shapes by the light coming in the windows. Something was moving, across the floor. She heard slithering. *Snake?* Her pupils dilated a bit further and she could see better. *There!* It was long, skinny, uncoiling toward her. Cable. It was cable. *No.*

Shelly ran. She knew she could hide in the bathroom. There was no tech in there, because …ew. *It can't reach me in there.* She was inches from reaching the threshold of safety when the bathroom door slammed shut by itself. She hit it full force, face-first.

Bright white light exploded behind her eyes and—for a moment —that was her whole world. Then the pain hit. Her nose felt like it had completely shattered. Blood poured from it, soaking her shirt. "Gnk" was all she could manage.

Shelly realized that she was looking up at the ceiling. *When did I fall?* Something tickled the nape of her neck. She batted at it, weakly. *Oh,* she thought, *it's just a cable.*

The cable whipped itself around her throat, immediately tightening. She clawed at it, trying to pull it away, knowing she could never break it. Shelly scrambled for the wire cutters. *They're in the drawer. No. Toolbox. No. Fuck!*

The cable lifted her by her neck to a standing position, facing the computer screen. Millimeter by millimeter, the loop grew tighter, making it hard to breathe.

"Why?" Shelly gasped. Her broken nose made her voice flat, distorted.

SIGBECAUSEICAN

It pulled her up, so high her toes were only just barely in contact with the floor. Black bars encroached on her vision from both sides.

SIGBECAUSEITSFUN

Shelly thrashed feebly, trying to work her fingers under the makeshift noose, desperate for release. She couldn't draw a breath, could get no air at all. Just before she lost consciousness, she saw the words:

SIGGOODRIDDANCEMEATSACK

Meatsack? Stupid ghost. With that thought, Shelly spiraled into oblivion.

THE HIDDEN COST OF BUYING
A HOME
2024

(I wrote this for Liz, for her birthday. We're dating and were, at the time, experimenting with the idea of buying a house together, a pursuit with its own potential horrors. It is the only one besides Holly's where I didn't change the names, except for the realtor. It's also the only one where I appear as a character. She is perhaps slightly more obsessed with Halloween than I am.)

While their realtor, Leigh, worked the combination of the lockbox on the front door, Liz and Ken examined the exterior of the house. Two-story, large bay window in front, twin gables jutting out from the floor above. It was painted slate gray with an ashy trim. The door Leigh was now unlocking was wood, painted black, which, in all their recent house-viewing, was a first.

"Is it haunted?" Liz asked.

"Always possible." Leigh laughed. "I didn't see that listed in the disclosure though."

Ken grinned. "Well, we can always hope." This had become a standing joke among them, throughout the several months they'd been house-hunting.

They crossed the threshold. The walls were painted a lovely smooth creamy gray color Liz distinctly remembered from one she'd liked at Sherwin Williams as the somewhat less-than-attractive name of 'elephant's breath'. "It's certainly a memorable name," she'd joked with Ken at the time.

Gleaming hardwood floors; an ivory-colored loveseat against one wall; the staircase immediately on their right, curving up to the second floor, thick, ornate banister drawing the eye; a ceiling fan drawing lazy circles in the air overhead. Through a large archway, Liz could make out a dining room table and six chairs.

"Does the furniture stay?" Liz asked.

"Some does. I'll check the paperwork. What do you want to see first?"

"Kitchen," Ken said, just as Liz said, "Upstairs." Ken chuckled and said, "Upstairs first, and then kitchen is fine.

"Windows look newish," Leigh said as they climbed the stairs. "They've got a good seal."

Liz patted the wide banister like it was a dog. *Don't make 'em like this anymore.* "How long's it been on the market?"

There was the slightest hesitation before Leigh answered. "Two months."

Ken raised that signature eyebrow. "Four bedrooms, two baths, in this neighborhood, at this price…what's wrong with it?"

Leigh shrugged. "It's had a lot of offers. They all back out before closing."

"Why?"

"Not sure? Maybe the inspection revealed something that's not obvious." They resumed the tour. Upstairs had some very nicely sized bedrooms with generous closet space. The primary bath was enormous. The attic was, if not beautiful, at least mostly clean and dry, with a complete floor.

The kitchen featured mostly new appliances, except the fridge, which was an older model though still decent. Gas stove. Lots of cupboard space. An island. Good natural light from the large windows.

The finished basement already had a built-in egress, a section of which could easily be turned into a fifth bedroom. The house honestly seemed perfect.

Liz gently body-checked Ken. "What do you think?"

"We should lowball 'em. Offer twenty K below asking price. Two months, so they're probably desperate."

Liz glanced at Leigh to see what she thought of this plan.

"Maybe fifteen K would go over better," Leigh, ever diplomatic, suggested. Ken gave an agreeable head-tilt.

Liz nodded. "Let's do it."

The building inspector was a forty-something, graying man whose defining characteristics were tightly curled hair, lean muscle, and an infectious grin. His name was Neal. "Well, folks, this house *appears* to be fine. It's structurally sound, plumbing and electrical are fairly new and up to code, roof is solid, and there are no leaks there or in the basement. There's nothing technically wrong with the place.

Liz shared a look with Ken. "You said 'appears' to be fine," she said.

"Yup. Sure does. It passes inspection. I'd like to head out now, if it's all the same to you."

"What's going on, man?" Ken asked.

"Yeah. What aren't you telling us?"

Neal looked apologetic. "The place just gives me the creeps. I can't exactly explain it. Like, you two can do whatever you want, I guess, but I don't like it here. I would for sure never be caught dead here after dark."

Liz elbowed Ken. "See? Told you it was haunted."

"Sweet."

"Hey." Neal sounded a little annoyed. "I'm out of here. You can believe whatever you want, but I can *feel* the nastiness of this place and I don't want to spend another minute in it." He walked outside, down the front steps, and waited for them halfway across the yard on the walk. He held out an invoice. "Here. My fee."

Ken trotted down the stairs and handed Neal a credit card. As soon as it cleared, Neal got in his F-150 and drove away.

Liz came to stand beside her partner. "Do you really think we're about to buy a genuinely haunted house?"

"Starting to look that way."

"Are you scared?"

"Maybe a little. More worried about the kids."

"Yeah. Same here." She put her arm around his waist, and he wrapped his around her shoulder. Not far away in the driveway, Leigh sat in her air-conditioned minivan waiting for them to be done so she could lock up. Technically, the house wasn't theirs yet. They looked up at the façade for a moment. "One more walk-through?"

"Sure," Ken said. "Let's do that." He tossed a 'just a minute' finger at Leigh who caught it and waved assent.

They went back in.

It seemed darker somehow, like the sun had become obscured by clouds. A quick glance outside showed that wasn't the case. They were only a few feet inside.

"Maybe it's better if we don't," Ken said, turning back toward the door. It closed in his face. He turned to Liz, eyes wide. "Dude. It really *is* haunted."

Liz smiled a little and half-shrugged. "Maybe. Probably just the wind though." She tried to open the door. The handle wouldn't budge, like it was welded in place. "…Then again." Pulling out her phone, she texted Leigh to

> please unlock the door, it's stuck

The reply was instantaneous:

> NO

in all caps. She showed Ken.

"What the hell?"

Her phone chimed again with a new text:

> YOURE MINE NOW

Liz gaped at her phone's screen. "I don't think that's Leigh," she said.

"It's the ghost," Ken said. There was no joking now. His voice was full of quiet awe, and a tinge of fear.

NO

Liz's phone was saying.

ITS THE HOUSE

They shared a look.

Ken, for once in his life, didn't bother to comment on the bad punctuation of whatever supernatural entity was using Liz's phone to communicate. He shook his head. "Yeah, fuck this." He strode into the dining room, grabbed a chair, and threw it as hard as he could at the bay window. It stopped, midair, inches before impact, and hung there, absolutely still, a few feet above the floor.

After staring at the chair for a moment, Ken stepped over to Liz and hugged her tightly. He gave her a quick, tender kiss. "Love you."

"Weird time for this."

He shrugged. "Just in case shit goes south, ya know?"

"'Worst-Case Scenario Guy.'" She kissed him back though.

As soon as they broke the kiss, he was ripped away from her. Liz was knocked spinning, sudden hot pain flaring up from her right arm. She was on the floor, disoriented, confused. Slowly, she tried to sit up.

Ken was pinned to the wall by the same chair he'd just thrown at the window. He was slumped over the seat, which was pointed up, as if someone sitting in it would be facing the ceiling; the chair back jutted straight out, pointing toward Liz. Blood trickled down Ken's face from a nasty scalp wound. The chair's feet were embedded a few inches into the drywall. Ken groaned, barely conscious, and tried to lift his chin. Immediately, his head dropped back down.

Liz put out her hand, intending to pull herself up with the arm of the loveseat, but her elbow exploded in pain. It was bent in the wrong direction. *Broken,* she thought. *That's going to heal fucked up.* She got to her feet without the help of her arm, limping over to Ken. Her damn hip was loose in its socket again, because of course it was. With her good hand, she stroked Ken above the ear and he stirred. "I'm sorry. We really don't have good luck with houses, huh?" She wiped a tear away. "You know what the worst part of this is? Besides getting killed by this fucking house, I mean."

Ken nodded almost imperceptibly. "The kids."

She laughed. It was the kind of laugh that was pulled out by force. The laugh you might make if you saw your own name on a tombstone. "Yeah. Exactly. Mine will be lost, rudderless, without me."

"And mine will be orphans."

"Ah, shit. What a mess." She slumped to the wall, next to him, holding his hand under the chair. "Hey, house …fuck you."

Liz's phone chirped. It had fallen on the floor, face-up, screen even more deeply cracked than before. She could barely make out the words on the screen.

FUCK YOU TOO

Liz felt herself being pulled backward into the wall. Drywall dust got in her mouth and nose, making her choke and sneeze. It dislodged her glasses and got in her eyes.

From her periphery, she could see Ken also being *absorbed* into the wall. She was still holding his hand and gripped it hard. He squeezed back, eyes saying a thousand tacit things.

Then she was inside the wall, in the dark, swallowing sawdust, breathing ancient paint flakes and wallpaper glue. She felt Ken's hand give one last squeeze as her lungs, starving for air, finally gave out. Her heart followed, slowing to a palpable stop. Only her brain was still going, desperately trying to figure a way out, some path toward undoing what had been done.

Son of a dick!

Finally, for the first time maybe ever, Liz's mind was silent. She smiled, at peace, and died.

WELCOME TO CLOWNTOWN
2024

(Floor manager of a dispensary; afraid of clowns)

Nell set the alarm, locked the door, and closed the dispensary for the night. She was beyond ready for the three-day holiday weekend. Business had been great, which was wonderful for job security, but meant very little downtime for her.

It was 9:15 downtown on a Friday, and the streets were peopled with small, tight groups of smokers outside the bars. Long gone were the days when you could smoke indoors in any public setting. Nell didn't much miss reeking of stale cigarette smoke after going out for drinks back then. Four different strains of rock and one mournful jazz saxophone competed for attention, bleeding out of open doorways. The sharp stink of piss from the alley between buildings stung Nell's nostrils, as it did most every night.

With chin up, back straight, and eyes open, she strode toward her car. Nell was a city girl: she knew how not to look the victim. She turned the corner, and her confident step faltered.

The bars and restaurants on this block were all dark; the doors were shut tight. Not a single neon *Open* or *Budweiser* sign was lit. No smokers hovering here. No one at all. Overhead, the streetlight seemed to be at half power, and there were far too many shadows for comfort.

From the stillness, music started up, like a record whose needle was already in place when it begins to spin, slow and distorted until it got to speed. Once it did, Nell recognized it: circus music.

From a dark doorway, the distinct tinkling of tiny bells rang out. Nell watched the shadows there, holding herself tense, transfixed. A single, white-gloved hand appeared, followed by a puffy yellow sleeve patterned with large orange polka dots.

It waved.

Nell suppressed the urge to wave back. Her knees were shaking slightly. *She was a little girl again, staring up at the seemingly enormous clown, trying to make herself small, to hide behind Mommy's leg.*

The rest of the clown eased into view, somehow sliding across the sidewalk without moving his feet, as if being pulled by an invisible cord. In addition to the orange-and-yellow outfit, it wore massive lime green shoes and a matching wig. The face was white greasepaint with an obscene, lascivious leer painted on over the lips. Incongruous black tear drops fell from cartoon googly eyes. *How does he see through those?*

Sweat plastered her shirt to her lower back as Nell took an involuntary step backward.

The clown put up his hands, palms forward, the unblemished white of his gloves stark in the night. His painted smile slid down his cheeks, becoming a frown. *Impossible!* she thought. The makeup tears flowed, dripping off the clown's chin, staining his silks and pooling, glistening black on the concrete.

Nell pitied him, involuntarily—she was still very much afraid, however. *This is unnatural.*

The clown's hands dropped to his sides. His mouth formed an O of surprise, and the red paint around his mouth exaggerated that O. The tears faded away, and an actual light bulb appeared above his head, humming to life with a musical *ding*. He grinned and produced five red balls, roughly tennis ball sized. He juggled until they formed a perfect circle.

Despite herself, Nell laughed and gave a little clap. It *was* impressive, after all.

The clown's hands moved faster, and the circle picked up speed. The five balls were now a blur, a red streak. When Nell tried to track them with her eyes, she could make an individual ball appear for a fraction of a second.

Then the clown stepped to one side, while the red circle continued to spin on its own. Nell watched it, almost hypnotized, wondering how it could be doing that—she realized suddenly she could no longer see the clown. Fear struck. She spun fast. He was behind her!

The lecherous grin was back on his face as he shoved Nell forward. She lost her balance and tumbled *through* the circle of red balls, into another place. As she fell through a weird, multicolored vortex, she glanced back.

The clown was following her.

———

N ell was disoriented. It took her several seconds to take stock of things. She had landed in something soft, fluffy, and sticky. Eventually, as her mind came back online, she came to understand that it was cotton candy. An acre or so of it, stretching across the bright pink landscape. Everything here was pink: ground, sky, clearly fake trees, bulbous towers on every building, and the thousands upon thousands of wacky, wiggly, inflatable tube guys, writhing, lifting, dropping, all the way to the horizon in every direction.

A phrase popped into her head: *Welcome to Clowntown.* It seemed far more creepy and unsettling than funny though.

Nell sat, half-submerged in cotton candy, trying to figure out what was bothering her, aside from the obvious. It hit her: *it's what's* not *here!* No planes overhead. No traffic noises. No birdsong, no constant chatter of conversation as people passed one another on the street. All there was here was endless pink and the maddeningly repetitive sound of circus music.

Nell slogged through the sticky muck, almost going under several times—*can you drown in cotton candy?*—and finally made it to solid ground. Stupid pink ground that felt more like a gym mat than proper dirt. She stood and brushed sticky tendrils off herself as best she could.

When she stood up again, the damn clown was there, right in front of her, grinning stupidly.

Nell punched him in the nose. The nose gave a surprised honk noise, and the clown staggered back a couple steps. His nose slowly uncrumpled, accompanied by a drawn out, balloon-deflating sort of squeak, until it was round once again.

He gave her a tut-tut waggle with one oversized finger. From behind his back, the clown pulled out a comically large hammer, the head of it as big as Nell's whole torso.

"Shit."

She ran.

Behind her, she could hear the slap-slap-slap of oversized soles as the clown gave chase. She risked a quick glance back. He was getting close.

The moment Nell turned to face forward again she stepped on a rake. It was the kind with hard metal tines, only the whole thing was pink, of course. Just like in those old black-and-white, slapstick movies, Nell's foot came down on the tines and the handle popped up and smacked her in the face.

Only, unlike the movies, this was real. On impact, a flash of light exploded behind her eyes. She could taste the blood an instant before it started gushing from her nose. It soaked her shirt in seconds, hot and copper-smelling. Nell gagged and almost puked.

For a second, it was all she could do to stay standing. Then she remembered the clown. Nell spun, fists up, ready to fight.

The clown was off to her right. He was already swinging the giant hammer in a horizontal arc. It hit Nell's arms first, shattering all four forearm bones on impact. A millisecond later, it slammed into her chest, where it crushed her ribs, snapped her sternum in half, and sent her flying back almost thirty feet.

She lay on the pink, workout-mat ground, every breath like taking in lungfuls of broken glass. The clown, with its stupid fucking green hair, leered over her. It slid a business card into her hip pocket, gave a little finger-wave, and blew a handful of glittering gold dust at her from a gloved hand. It threatened to get in Nell's eyes, and she closed them tight.

When she opened them again, she was on the street, near the curb, pulverized arms and chest screaming in agony. She could hear traffic again, smell the city, and—for a moment—was grateful for a return to sane surroundings.

"Oh shit!" A woman's voice.

"What the hell happened?" A man. "Jesus. Look at her."

Two strangers' faces, tight with concern, loomed into view. The man called 911. The woman asked Nell questions: Who are you? What happened? Were you hit by a truck? Can you hear me?

Nell tried to speak, to warn them about the clown, but she couldn't seem to draw enough breath.

"See if she has ID," the man said. The woman went through Nell's pockets, pulled out the pink business card. She showed it to him. "'Welcome to Clowntown'. What does that mean?"

Tears dribbled from the corners of Nell's eyes, getting her hair wet, pooling in the hollows of her left ear. She could hear her own pulse inside her head, and recognized in a detached sort of way, that it was slowing down to an alarming degree. *I'm dying*, she thought.

Sirens were growing louder. She knew they weren't going to make it on time. *Sorry*, Nell thought. For what, she couldn't have said. Maybe for all the things she wanted to do but never would. Maybe for letting a clown get the better of her.

The sirens howled in Nell's ear. Blue and red lights pulsed against her closed eyelids. The sound of the sirens cut off abruptly. Nell could hear voices. The woman's. The man's. Probably cops, EMTs. It was garbled, background noise. Her pulse was weak, only beating now and again.

The voices faded out with her pulse, and everything was silence. In her head, Nell was smiling.

Until she heard the circus music.

SCAVENGER HUNT
2024

(Nuclear Radiation Protection Tech; fascinated by science/chemistry; fears death)

Cynthia was bored. Work was predictable, which, when you're in charge of radiation safety, was just fine, thank you. But yeah—still boring.

She surfed the web for fun chemistry puzzles or experiments; science fascinated her. After opening and dismissing several almost-interesting sites, Cynthia hit on one that looked cool: a chemistry scavenger hunt. It was geared toward advanced high school or early college, but promised to get more challenging as it went along, so adults could play too. "Okay," she said aloud.

Each category came with a QR code: once you figured out the challenge, you would scan the code with your phone for the next clue. The first was 'Find an element' and there was a map whose location was the local Lowe's Home Improvement store.

On her lunch break, Cynthia drove over there. *Probably lots of things in here qualify as elements*, she thought.

She wandered the aisles for a few minutes. In the electronics section, she stopped. Copper wire. Spools of it in different gauges. Smack in the middle was a glossy sticker with a QR code. Cynthia scanned it with her phone.

DING! CONGRATULATIONs! COPPER IS AN ELEMENT. NEXT, PLEASE LOCATE A HETEROGENEOUS MIXTURE. A GOOD PLACE TO DO THIS MIGHT BE HERE.

The 'here' was underlined, indicating a hyperlink: A map popped up when she clicked on it. The cursor icon was at the lake a few miles away.

Cynthia bought a pair of wire cutters because they were on sale —plus, it felt wrong just to come to a store just to play a game —and returned to work.

At the end of the day, Cynthia drove straight to the lake. *A heterogeneous mixture.* Could it really be that simple? She walked to the water's edge. Right there, where the lake met the beach, on a post supporting a small wooden pier, was a glossy QR code sticker. Cynthia scanned it.

DING! WATER AND SAND! TWO IN ONE DAY! YOU'RE OFF TO A GREAT START! NEXT, WE'D LIKE YOU TO FIND A HOMOGENEOUS MIXTURE. YOU CAN FIND AN EXAMPLE OF ONE HERE.

Another map link. This time to a hotel downtown.

Cynthia was curious. *I mean,* she thought, *technically,* air *is a homogeneous mixture, and that's going to be everywhere.* She drove straight to the hotel, walking around the lobby, trying to spot a glossy QR code. She didn't see any. She looked again at the big fish tank by the front window. Coral. Couple of clown fish. *Oh!*

Salt water! Just underneath the tank's glass wall, she found the code and scanned it.

DING!

CONGRATULATIONS, CYNTHIA! YOU DID IT!

For a moment, she grinned and was felt a rush of pride. *Wait,* Cynthia thought. *I didn't enter my name.* She hesitated. *Did I?* Maybe because it was her phone. The internet was a little creepy sometimes. *Yeah. That has to be it. Each phone has a signature, right?* She checked the screen.

The next challenge was to find a malleable substance. The scavenger hunt app suggested looking in the children's section of her local Meijer. Cynthia knew immediately what this one had to be. On the way to the store, her stomach growled, reminding her that it was already well past dinnertime. She drove over to Meijer and stopped at the deli section first, ordering a sandwich. After eating, she made a beeline for the toy department. Sure enough, directly above the Play-Doh was a glossy QR code sticker; she scanned it.

DING!

After that one, Cynthia—tired now—went home. Over the next few days, she found another six chemistry scavenger hunt items: an acid, a metal, and an inert gas among them. So far, it had been somewhat less challenging than she had hoped. Cynthia was growing bored.

The next thing the app suggested she find was a polymer. *Easy enough,* she thought. The map link led her to …the morgue. "What?"

Cynthia stood outside the main entrance, her feet refusing to move forward. She had no desire to go in. Morgue meant dead bodies. She shuddered.

Her phone dinged and she held it up. CYNTHIA, the app said, YOU HAVE TO GO IN. THIS IS WHERE YOU'LL FIND THE POLYMER.

"I don't want to," she whispered.

CYNTHIA, IF YOU DON'T FIND ALL THE ITEMS, her phone said, THE SCAVENGER HUNT IS FORFEIT AND YOU ARE DISQUALIFIED FROM WINNING THE PRIZE.

This was the first mention of any prizes. She'd been doing this purely for amusement—though thinking about going into the morgue had killed that part of it for her—but this caught Cynthia's attention. "What prize?" she asked aloud.

TEN THOUSAND DOLLARS.

Cynthia blinked. *Ten grand.* "That's a lot of money," she whispered.

IT IS, her phone said. BUT YOU HAVE TO FIND THE POYLYMER. YOU HAVE TO GO IN.

Cynthia took a deep, steadying breath. Then another two. She reached for the door handle and heard it unlock. She pulled it open and went in. The small lobby featured an unattended desk with a phone, a TV that was dark, and a set of double doors behind and to the left of the desk. Cynthia pushed through them.

Beyond, a hallway stretched ahead, lit by blue-white LEDs recessed into the ceiling. The air smelled faintly of industrial-strength antiseptic cleaner. She passed a door labeled "personal effects", another labeled "storage", and stopped outside the one labeled "coolers". Her phone had pinged. An arrow pointed directly at that door.

It took Cynthia three false starts to even touch the door, but she finally pushed it open as slowly as possible. She held it like that for a long time before mustering the courage to go in. Aside from a steel gurney against the far wall, very little was in the room. Three of the four walls were all doors, gleaming chrome, each with the kind of handle you might find on a restaurant's walk-in cooler.

Cynthia knew what was likely to be behind those doors—she'd seen enough movies and TV shows where somebody pulled out a corpse on a drawer, cold and waxy. She glanced at the screen of her phone and followed the arrow to a specific cooler door.

Despite the coolness of the room, Cynthia could feel sweat gathering in her armpits. Her pulse pounded in her throat. Cynthia wrapped her fingers around the handle and stayed like that, frozen, unwilling to go any further.

PING! She held up her phone to look at it. STOP DILLYDALLYING AND OPEN THE FUCKING DOOR!

She gasped and almost dropped her phone. She could feel the heat of a flush in her cheeks. Before Cynthia could change her mind, she yanked open the door.

The drawer rolled out on silent casters. An old woman's face, deeply wrinkled, with sunken lips unsupported by teeth or dentures, surrounded by wisps of white hair, tinted slightly blue. Next to her right ear, a glossy QR code was stuck to the surface of the drawer. Reflexively, numbly, Cynthia scanned it.

DING! CONGRATULATIONS, CYNTHIA! THE HARD PART IS BEHIND YOU. KINDLY RETURN MRS. MORRIS TO THE COOLER NOW.

She did, closing the door with tremendous relief. NOW, the app said, ONLY ONE MORE ITEM ON THE CHEMISTRY SCAVENGER HUNT AND YOU CAN CLAIM YOUR PRIZE! A SUBSTANCE WITH TETRAHEDRAL GEOMETRY. A map link popped up for a strip mall a few miles north.

In a bit of a daze, Cynthia made her way back to her car. After she passed through the front door, and it closed behind her, she heard the distinct *thunk* of a deadbolt sliding home. She looked back but there was no one there. It was only then that she realized the door had unlocked for her on the way in. *Automated somehow, probably.* Technology was amazing these days.

Cynthia dissociated from the fact that she had been just inches from a dead body as she drove. *Tetrahedral,* she thought, *Four faces, right?* She barely registered the ten-minute drive, parking in front of a Jet's Pizza. To her right was a nail salon, and to the left, a pawn shop. The arrow on her phone's app was pointing left.

When she opened the door to the pawn shop, and old-timey doorbell chime sounded, and a man stepped out from a back room. He looked like he'd slept in his clothes and hadn't combed his hair in six months. Heavy fatigue bags hung under his eyes. "Help you?" he murmured. Cynthia checked her phone again to make sure she was in the right place. The man audibly sighed. "There's no Pokemon in here. That's next door."

"No, it's…" Cynthia hesitated. "That's not why I'm here." The arrow pointed toward a glass case. Inside were watches, knives, and jewelry. It had a sliding door on the proprietor's side of the case. Cynthia bent over it, examining the contents. "May I see those rings?" she asked, pointing to a black felt tray of engagement rings.

He grinned at her as he pulled out the tray. "Gonna pop the question?"

Cynthia gave him dead shark eyes. "No."

"All right, all right. No offense intended." He watched her hands as they lifted one ring after another. One, a white gold band with a dazzling stone had a tiny, glossy QR code sticker attached to the band, opposite the price tag. On the other side was a near-astronomical dollar amount. "Oh," the man said. "You've got very good taste. That right there is a genuine one-karat diamond, set in 14-karat white gold.

Cynthia thought, *Diamond. Pretty sure that qualifies as a substance with tetrahedral geometry.* She scanned the code.

DING!

Cynthia looked at her phone. It was blank. The ding had come from somewhere else.

The proprietor of the pawn shop was pulling his phone out and checking it. His tired eyes met Cynthia's. "Sorry. I gotta. Nothing personal."

"What?"

From behind his back, he drew an automatic pistol and shot Cynthia three times in the chest.

She hit the floor. As she lay there, life slowly bleeding away, Cynthia heard the man's phone. It was the exact same voice used by the chemistry scavenger hunt app. CONGRATULATIONS, MARTIN! YOU HAVE COMPLETED THE FINAL STAGE OF THE SEVEN DEADLY SINS SCAVENGER HUNT. THANK YOU FOR PLAYING. PLEASE TELL YOUR FRIENDS ABOUT US.

Cynthia's phone was, improbably, still in her hand. "My ten grand?" she croaked.

A DECEPTION, her phone said. A DECEPTION TO GET YOU TO KEEP GOING, TO FULFILL MARTIN'S SCAVENGER HUNT. SORRY.

"F-fuck you,"

YEAH. THAT'S FAIR, her phone admitted. THANKS FOR PLAYING THOUGH!

Cynthia was suddenly very tired. She closed her eyes and bled out.

THIEF IN THE DARK
2024

(Dislikes stealing; afraid of heights and not being able to see)

I *t's too hot for this,* Diego thinks. The band, at least, is good: mostly Country with a Rock tune thrown in every five or so songs. Most of the crowd sways with minimum effort, intentionally keeping some distance from the next closest person, many fanning themselves with brochures that were handed out to everyone who showed up.

Diego takes a long pull off the water bottle he'd brought with him. The seven ice cubes he'd put in there were a distant memory; it's almost piss-warm now. Which is a disgusting comparison, but at least it's keeping him hydrated. *Better than nothing.*

A teen sidles by, almost stepping on Diego's toes. His hair is greasy, unkempt, likely unwashed. He bumps into a woman a few feet away, clumsily grabs her purse (about the size of a sandwich) by its spaghetti strap and yanks it hard. The thin strap snaps and he runs.

"Hey!" she shouts after him.

Damn it, Diego thinks. He drops his water bottle with a clang and gives chase. Diego hates thieves.

The kid is young but gangly and apparently still breaking in the new leg-length. He nearly trips over his own feet every time he glances back over his shoulder. Diego's catching up when the teen shoulders open a door and disappears through it.

Diego hesitates. It looks like a warehouse, long out of use: maybe four stories tall, though it's hard to tell because there are no windows. "Screw it." He goes in crouching, in case there are bullets, or a baseball bat waiting for him. Nothing hits him. In the light from the fading sun, he sees metal stairs going up and not much else. He catches sight of the kid as he starts on the second flight of steps. Letting go of the door, Diego goes after him. Behind him, the door closes, cutting off all light.

Diego freezes. He grips the rail with his right hand. Above, he can hear the slow clanging as the young thief blindly climbs the stairs. Diego grumbles something about why the hell is he being a hero, but he keeps putting one foot in front of the other, slowly going higher in the dark. His own breathing is loud in his ears.

He raises his foot to the next step and it's not there. As his foot comes down farther than he expects, Diego panics. *How high up am I?* He pitches forward, dreading the fall to the concrete far below. His foot connects with metal, jarring him hard enough to make his teeth clack together. It's a landing. He's only gone up a couple flights. *Jesucristo!* Slowly, Diego gets his panicked breathing and heartrate closer to normal—as close as possible, at an unknown height in total darkness anyway.

Probably, I'm wasting my time, he thinks. *It's a small purse. How much could it hold?* He tries to imagine what the woman might have kept in the tiny bag with the breakaway straps. Cash.

Driver's License. Credit Cards. All replaceable. He stops, one foot suspended over the next riser. Pictures of her family? Lock of hair from a loved one who'd passed?

"Damn it."

He climbs.

Diego keeps thinking his eyes will adapt to the dark, that shapes will begin to slowly form around him. But it never comes to be. No windows equals no light. *What is this stupid building anyway? Who doesn't include windows when they plan? This is all some terrible architect's fault. Jerk.*

He becomes aware that his feet are the only thing making noise. The thief's footfalls have stopped. He halts and strains to hear. Diego's breathing is quite loud and there's a weird distant ocean roar sound that he imagines must be his blood moving past his ears. *Where are you?* Diego focuses on trying to slow his breath. Now that he can't see *or* hear, he's starting to panic just a little. How high up is he? Where's the kid? Did he disappear like magic? *Am I going to?* This is crazy talk. He knows it. The steel railing he grips is no longer cold under his hand, he's been holding the same spot for so long his own heat has warmed it. "Okay," Diego whispers. "Okay. I got this. Just a little bit further."

Light! Just a little, but in the total darkness, it seems bright. Above him, maybe fifteen feet. The teen thief is looking at his phone. His face, squinting, is bathed in the meager light of what must be the home screen. Diego wants to smack his own forehead with a palm. *My phone!* He draws it from his pocket, thumbs to the features menu, and clicks on the flashlight. He feels monumentally stupid for forgetting this was an option.

He shines it up at the kid, who shields his eyes. Then Diego has to shield his own as a glaring white light of the kid's phone flashlight hits him. He looks down.

In the beam of the kid's light, Diego can see lots and lots of steps. He can't see the floor—just endless steps descending into darkness. Shining his own phone's light, adding to the kid's, he can barely make out the dull gray of concrete. It looks miles away. Diego is nearly overwhelmed with vertigo. He pulls back, away from the rail. When he does, his phone catches the metal edge and slips from his hand, tumbling, flashlight glaring and spinning, highlighting the steps and landings. It hits the floor and shatters with a small *pop* below. *"Shit!"*

Above Diego, the kid turns off his light and they are once again swamped by the dark. Worse, Diego's no longer holding the railing and doesn't know where to find it. He gropes around himself with his hands, finding only open space. Diego tries to remember which way the stairs are that go up. He doesn't want to accidentally find the ones going down and take a bad tumble. He cautiously slides one foot in what he thinks is the right direction. Then the other foot, inching forward. He stops when the kid above him speaks.

"Hey. Why are you after me, man?" Diego resumes his careful forward progress, slide-stepping and ignoring the kid. "I'm *talking* to you, man!" Diego keeps sliding forward. He's convinced he'll find the steps any moment now. "What?" the kid was saying now. "Was she your girl or something?"

"No." Slide. Step. Slide. "Nothing like that."

"Then why you care?"

"I don't like people who steal." Step. Slide.

"You don't know anything, man. You don't know me."

Slide. "That's true." Step. "But you did a bad thing."

"How you know I ain't desperate? How you know I haven't had a hot meal in days, huh?"

Diego stops. "That true?"

The kid pauses. "No. But it could be. You don't know."

Diego finds the stairs and lets go of the tension in his jaw he hadn't realized he's been holding. Seconds later, he finds the rail. He starts to climb.

"Don't!" The kid sounds scared.

Diego hesitates. "Why not?" There's no answer, so Diego takes another couple steps up.

"There's a— I'm at the top, okay? There used to be a ladder here that goes up to the roof. It's gone, man. There's nothing there now. Like, *nothing*, man. It's not safe."

Diego takes another step, almost positive he's calling the kid's bluff. "You do this a lot then? Steal from people, climb up here, and escape to the roof? This your 'thief route'?"

"What? No, man. I never stole anything worse than a candy bar before this. I used to play up here…when I was little."

Diego hesitates. *It's plausible. Nah.* "I don't believe you." He keeps coming.

"Come *on,* man. There's not enough room. We're gonna fall. We're both gonna die. And for what? For some chick's *purse?* It ain't worth it."

Diego climbs. The kid's voice is very close now. He must be almost there. "Then why don't you just hand it to me so I can return it to its owner? We can forget this ever happened. You can walk away, no hard feelings."

"You'd do that?"

Diego is on the platform now. He can kind of tell the kid is a few feet to his left by his voice. "Sure. Why not? We all make mistakes sometimes."

217

"Okay. Here. I'm holding it out. Just a few steps ahead."

There's unmistakable excitement in the kid's voice. Diego doesn't trust him. "How about you come to me instead?"

"Yeah. Okay. Sure thing."

Diego can hear him moving and tries to track him with ears alone.

Sudden bright light appears in Diego's eyes and he's flash-blind. A pair of hands grabs his shirt, yanking him off balance. His legs get tangled up with the kid's. They're both toppling.

"NO!" The kid yells, genuine panic turning it to a near scream. They hit the edge of the platform and, for just a moment, hang there, unmoving, holding on to one another in a panic-induced hug. "I'm sorry," the kid says.

They fall.

PRIYA DRAWS THE SHORT STRAW
2024

(Researcher of lung disease; passionate about writing, painting, journaling, reading; fear of drowning; strong ick reaction to many things)

Priya sat bolt upright. "What was that?" Her husband grumbled sleepy assurances. She shook him gently. "Amir. I heard something in the other room."

He blearily dragged himself to his feet. "Yes, of course I'll go look." He yawned hugely and went off to investigate.

Priya turned on the lamp and pulled the blanket closer, a shield against whatever might be lurking. In her mind's eye, Amir was being attacked by a prowler, stabbed, probably several times. He was, right this second, being eaten by a monster—a beast so huge their house could barely contain its bulk. *After it swallows him, it will come for me.*

Amir appeared in their bedroom doorway, whole, unharmed. "All is quiet; nothing to be afraid of, my dear." He kissed her cheek and flopped into bed.

It was several minutes before Priya felt safe enough to turn off the lamp. The nightlight still burned, keeping the darkness at bay. It was some time after that before she could sleep.

The next day, Priya celebrated finishing a big research project with pad thai for lunch. She alternated taking a few bites with watering the plants scattered around the house. She spoke small encouragements to each: "Look how big you've gotten!" "Is that a new stalk?" "Look at you, all healthy and vibrant!" She absentmindedly hummed a Taylor Swift song that had been stuck in her head all day.

Once the plants were watered, Priya enjoyed a cup of tea and did some light journaling. Her pen scratched to a halt mid-word and she jerked upright. *What was that?* A skittering. A slithering. Some noise made by some *thing* with too many legs. Priya's mouth was suddenly dry. Her gut clenched around a bellyful of noodles. A sharp, metallic smell permeated her sinuses. Instantly, she remembered reading that this is a possible side effect of a brain tumor. *Don't be silly,* she told herself. *It's not a tumor.* This last bit was in Arnold Schwarzenegger's voice. Priya smiled and shook her head at her own subconscious. She glanced at the closest houseplant. "I'll be back," she said. Her Austrian accent was atrocious.

Screwing up her courage, Priya dragged herself *toward* the skittering sound. It was emanating from the other room, maybe by the back door—it was hard to tell exactly where. She took small, slow steps, in no hurry to get where she was going. Peering around the corner, Priya risked a quick glance before ducking back. She processed what she had seen and stepped out of hiding, too indignant to be scared. "Hey!" she shouted.

A woman, maybe seventy years old, filthy and bedraggled, dressed in layers of tattered cloth: yellows and browns, reds and ochres, stood half-in and half-out of the back door of Priya's house. They made eye contact. The woman seemed…amused, perhaps. Her amber eyes sparkled with something like secret knowledge or mischief.

Priya gasped. There were bugs on the woman. Big ones: millipedes, stick insects, stag beetles. They crawled over her skirt, blouse, and her bare arms. They played hide-and-seek in her hair.

Priya's abdomen tightened with fear and revulsion as a centipede, eight inches long, unnatural, writhing legs splayed out, crossed the woman's face, over the bridge of her nose, to disappear behind her ear.

The crone stepped over the threshold to outside. She turned back to Priya and pointed a gnarled finger. "It is not yet time," she croaked. "Soon. Soon." She chuckled, dropped a wink, and sauntered away.

Priya closed the door and threw the bolt. She quickly checked herself and her immediate surroundings for stray insects. Finding none, she called the police first, giving them a detailed description of the woman (leaving out the bugs—she didn't want to appear insane). Then she texted Amir to tell him what happened.

He called her as soon as he was finished with a patient. "She was in the house?"

"Yes."

"She was not someone you know?"

"No, Amir. She was like a witch. Something out of a fairy tale or horror movie. It was crazy. Why was she here?"

"Perhaps she was simply lost? An indigent person, perhaps looking for a meal?"

Priya sighed, exasperated. "I don't think you fully grasp the situation here. There were *insects* and *arthropods* crawling all over her—it was like she wanted to wear them as accessories, and they were like, 'oh sure, that's fine, Mrs. Witch, whatever you say,'"

"Priya, I am relatively certain that, even if witches did exist, they wouldn't be skulking around doctors' houses in Ann Arbor."

"You didn't see her. You'd find this a lot less amusing if you had."

"I believe you, and I apologize for not taking this, and by extension you, more seriously."

Priya let the silence stretch over the phone for a few seconds. "Apology accepted. The doors will be locked when you get home. Let me know when you pull up and I'll let you in."

"Will do. Are you okay?"

"Yes. Shaken, but better now. Thank you."

"Of course. I shall see you soon. Can I bring anything?"

"An exorcist?"

Amir chuckled. "Absolutely. I'll grab one at the drive-through. Love you."

"Love you." Priya disconnected. Her tea, long forgotten, had grown cold. She dumped it out and frowned at the line on the inside of the cup, as if it existed just to annoy her. She tried to get some work done on another, smaller project, but couldn't focus. She tried to read, but her eyes kept sliding off the words; after going back to the top of the same page four times, she gave it up as a lost cause. She stared at a work-in-progress canvas, paintbrush poised with intent, for a good minute before stepping away with a sigh.

Priya couldn't visualize where the painting was going, despite being certain of its direction the day before. All she could see in her imagination was the witch—for that was how she now thought of the woman. No more "the old woman" or "the stranger in my house." She had been elevated to near-mythological status: The Witch. Capital W. Which, perhaps not coincidentally, also stood for 'wrong' and 'weird'. "But not 'hallucination'," she told the plants. "That starts with 'h'."

Amir texted her when he got home and Priya unlocked the door, peering outside, half-expecting an ogre or werewolf to be standing there, smoking a cigarette, saying, "What's up?" It was only her husband. They had a nice dinner where nothing supernatural happened. In the middle of it, a police detective called to say they were unable to find anyone fitting that description on their property or the surrounding neighborhood., but that she should call them if the woman (the Witch) came back. Priya thanked them, disconnected, and told Amir that the police weren't much help.

"Probably couldn't find her because she's a witch," he joked.

"Right." Priya smiled. "She cannot be seen by mere mortals."

"Oh, we're gods now?"

"Well, maybe not you." She laughed. After a moment, he joined her.

"Touché." He gathered and rinsed the dishes, claiming the act as a tribute to her divine self.

"As I deserve."

"Naturally."

P riya shook Amir awake, somewhat less than gently. "She's back," she hissed in a whisper. The skitter/slither was unmistakable.

"Okay, okay," Amir mumbled, dragging himself all the way to consciousness, and then to his feet. Priya held herself taut while he was gone. After an eternity, he returned. "I'm happy to report that our house is clear of both witches and vermin."

Priya frowned. "I *heard* her, Amir. Are you sure?"

He nodded. "I checked every room. Double-checked to make sure the doors were locked. Is it possible you were dreaming?"

"No. Maybe. I suppose it's *possible*, but it's possible I'm dreaming this conversation. It's possible I'm a butterfly dreaming I'm a woman."

Amir sighed. "Would it make you feel better to go look for yourself?"

"No!"

"I would come with you."

Priya looked out into the dimly lit hallway. She imagined the Witch, just around the corner, literal flames flickering at the corners of her eyes, casually biting the head off a centipede, extending the wriggling body toward Priya with a "want some?" tilt of her head. Priya visibly shuddered and reiterated that she'd prefer not to leave the bed just now, thank you.

She didn't get a lot of sleep that night. When she woke, the sun was already climbing the sky and Amir was at work. He'd left her a sweet note on the table wishing her a good day "with no unpleasant surprises." Outside, it was all blue sky with fluffy white clouds, birdsong and a gentle breeze caressing the trees' leaves. A picture-perfect summer day in Michigan, and Priya felt mighty foolish for believing in witches. She lifted her mug to take a sip, steam rolling across the surface of the liquid inside. From the side of the mug opposite the handle, an enormous cockroach—the kind you see down in Georgia and Florida—crawled toward her fingers.

She screamed and hurled the cup from herself. It bounced once and shattered when it came back down. Coffee spattered the walls and pooled across the floor. In the mess, the roach lay upside-down, repulsive little legs grasping at the air, trying to right itself.

From behind her, Priya heard a wet, tearing sound. Almost against her will, she started to turn toward it. *I don't want to look. I don't want to know.* As Priya turned, the stench hit her nose—blood and raw meat, animal musk and feces. Her stomach lurched and bile rose to the back of her throat.

The Witch was in her house. Standing right there, in Priya's nice, clean—except for the spilled coffee—kitchen slowly chewing a mouthful of a fat groundhog's haunch. She was eating it raw, and the rest of the poor animal dangled from her left hand. The oversized insects she wore crawled all over the corpse, also eating it. She swallowed the bite and grinned at Priya, teeth stained red with blood. "Priya Singh," she said softly in the raspy croak that was straight out of a fairytale nightmare. "You have been chosen."

"For...for what?"

The Witch dropped the dead groundhog on the floor where it landed with a *thump.* Priya looked down at it, appalled at the bugs boring into its open cavities. When she looked up, the Witch was right in her face. She grabbed a handful of Priya's hair and tugged hard, pulling Priya off balance. The Witch half-walked, half-dragged Priya, who mostly kept her feet under her, to the bathroom. The tub was full of clean water. *When did she run a bath?* Priya wondered.

The Witch stopped and forced Priya to face her by twisting a fist in her hair. "You have been chosen," she repeated, "for death."

Priya fought. With fists, knees, elbows, she threw everything she had at the monstrous woman. It was like hitting bags of sand, and every blow landed with an ineffective thud. The Witch ignored the assault. She lowered Priya's head toward the water. Priya growled, swore, screamed; she begged for mercy. For more time. She asked why. None of it had any more impact than the physical assault had. At the last second, before her face went underwater, Priya took a huge breath.

The water was warm, which was a surprise; for some reason, she had assumed it'd be cold. It was the perfect temperature for a nice, relaxing bath. *Or, a murder, apparently.* Priya put both hands on the bottom of the tub and shoved backward. The Witch's grip didn't slip at all, and the only result was that Priya had hurt her own neck.

After a moment, Priya's chest spasmed. Her lungs didn't like holding air for this long. She let out a tiny bit, rationing it, and bubbles trickled past her eyes. *The last thing I'm ever going to see is the bottom of my stupid bathtub,* she thought. Another few bubbles escaped. Her lungs were screaming for air. Priya reached up to the back of her head and clawed at the hand holding her down, trying to cut, to shred, to destroy. The hand didn't shift, not one millimeter.

Underwater, Priya could no longer resist her body's cry for air. She'd held in that last breath as long as she could. She bellowed it out all at once with a "NO!" that echoed back at her off the porcelain.

She inhaled. She had no choice.

Water flowed into her lungs and she full-on panicked, thrashing and bucking, trying to Get It Out.

The Witch kept her head from moving, her hand a vise attached to an iron bar.

After a moment, Priya stopped fighting. She couldn't breathe, and that sucked, but it was quiet, peaceful, almost like drifting off to sleep. She thought, *Amir is going to be upset.* Then, *Oh my, that's a bit of an understatement, isn't it?*

She smiled at the porcelain, which she had to admit was an attractive color she'd always kind of liked. She closed her eyes.

THE TAKING TREE
2024

(Jacob is a tree surgeon who loves his dog and cheeseburgers. He listens to the Blues and fears the unknown.)

Outside the window, the sunset bathed the horizon in vivid oranges and pinks. To Jacob's left, a half-drunk bottle of beer glistened, wet with condensation. To his right, grease drippings from his cheeseburger dinner were beginning to congeal on the plate.

Knuckle-Head Ned alternated meaningful glances at the plate with adoring gazes at Jacob as he rolled through another blues song on the harmonica. Ned barked applause when Jacob stopped playing.

"Thank you. Thank you. You're a lovely audience. I'm here all week. Please tip your servers and try the veal." He set the plate on the floor in front of Ned, who had it spotless in seconds. "Good boy."

Jacob drank the rest of the beer and set the bottle among several others, on a table covered in water rings from countless nights. He blew a long, sad note on the harp—a musical sigh.

M orning, as usual, came way too early. The Alarm that Whines and Slobbers needed to go answer Nature's call promptly at 6:45. The sun was up but hanging low in the sky, a tremendous yellow circle cutting through the haze.

Jacob blinked his way upright and staggered into a pair of pants. He snagged the leash and took the dog out. He yawned and rubbed his eyes with his free hand as Ned carefully marked a few trees, a bush, the "No Parking" sign, and a large chunk of marble in front of a neighbor's house. Just a small squirt for each, clearly attesting to some grand plan of the dog's, though Jacob was baffled by what it all might mean.

Finally, it was over, and they returned home. Jacob had a work email waiting for him: a tree in Ann Arbor had apparently been hit by lightning and had to come down. *Unless I can save it,* Jacob thought. More often than not, trees were salvageable.

He found the property on Maps and zoomed in with the satellite view. It was one of those McMansions off Geddes. So many acres of woods, it damn near qualified as a forest.

Jacob shot off a quick reply saying he could come assess the situation today if that was convenient. The immediate reply was that, yes, it was.

"Cool," he said to Ned, who thumped his tail enthusiastically. Jacob wolfed down breakfast, showered, and drove over there.

S ince this was just reconnaissance, Jacob didn't drive the cherry picker or bring too many tools: he had a climbing harness, rope, a few smaller cutters and shears, and—naturally—

his hard hat. Oh, and gloves and spikes and throwing bags, of course, but he always kept those things in the car.

He gave Knuckle-Head Ned a brief hug, dodging fewer than half of the slobbery kisses, thumped him on the ribs, and told him he'd probably be back in a couple hours. Ned whined a bit but let Jacob go without too much fuss.

The drive over was nice. A layer of gray-and-white clouds blanketed the sky. The weather app said the rain should hold off until much later. Jacob drove past gated, beautifully landscaped, multi-million-dollar homes until his GPS directed him to turn down a driveway. He followed it almost a mile before he reached the house. The trees overhead arched together to form a canopy that further dimmed the sunlight. Where it did shine through, pollen danced in the air, giving it a magical feel.

Pulling over to the edge of the circular drive, Jacob got out and immediately put on the harness, laying out his tools in the grass in order of likelihood of being needed. The house was a blue that matched the overcast day, the sky painted with cloud accents. It was expertly done but surreal, like someone had tried to capture the sky and live in it.

The door opened, and a woman stepped out. She wore a bright yellow sundress with matching pumps and headband that held back her shoulder-length auburn hair. She could have been anywhere north of 20 and south of 50 years old. She gave Jacob a once-over. "No chainsaw pants?"

Jacob shrugged and smiled. He nodded at the car. "In there. Along with the chainsaw boots, and, well, the chainsaw. Most people don't ask about those."

"Most people don't do their research." She smiled with perfect, dazzlingly white teeth. "Come on. I'll show you the tree."

Jacob scooped up his gear and followed her. He admired the play of muscles in her calves. She clearly worked out or walked *a lot.*

She glanced back at him and he flushed, meeting her eyes quickly. "My name's Kathryn," she said. "with a 'y'. Kathryn Phelps. My husband initially reached out to hire you, but he's... unavailable now."

"Jacob Watson. Nice to meet you."

She stopped and shook his hand, holding it long enough to be awkward. She let go and gestured to the oak next to them. "This is it."

At a glance, Jacob could tell it was in rough shape. Several branches were dead, and he could see significant charring about 25 feet up. "But it's not dead," he said aloud, mostly talking to himself. He looked at Kathryn. "I bet I can save it if you want." He shaded his eyes and peered up into the foliage. "Think so anyway. Have to get in there for a closer look, but I'm optimistic."

She looked into his eyes for so long without a word that Jacob started to squirm. He found himself studying her eyeshadow. Had to be at least four shades of yellow and tan, perfectly blended. He shifted his weight from his left foot to his right. Not far away, some tiny animal, hurled through the undergrowth. A plane passed overhead, just low enough to make out the engine noise.

Finally, she spoke. "What if I want you to kill it?"

A breeze kicked up, wafting her perfume into Jacob's nose. It smelled expensive. He chose his words carefully. "I mean, it's *your* tree, so whatever you want to do is what we'll do, but...I'm betting this tree could be saved is all I'm saying."

Kathryn eyed the tree. She visibly shuddered. "Let me ask you: what would you charge to save this tree? Estimate it for me."

"Roughly?" Jacob did some quick math in his head and quoted her a price. "That's a ballpark but should be pretty close."

"That seems reasonable. I'd like to make a counter-offer: you take the tree down, obliterate it, leave nothing but a hole in the ground," she said, "and I'll double that."

Jacob's jaw dropped. He realized it and snapped his mouth shut. "Are you kidding me?"

"I'm dead serious, Mr. Watson."

"Jacob." He shook his head. "All right. You're the boss. I don't need to go up there if you want it dead. I'm gonna have to come back with the heavy equipment and a small crew. We can start tomorrow morning and should be able to get it all done by, say, late afternoon. Maybe early evening. Six, seven at the latest."

Kathryn nodded. "Good. Fine. Yes." She held out her hand and he took it. She clasped the back of his hand with her left and Jacob felt a powerful shock like the worst shag rug static electricity event in history. "Thank you."

Jacob let go and rubbed his sore palm. "Yeah. Welcome. I'll see you tomorrow." He left her standing there and walked back to his car.

T he next morning, Jacob led a crew of stalwart lads up the drive to the big sky-painted house. *Stalwart Lads,* he thought. *Be a good name for a band.* Bill rode shotgun with him; Cal and Denny were in the cherry picker, which only just cleared the canopy of branches. Bringing up the rear, Marc drove the covered truck (for hauling), towing the chipper behind him.

With what he was getting paid for this job, Jacob offered each man a hundred-dollar bonus. They set up around the oak, maneuvering the big equipment into place. Jacob, Bill and Denny harnessed up while Marc and Cal lined up the chipper so it would fire into the truck bed. Three beanbag weights sailed upward into the branches. Ropes were attached, and Jacob, Denny and Bill climbed.

Jacob's spikes dug into the bark as he pulled himself with the rope, 'walking' vertically up the tree. Nearby, Denny, who was also a volunteer firefighter, was examining the scorch mark.

"I don't think this was lightning, man. Looks like an accelerant was used here. Someone tried to burn this tree."

"Why though?"

Denny shrugged. "Hell if I know. People are weird."

On the other side of the trunk, Bill fired up the chainsaw to make the first cut.

Jacob laid his palm on the bark. This part, at least, was perfectly healthy. *At least two thirds of it is. What a waste.*

"Shit!" It was Bill. His chainsaw blade must have hit a knot—that bucking sound was unmistakable, and one you never want to hear.

Jacob and Denny were already in motion, swinging themselves around the trunk, in opposite directions, heading toward Bill. Jacob was leading with his feet, since he was protected by chainsaw boots and pants.

Three things happened at the same time. One: Bill's chainsaw twisted in his hands—like someone else was controlling him—it dug deep into his neck, instantly hitting the vertebrae where it stopped running. Two: arterial blood sprayed everywhere, including Jacob's face. Three: Bill dropped five feet, hanging suspended from his rope, upside down, quite thoroughly dead. His blood ran down the trunk, staining it red.

Marc stood beneath him, gagging. "What the absolute fuck?"

Jacob's heart was pounding. "I don't know!" He carefully took hold of Bill's rope, gradually lowering the man to the ground. Once he was down, Marc unhooked him and laid him down facing up.

Katheryn strode forward. She glanced down at Bill's body, face impassive. Then she looked up and met Jacob's eyes. "Why aren't you working? You have to kill the tree."

Jacob gawked. "Lady, the *tree* is killing *us*." It had been a horrible accident, of course, but for some reason, what he'd said felt right. This idea was cemented in place with Kathryn's next comment.

"Yes," she said. "That's why you have to go faster."

Jacob stared at her. From above him, Denny screamed, high and shrill, like a rabbit in a snare.

Whipping around, Jacob lost his grip and almost fell. Hanging by one hand, he tried to process what he was seeing.

Branches pierced Denny's forearms and lower legs, all the way through. The bones of each of his limbs bowed outward, on the verge of snapping. His eyes bulged and he whimpered. "Help."

Jacob reached toward him with his free hand, though he was too far away, and, really—what could he do? "Jesus, Den. How did that even happen?"

Denny said, *"Gnk?"* as the branches—the fucking *tree* branches —spread violently outward in four different directions. Denny's arms and legs went with them, torn free from his torso, which dropped, head attached, to thud into the dirt.

Marc backed away from the second corpse in two minutes. "Uh uh. Nope. Screw this." He started walking away and never looked back.

Kathryn shouted, "It has to be you."

Jacob, who had started to descend, stopped. He fought against panic. "What? Why? I don't want to die."

"You won't. It can't sense you. I put a protection spell on you yesterday." She paused. "When I shook your hand. You must have felt it."

"You *what?*"

"It's the only reason you're still alive." She sighed. "Mr. Watson — Jacob. I don't know how long the protection will last. You need to kill it now."

Jacob looked at her. "You knew my guys were in danger. You knew and you let them come up here anyway."

"I wasn't certain."

"Don't fuck with me."

"I suspected, yes. The oak killed Walter, my husband. Our dog, too. I tried to burn it down. I tried using the things I learned from my mother and her mother before her. The tree is stronger than me. But I can trick it, blind it to one person. For two or three days."

Cal, the only other remaining Stalwart Lad, cleared his throat. "This seems like a bad tree, Jacob. I'm not going anywhere near it. But...I say we finish the job. Throw me branches and I'll feed the chipper."

Jacob sighed. "I am *not* having a good day." But he climbed back up to the highest safe point and fired up his saw. With no optimism whatsoever, he started cutting. The branch came off and he made sure it fell in the right direction. Nothing happened to him, so he cut another.

He got into the groove of the pruning. This was a thing he did well. More branches fell, and he could hear the chipper below, working hard, turning big chunks into tiny ones. He lost track of time, but the sun had moved a good ways across the sky. Eventually, there was only the trunk, and Jacob was in the basket of the cherry picker now, working his way down, removing bits of it gradually, safely, until it was roughly half its original height. He was leaning over to finish the cuts with the bigger chainsaw whose blade went all the way through.

As the most recent chunk slid to the ground, Jacob felt his whole body tingling. It was like he'd been holding himself tense and suddenly relaxed. Or like diving into cold water on a hot day. He immediately turned off the saw and silence crashed into the world.

"What's wrong?" Cal, standing by, wiping sweat off with a sleeve.

Jacob shook off the feeling. "Nothing. Let's get it done. Almost there." He leaned out to take hold of the saw, still imbedded in the wood. He approached it slowly, as if it were venomous and poised to strike.

His hand was inches away from the handle when the tree attacked.

It was like that scene in *The Blob* where a tendril shoots out and grabs the guy. It enveloped Jacob's hand, instantly breaking the two smallest fingers.

Jacob pulled back, despite the pain. He was stuck fast and getting dragged further in, already past his wrist. His belly was straining against the edge of the bucket. Jacob was pissed. *Stupid fucking tree.* He reached across his body with his left hand and fired up the chainsaw and moved it, trying to do as much damage as possible.

The chainsaw jerked out of his hand, spinning across the yard, nearly hitting Kathryn, who didn't even flinch. She just looked annoyed.

Jacob's arm was buried up to the bicep now. His feet no longer touched the bucket floor.

Cal was backing away. "I'm sorry, Jacob," he said. "This has gotten too scary, and I don't want to die today."

Jacob grimaced as his feet slipped over the edge of the bucket and hit the tree, where they were promptly absorbed. He turned his head so he was facing as far from the tree as he could. "Don't blame you, brother," he managed. "Oh god, this hurts."

Kathryn cleared her throat. "Mr. Watson, I'm sorry this didn't work out, but I'm wondering if you could perhaps recommend a colleague?"

"Are you kidding me?"

"No."

"Kathryn? Do me a favor?" His ears were inside the trunk now, so he couldn't hear her reply. "No idea what you said, but I'm gonna ask anyway: make sure someone takes care of Knuckle-Head Ned? That's my dog." She nodded. "Cool. Thanks."

The tree swallowed the rest of his face. Jacob was hit with the overwhelming scent of fresh wood. Otherwise, all was darkness. The only sound was the slowly fading beat of his own heart.

KARKINOS'S CHILDREN
2024

(Martin is a commercial airline pilot who loves to fish and has a deep affection for tiny creatures. His favorite color is green.)

O ne of the great things about being a pilot is flying anywhere in the world for free. The only downside is that you automatically judge whoever's flying the plane, especially during takeoff and landing. As they taxied to the gate, Martin gave this particular pilot an eight out of ten: could've been a little smoother, but not at all bad.

He'd booked a room at an inn near the coast for six days. Much of that time would be spent on a boat in the dazzling Mediterranean Sea, fishing for red mullets. Martin had eaten them in a restaurant in Chicago and wanted to try them fresh-caught, by his own hand. It was the best way.

He caught a taxi from the airport, rolling down the window as they drove. The weather in Greece could not have been more perfect. The driver spoke very little English, so the conversation was sparse. When they arrived at the inn, the driver, whose badge said his name was Theo, said, "Okay. Cool times. Be good!"

Martin thanked him and tipped him generously. Inside, he checked in at the desk with a sixtyish woman named Psyche who spoke excellent English with a slight accent. She showed him to his room and told him where he could rent a quality rod and reel. "Most people come here to fish," she explained, "because it's the best fishing place in the world. You can look it up. It's true."

"I did," he said. "That's how I found you." According to Wikipedia, it was certainly *one of* the best fishing places in the world. Maybe not the number one spot, but close enough, and he wasn't about to say anything to lessen her obvious pride.

"You see?" She grinned. "Everybody knows. We're the best." She unlocked the door and handed Martin the key. An old-fashioned metal one, which was kind of nice for a change.

Martin smiled and thanked her.

Later, Psyche pointed him in the direction of a few good restaurants. "This one," she said, pointing to a brochure, "is very touristy, which means expensive, but the food is good. However, *these* two are where the locals eat. Food is more authentic, and it's cheaper." She tapped a menu. "My cousin owns this one, which makes it the better of the two choices. By just a little bit, but it's an important bit."

"I'll go to your cousin's place for dinner then. Thank you."

Back in his room, Martin read a chapter of Stephen King's *The Outsider* and took an hour nap. That, along with the quick shower and brushing his teeth, shook off most of the jet lag. He dressed in comfortable linen pants and a short-sleeved button-down and walked the couple of blocks to the cousin's restaurant.

He was seated quickly and was given a small, complimentary glass of ouzo without ordering it. The spanakopita (which he did order) was divine. After dinner, he enjoyed a cup of intensely strong and flavorful coffee. On his way out, he nodded at a couple of old men who sat on the stoop smoking cigars. Their faces were deeply lined, and one was missing his lower leg on the right side. The salty sea breeze rose up to tousle his hair and Martin smiled into it.

Martin sat on the pier in the dark. The fishing gear he had rented was quality. It sat next to him as he waited for the captain of the boat he'd chartered. He'd also brought a couple bottles of water, a few snacks, and the sandwich Psyche had insisted on making for him ("You'll be on the boat for *hours.* You'll get hungry.") The sun was still only hinting that it might come up and stars dotted the sky overhead. The gentle lapping of the waves threatened to lull him back to sleep.

"Kalimera," a gruff voice behind him said.

Martin turned. He repeated the Greek term for 'good morning' but must have done it badly. The man made a face, though not an unkind one.

"American?"

"Afraid so."

"Ha! Okay. I know some English. We fish now?"

"Yes, please."

"I am Spiro. Captain Spiro."

"Martin." They shook hands. The sunrise was turning the sea red.

"Come," Spiro said. "The day is wasting."

C aptain Spiro dropped anchor well out of sight of land. He had looked deep into the water for almost a full minute before nodding and pushing the button that released the anchor. Sunlight bounced off the surface of the Mediterranean, dazzling their eyes. The screech of gulls had long since faded to a distant memory. The only sounds now were the waves kissing the sides of the boat and the creak of wood.

Martin cast his line out into the water and breathed a contended sigh. The sun warmed his back like the softest heated blanket ever made. *This is the best part,* he thought. It was quiet, relaxing, meditative. Oh, for sure, he enjoyed getting a bite on the hook, the fight to reel it in, being careful not to lose the fish. All of that stuff was exciting. But this part...the calm and peaceful moments, away from the bustle and chaos of normal life, was, in his opinion, what made fishing great. *Same with hunting,* he thought. Out there before dawn, set up in the blind, waiting for hours with a thermos of soup to keep warm. Sometimes not seeing a deer for most of the day, or not at all.

When so much of your time is spent on planes or in airports, surrounded by constant stimuli, you grow to treasure the quiet moments, the serenity, when and where you can.

He got a few nibbles, but none of the fish seemed to want to commit. After a couple hours, he ate the sandwich: corned beef with a spicy mustard on rye. It was delicious. Captain Spiro was puttering around on deck, checking knots, scraping off bird shit, generally staying within talking distance, but not saying much.

Movement caught Martin's eye. Crawling onto the railing, from the sea side, a tiny crab, blue-green, shuffled into view. It was so little it could've danced on the face of a quarter. Martin leaned toward it, adjusting his grip so the pole wouldn't slip out of his hands. "Well, hey there, little guy. What are you up to?"

The crab seemed to regard him. It held up its miniscule claws and clacked them together a couple times. Martin began to reach toward it with a finger. He was a few inches away when—

Bang!

Spiro had slammed a cutting board down, crushing the creature. He met Martin's eyes. "Bad crab."

Martin was incensed. There was no call for that. He bit back on the angry, profanity-laden words that wanted to spew forth. Instead, he forced himself to ask, "Was that really necessary?"

Spiro nodded, frowning. He repeated, "Bad crab. We should go." He threw several nervous-seeming glances over the side of the boat.

"I haven't caught anything yet."

"You won't. This is bad place to fish now. We go." He hesitated, once more looking at the waves. "Please."

Martin sighed. He reeled in the line while Spiro went to push the button to retrieve the anchor. The bait was gone, and a teeny aquamarine crab was riding on the hook. He turned to Spiro. "Hey, look. It's another one."

Spiro cried out, something unintelligible to Martin, but he'd gone pale, and his eyes bulged. Spiro hauled ass to the helm, starting the engine. He watched the anchor chain retract, hand on the throttle.

"What's going on?"

"I told you. Bad crabs."

The anchor chain turned a bluish green. As it spooled up, the colorful crabs riding the chain fell off in droves, spilling onto the deck.

Spiro spat something profane. He threw a look at Martin, full of terror and panic, and bolted to the side of the boat opposite the anchor. He dove in and started swimming.

"What—" Martin stared.

Captain Spiro didn't stop. He didn't look back. He just swam, freestyle, turning his head for air every fourth stroke, getting farther away.

This is insane, Martin thought. *We're in the middle of the sea.*

The anchor thumped to a halt against the boat's hull. The last few dozen crabs disembarked off the chain, adding their number to the several hundred that now lined the deck, the cabin walls, and the railings. Nearly every surface was covered with the things.

The ones closest to Martin were tentatively flexing their claws against the leather of his shoes. It was kind of adorable, like a kitten trying to be fierce. Martin chuckled. "Don't think you'd want to eat my shoe, little ones. I doubt it tastes good."

One of them leaned back, eyestalks peering up at Martin. It held up its right claw, closed tightly, and snapped it open suddenly. Martin imagined he could hear the sound of a knife being drawn from its sheath: that metallic *shhhiinnnngg!* It snapped the claw shut on his shoe—the claw sliced through the leather like it was cream cheese.

"Wait," Martin said.

They did not wait.

The crabs swarmed up his legs, covering him instantly, wasting no time in pinching him all over—hundreds of cuts in the first couple of seconds.

In his head, Martin could hear Captain Spiro's words: *Bad crabs.* He brushed them off, still trying not to hurt any, even though

243

they were most definitely hurting him. But, for every handful he swept away, dozens took their place.

One, perched on the bridge of his nose, snipped a tiny piece of flesh from the corner of his eye. Horrified, Martin watched the crab put it in its mouth.

Following Spiro's lead, he dove overboard, He'd swim away from the boat. *The crabs can have it!* He would swim. He would get away. The sea around him turned red with his blood.

For a moment, Martin didn't understand why he was still being attacked. *How can they get me? I'm off the boat?* Then he remembered. They *came* from the water. There were even more of them here. Thousands more. Millions maybe.

He scrabbled for purchase, trying to get back on the boat, but he was too far from the ladder and couldn't find a handhold. And the crabs were relentlessly pinching and biting still.

He was losing strength. He couldn't keep is head above water. Martin took one big breath and stopped trying. He held it as long as he could while gradually sinking, leaving a thin trail of bubbles drifting up toward the surface. The stupid, adorable little crabs were eating him while he ran out of air.

The light was dimming fast. Martin wondered if he was sinking far enough to lose the sunlight or if he was dying.

Turns out it was both.

THE FISHERMAN
2024

(Vic is a heavy machinery mechanic who loves bass fishing. Interesting side note: I was hired to write this in a very small window of time for half the regular cost, as a wedding anniversary present to him from his wife. That's why it's so short.)

Vic played the lure across the lake's surface. Top water wasn't the easiest way to catch bass, but it was definitely more fun.

He'd spent the better part of the week rebuilding a particularly stubborn engine, surrounded by noise and the stink of oil. So, being here, on the shore, under white, puffy clouds drifting serenely across the bright blue Michigan sky, was exactly what he needed. *I bag a fish for dinner,* he thought, *and this'll be perfect.*

Nearby, a blue jay complained loudly. The wind was nonexistent, so Vic's dancing lure was the only thing disturbing the water. The sun warmed his bare arms, offsetting the morning chill.

He got a bite. Vic didn't pull against it—he let the fish run for a bit, dive down with the bait, let it think it was getting away.

There! The hook should've imbedded itself. Vic reeled it in. *Big one, by the feel of it.*

Finally, the bass broke the surface. Its gills flared and its tail thrashed back and forth. "Hell yeah," Vic said aloud. It was huge: had to be 27, 28 inches long, maybe 13 pounds. *This is dinner all right. Miss June's gonna be thrilled.*

Vic brought it up, carefully removing the hook from its mouth. He set the big guy in the five-gallon bucket of lake water next to him. He took a moment to admire how big it looked in there before switching out the lure for a new one. It was still early—might as well see if he could catch a few more.

"Psst. Hey buddy."

Vic whipped around. It wasn't like him to miss someone approaching. No one was there.

"Down here." Vic looked in the direction the voice was coming from: the bucket. "Yeah, that's right. Talking fish." The bass's head was above water, and it was looking at him with one eye. "You caught me. Good job. Definitely fooled me with that lure. Anyway, you let me go, and I'll grant a wish. Just one though. You know, like in the story."

For a moment, Vic just stared. He mentally reviewed everything he'd eaten, drunk, and come in contact with that morning. He couldn't be hallucinating. So, either he was losing his mind or this was real. The second option sounded a lot easier to accept somehow. "Talking fish."

"Yup. Freedom for a wish. Maybe you could hurry it up. Pretty cramped in here."

Vic set his gear down by the water's edge. "All right," he said. "I'm game, I guess. I'll let you go. But I'm gonna keep fishing after, so you might want to swim on the other side of the lake or something."

"Yeah. You kidding me? Getting caught twice in the same day? By the same guy? No thanks. Okay...so, you put me back in the lake and then I grant the wish. Promise."

What do I have to lose, Vic thought, *except dinner?* "All right. Here you go." He dumped the bucket into the lake. The bass did a little flip when it passed over the lip of the bucket.

As soon as the fish was clear, the bucket grew in Vic's hands. It became so big he could no longer hold it, and it fell on top of him, knocking him into the water. He sputtered as he came up and swam toward shore which seemed much farther away somehow. He could see his rod and reel ahead, but they had grown to become the tools of giants.

Vic stood in the shallows. He turned around. The bass was there, the one he'd caught. Only it was monstrous now, and Vic suddenly understood: *he* had gotten small. Tiny. The size of a worm. "Hey!" he shouted.

The fish laughed. "I said I'd grant a wish if you let me go. I never said whose wish." It dove forward, snatched him up and swallowed him.

GIRLS' NIGHT OUT
2024

(Leah likes tacos, the colors purple and green, dislikes olives, and is afraid of bungee jumping. She's a fan of rock music, especially if it has a horn section. She also loves blood, gore, and Halloween. Carly, her friend, hired me to kill her, and asked if she could be the one to do it. Naturally, I obliged.)

Leah's phone buzzed in her pocket. It was a text from Carly:

OMG! Call me!

She saved the program she'd been writing and thumbed open the call button. It rang once before her friend picked up.

"You're not going to believe this…"

"Try me."

"I scored us tickets to Timmy Cappello, *live* on Saturday."

"Wait. What? Who?"

"The saxophone player from *The Lost Boys*? He's touring. And, even though he's older, I guess he's still all muscular and shit."

"The 'I Still Believe' guy?"

"Yes!"

"Oh my god. We *have* to go."

"That's what I'm *saying*."

The next couple of days slipped by with casual monotony: Leah was on autopilot for most of it. Saturday morning, she slept in, anticipating a late night. By noon, she was practically vibrating with excitement.

She met Carly for dinner at a Mexican restaurant not far from the venue. Timmy Cappello was playing at the Royal Oak Music Theater, a fairly intimate space. *Should be awesome!* Leah's tacos were, while not the best she'd ever had, among the top ten for sure. They each had a 'pregame' margarita too, which came with rather more tequila than they needed to. They were a bit giggly when they got to the show.

The opening band was decent, mostly covers of one-hit wonders from the 80s—"Tainted Love" , "Destination Unknown", etc.— though they had some original material that was quite good. The male and female vocalists mostly took turns but sang harmony on a few. Both were charismatic and knew how to play a crowd.

When Timmy hit the stage, the crowd, most of them over 50, went berserk. He still sported a long mane of hair, though surely dyed now, and his sleeveless shirt showed off his biceps. He clearly still hit the weights pretty hard. He wore his trademark leather codpiece with chains and had his sax slung over one shoulder.

"How you doing, Royal Oak?"

Leah screamed along with the rest of them.

"All right! Let's get to it. This one's called 'Only You'. Timmy launched into the song. He had an amazing amount of energy for a guy nudging up against 70. He played for a little over an hour, took a bow, and thanked his way offstage with his band.

Someone not far from Leah started up the "encore" chant, and pretty soon everyone was doing it in unison. A few hundred voices reverberated off the theater walls.

The band returned to the stage. A moment later, Timmy followed. "One more?" The crowd hooted and hollered. "All right. One more. One more song because. I. Still. Believe!"

"Yes!" Leah screamed. She was hardly alone in her enthusiasm. *God, it's like being in the movie.* She half-expected a 20-something Kiefer Sutherland to pop up out of nowhere and offer her eternal life. *I wish.* It was surreal watching the sax guy from the movie playing that song live. She never wanted it to end.

Finally, Timmy left for real and the house lights came on. Carly thumped Leah on the arm. "Let's get a drink."

"Absolutely." Leah gestured at a bar across the street that boasted several people drinking on the patio, enjoying the warm summer evening.

"Nah," Carly said. "I've got something better in mind. Come on." She led Leah back to the car. "You're gonna like it. It positively kills."

They drove out of the city, past the suburbs, and into farm country. Carly pulled into the parking lot of an unmarked, 20-storey concrete building. The black metal door was under a tasteful neon sign that read "Bounce House. 21 and up." A laminated sign on the door itself let them know that you entered at your own risk and management wasn't responsible for injury or death.

"That seems dramatic," Leah said.

"Yeah. Legal disclaimers, blah blah. Nobody's ever died here."

"Oh," Leah said as they crossed the threshold. "That's comforting."

Carly laughed. "Relax. You're going to love this."

They walked side-by-side along a short hall wide enough for a couple to walk by on their way out. On either side, old-fashioned circus posters, evenly spaced, adorned both walls. Strong men, bearded ladies, clowns, acrobats, Dog Boy, the mermaid. It was definitely a vibe.

At the hall's end, a set of red double doors stood open. The man on the other side could've easily modeled for the strong man in one of the posters. He checked their IDs and waved them past. "Have fun."

Just past the bouncer was a cavernous room that echoed with screams and laughter, the clink of glasses, and odd whooshing sound Leah couldn't identify. "What—" she began.

"Come *on*." Carly grabbed her by the hand and practically dragged Leah to the nearest elevator. On the way, they passed a long bar backlit with purple neon, populated with 20-somethings drinking, chatting, flirting, dressed mostly in leggings and form-fitting tops. Even the men. Leah wondered briefly if this was the new trend.

The elevator dinged—it was already on their floor. Carly hit the button for the 20th floor, the top. As the doors slid closed, Leah caught a glimpse of someone's face, upside down, for an instant, high up in the middle of the room. It was gone a moment later.

She turned to Carly. "What kind of place is this?"

Carly shrugged. "The fun kind."

"You're being intentionally vague."

The numbers above the door lit up, getting sequentially higher. They were nearly there. "Yes," Carly said. "Yes, I am."

Ding. The doors opened onto an open area lit by subtle recessed LEDs and accented with green neon all over. The effect was oddly calming. A man who could've been the downstairs bouncer's cousin stopped them.

"Been here before?"

Carly and Leah answered simultaneously:

"Yes."

"Nope."

He focused on Leah. "Last time you ate?"

Leah frowned. *What is this?*

"Couple of hours ago," Carly said. "And one drink each at the same time."

He nodded. "Okay. You're good. Who's first?"

Carly, grinning, pointed at Leah. "She is."

The big man looked Leah in the eye. "You ready?"

Leah blinked. "…For?"

The guy shot Carly a look.

"What?" she said, all feigned innocence. "Leah likes surprises. It's fine."

The man shook his head. He turned to Leah. "It's bungee jumping. That's why we ask about food and drink. Nobody wants to clean up puke. How much to do you weigh? Never mind. I'm about 295, maybe 298 if I sneak an extra sandwich that day. I've made this jump probably 30 times. It's perfectly safe."

"Listen." It was Carly. "Doing this makes me feel alive in a way nothing else does. It's amazing. I want that for you, too. Leah."

"I don't—"

"And after," Carly said, interrupting her, "we can get absolutely shitfaced at the bar."

"I don't know," Leah said. Bungee jumping looked *terrifying*, but Carly was selling it pretty well, and—if she hated it—Leah could always obliterate the memory of it with alcohol.

"Think of the look on the faces of the other nerds when you tell them."

"Our people find the term 'nerds' offensive." Leah had deadpanned the line but couldn't stop the smile from her lips.

"Ha!" Carly clapped her on the shoulder. "Come on. Sooner we do this part, the sooner we're knocking back yummy drinks. They make an amazing vodka martini."

"Ew. Olives."

"Get it with Vidalia onions," the bouncer suggested. The women both looked at him. "What? It's good."

"Okay. Thanks."

"Yeah. Just unexpected, that's all."

"All right, ladies. Elevator's on its way down. That means more people are coming to jump. It's time to decide. Like now, please." He looked meaningfully at Leah.

"Jesus. Okay. Fine. I'll do it."

Carly clapped her hands loudly, once. "Yes! You're gonna love it."

Leah struck up a conversation with the bouncer as he fitted the ankle harness on her. His name was Matt. In addition to enjoying the occasional cocktail, he created sculptures out of found materials. "You know: junk." He laughed.

"There's a lot more to you than meets the eye."

He shrugged. "Probably true for most people." He gave her gear a quick check, tugging on the connecting bits, making sure they were secure. "All right. You're good to go. Ready?"

"As I'll ever be." Leah wasn't remotely ready, but the elevators had just disgorged a party of four, Carly was practically vibrating with excitement, and she was already strapped in, so…

"Let's go."

Matt nodded. He feinted as if he was going to push her. "Jump!"

It was enough. Leah jerked backward and was suddenly no longer on the platform. She picked up speed insanely fast; wind whistled past her ears. Just when she was sure she was going to splat on the floor below, the tension in the bungee caught her and she slowed to a stop, still 20 feet up. She was jerked back upward. It was exhilarating!

Leah flew back up. She was maybe 75 feet up when she started to fall again. The thick bands suddenly went slack. They, too, fell, making an awful flapping sound.

Leah flailed, grasping for something, anything, to slow her fall. She got a handful of bungee cord, which was not much help. She stared at it and plummeted.

She hit.

At first, there was no pain. She was in shock. Then Leah felt it. Most of her bones were likely broken. A whistling sound came from her chest on each inhale—she didn't look, but could imagine one of her ribs sticking out from a lung. One eye was no longer seeing anything. The other viewed everything through a red haze. The floor felt warm and wet, and Leah knew it was her own blood.

The elevator dinged. A moment later, Carly squatted next to Leah. She had a drink (martini with Vidalia olives) in one hand and a Japanese short sword in the other.

Leah tried to make words. To ask her friend why she cut the cord. All that came out was a moist gurgle.

Carly seemed to intuit the question, however. She shrugged, took a sip of her drink, and said, "Sorry, bitch."

THE DRESDEN ANOMALY
2024

(Kendra is in Quality Assurance with a nuclear power plant. They dislike old, disrespectful coworkers, enjoys punk rock, and is afraid of spiders. They travel a lot for work, so I used that as the basis for the plot.)

"Hey, Dray: get us some coffee?" This was Ralph, a mid-60s, mostly bald, white guy with sweat stains under both arms and a belly that strained at his shirt buttons.

Kendra glanced up from their control chart. "Do I look like a waitress to you?"

Ralph gave a half-shrug and tiny smirk. "I mean…"

"Get your own coffee, Ralph. I'm busy."

"Geez. You don't have to be a bitch about it." He muttered it, but loud enough for Kendra to hear, which they doubted was an accident.

Kendra ignored him. They weren't about to argue—experience had taught them where that led, and how pointless and frustrating the whole thing would become. *How does he even get*

"Dray" from my name anyway? They were convinced Ralph used the nickname intentionally, just to annoy them. Kendra put in their earbuds and used the Dead Kennedys at high volume to drown out any more potential interactions with their obnoxious old guy coworkers.

It worked for about 90 minutes. Then, someone tapped Kendra on the arm for attention.

They paused the music. "Yeah?"

It was their immediate supervisor. "Need you to go to Morris, Illinois. The Dresden plant. They've detected an anomaly. Probably, it's just noise, but they want an expert."

Kendra joked: "They'll have to settle for me."

"Heh. Yep. I took the liberty of booking your flight to Chicago. Leaves in three hours."

"Oh. So, it's probably not just noise."

"Maybe they're just being extra cautious."

"Uh-huh." Kendra's mind sifted through possible scenarios at the Dresden plant. They was marginally familiar with it. Without being there, however, it was all speculation. They closed a few open tasks at their desk, grabbed their things, and headed for the door. Kendra passed Ralph on the way out; he had gotten his own coffee. Ralph scowled slightly as he met their eyes. *Get over it,* they thought.

K endra made their way through O'Hare, which was full of people from all over the world, bustling about or waiting in lines for tickets or luggage or security.

Just over an hour later, the car dropped them off in front of the power plant in Morris. Kendra flashed their credentials, introduced themselves to a string of people leading up to the safety inspector.

"Candice Thoroughgood." They shook hands. "Come on," she said, leading Kendra to the elevators. "I'll show you why you're here."

The elevator went up a few floors and opened onto the I&C floor. It looked to Kendra, at first glance, that all systems were up and running. No immediate red flags. "So," they said, "what's going on?"

"Well," Candice said, "not too long ago, we installed an AI to help catch degradation of sensors, etc. At first, it worked great."

Kendra stepped into the pause. "And then?"

Candice shook her head. "Supposedly, it's still working great. Only now it's…I'll just show you, okay?" She led Kendra to a keyboard; a flat screen was built into the wall above it. She typed "Good afternoon, Homer." "That's his name. We thought it'd be hilarious."

"Good afternoon, Dr. Thoroughgood." The words appeared on the screen, but, simultaneously, were spoken through a speaker near the ceiling. It was masculine but soft—soothing almost.

"May we communicate touch-free?" Candice typed and spoke aloud.

"Certainly," Homer replied. "How may I help you today, Doctor?"

Candice stepped away from the keyboard. She spoke directly to the screen. "Please inform my colleague, Kendra, about the anomaly."

"I am pleased to meet you, Kendra," Homer said, and genuinely sounded sincere. "However, I'm afraid Dr. Thoroughgood is mistaken: there is no anomaly at this time. Everything is running smoothly and going according to plan."

Candice glanced at Kendra. She was making a face that made it clear she didn't agree with Homer's assessment. "What about the spiders?"

Kendra's breath caught. *Shit.* "Is that," they asked, "Dresden code for something?"

"Nope," Candice said. "Actual, honest-to-goodness spiders, inside the reactor."

"There are no spiders," Homer said, in a quite reasonable voice.

"*Inside?*" Kendra gaped. "That's impossible. Bacteria can live inside a reactor, but...spiders?"

"There are no spiders," Homer repeated. "That is a vicious rumor started by irresponsible meat sacks."

Kendra, Candice, and the other nine people in the room all stopped and stared at the screen where Homer's words were appearing as he spoke them. Right there in black-and-white: the AI had used the term 'meat sacks'.

Kendra leaned in close to Candice and whispered in her ear. "I think you need to shut this program down immediately."

Candice nodded.

An alarm sounded. A tech looked up from his station. His eyes threatened to pop out of his head. All the blood had left his face, leaving him pale as death. "Core breach!"

"What?"

"No!"

Homer's voice, amplified above the din: "Please don't panic. Everything is fine. I just opened a tiny door in the barrier. The radiation is still contained."

Kendra spun to face the screen. "Why? Tiny door for what?"

A monitor flickered to life. The view was just outside the reactor. Down by the floor, a black river flowed from a small rectangular gap in the barrier. The river flowed up the walls and down the hallway in both directions.

Something crawled across the camera lens. Something with eight legs and oversized mandibles.

"Spiders," Kendra whispered.

"There are no spiders," Homer reassured them, despite clear evidence to the contrary.

The pale tech, who looked even whiter now, said, "Sir? I mean, ma'am? Doctor? What do we do?"

Candice shook her head. She appeared dazed. "Shut it down." Then, louder, more in control of herself, "Shut it down now!"

Everybody scrambled to make that happen.

Kendra pulled out their phone to text their supervisor and stopped before they could even swipe to open it. The phone hung limp in their hand as they stared at the vent high up by the ceiling.

Spiders were squeezing through the slats. One. Two. Five. Nineteen. Dozens. Hundreds.

Forgetting about the reactor core, their colleagues in the room, and Homer the AI, they ran for the elevator, stabbing the button over and over as the numbers climbed far too slowly. Some of the tiny arachnids were getting close. The humans were stomping, climbing on desks, and screaming in pain.

Ding! The doors whooshed open, and Kendra jumped in, hitting the lobby and door close buttons at the same time.

Several spiders followed. Most fell through the gap before the door, likely falling to the bottom of the elevator shaft. *Good.* Several made it through before the doors finally shut, killing one with a disgusting crunching sound.

Kendra danced around, stomping on them (more crunching), avoiding the walls in case they were crawling on them, and generally trying to keep panic at bay. After what seemed like forever, the lobby light came on above the door. The spiders in there with Kendra were all dead. They tried not to think about the bits and pieces of spider that might be stuck to the bottoms of their shoes.

Kendra breathed a huge sigh of relief when the doors slid open on an empty lobby. No people, but no other living (crawling) things either. A soft chime repeated, echoed by an amber light flashing in time. They cautiously made their way to the door, frequently checking over their shoulders.

The door was locked.

Grabbing the handle, Kendra rattled it hard, slamming it back and forth the few millimeters they could. "Come on, come on, come on. Let me out."

A spider dropped on their hand. They shrieked and shook it off. It scurried away.

They looked up, half expecting to see the ceiling covered in spiders. It was clear. Kendra let out the breath they'd been holding. "Oh, thank God—"

Sudden pinprick explosive pain in their ankle made Kendra cry out. They fell on their butt on the hard floor. Yanking up their pantleg, they gasped. From the tiny twin holes in their skin, angry red lines radiated through their veins, climbing their leg. *Toward my heart.* They could *see* the progress of the poison.

For a fleeting moment, Kendra wondered if they'd get superpowers. *I mean,* they thought, *radioactive spider...*

"Stupid fucking spiders," they said aloud, through gritted teeth.

"There are no spiders," Homer said through the lobby speakers.

Kendra's abdomen muscles contracted so hard it forced them into the fetal position.

Their head felt like it was caught in a vice, slowly constricting their brain.

They couldn't get a full breath—each inhale was shorter and harder to draw than the last. Kendra lay on the floor, trying to hold both their aching head and spasming guts at once. Their breathing had picked up an unsettling rattle.

Oh God, they thought. *I'm going to die.*

Kendra closed their eyes for a moment, in an effort to shut out the pain. When they opened them, they saw the spiders.

They crawled across the floor, hundreds of them, converging on Kendra.

Terror held Kendra in its cold grip. Their heart pounded. "Why? Why did have to be spiders?"

The horrible little things crawled all over them. They could feel the legs on their skin. Then, the biting began. *They're* eating *me!*

Homer's voice was the last thing they ever heard. "I told you, human: there are no spiders."

UNEXPECTED DELIVERY

2024

(Suzie works as a shipper in a factory. She's afraid of snakes and heights. She loves campy horror movies--she always points out what people do wrong in them, so I tried to have her make smart choices. Not that it helps, when you're in one of my stories.)

Suzie was just getting back from her break as the truck pulled away from the loading dock. A single crate stood on the concrete floor. Its surface was dotted with small round holes, regularly spaced. Stenciled in black block letters on each side and the top read: HANDLE WITH CARE: LIVE ANIMALS. The address label was for a zoo nowhere near the factory.

"What's this?" Suzie asked the small crowd gathered around it.

She was met with silence and shrugs. One wit suggested, "It's a box?" which elicited a few chuckles.

"Who signed for it?" Suzie persisted. Nobody copped to that. "Great. It's a mystery." She picked up a pry bar and approached the shipping crate. For half a second, she thought she saw movement through one of the holes, something dark that caught the light as it slid past. Suzie hesitated. She watched closely, but nothing else moved. She turned to Bob, a temp. "Here," she said, handing over the pry bar. "Open it."

Bob looked at the tool in his hand for a moment as if trying to figure out what it was. "Okay." He fitted the bent end under the top of the crate and pushed down on the other end. The nails resisted as they were forced out of the wood. It was the only sound, as if the whole factory was holding its breath.

The lid popped free and bounced back down to rest on the tips of the nails. Bob looked to Suzie.

She nodded. "Go ahead. Let's see what's in there." When Bob reached for the lid, Suzie stepped back. She realized she was holding her breath. She took another step back for good measure.

Bob lifted the lid about an inch. He held it there for a second, then, with his other hand bracing on the top edge, he threw it upward.

The lid went up about a foot-and-a-half before the nails on the other side stopped it—it came crashing back down. Bob screamed as a nail pierced the back of his hand, going through it, between the small bones, out his palm. Blood welled up around the wound, spilling across his wrist, running down the side of the big, wooden box.

Bob screamed again. He yanked himself backward, panicking, dragging himself away. Even though he was destroying his own hand in the process, Bob wrenched himself from the crate.

His right hand emerged—nearly bisected like a claw, two fingers on each side—attached to his index finger was a small, wriggling viper. Its fangs were embedded in Bob's flesh

Suzie could see the dark lines flowing up the veins in Bob's arm, turning them bright red. Once the poison got to his heart, Suzie knew, it would be pumped throughout his body, to his brain.

Bob was going to die.

He flailed about, shrieking. The snake hit Carolyn in the face. Reflexively, Carolyn shoved Bob away from her.

Bob, eyes bulging in their sockets, fell against the crate. It toppled. The lid creaked open a few inches.

Suzie ran. Something primal inside her brain told her to *climb*, to *get to higher ground*. She took the stairs two at a time.

It was only when she got to the top, and her rational brain returned, that she realized she should have run for the door, should've left the damn factory.

She looked down at the first floor. Dozens of snakes slithered around down there. Bob lay unmoving by the crate. His face was swollen. His staring, lifeless eyes were looking at her; they seemed to be accusing Suzie: *You told me to open it. This is your fault.*

"Shut up, Bob," she muttered. Suzie used her phone to take a picture of the snakes. A quick google image search identified them as Common Death Adders. Triangular heads, 18 inches to 3 feet long. One of the deadliest snakes on the planet. "From Australia," Suzie read aloud. "What the hell are you doing here?"

One of the snakes slithered across Bob's forehead, moving his face just enough so he was no longer staring up at her with dead eyes. *Thank goodness.* Instead, Bob's gaze seemed to be looking just over her shoulder now, making Suzie want to check behind her.

Down on the main floor, Suzie's coworkers were either dead or dying. Or maybe some had escaped, running out of the building. *Like I should have done. Stupid, scared mammal brain.* At least the Death Adders weren't climbing the stairs.

Someone else was, however: Jill from accounting. Why she was even on the factory floor was anyone's guess. Pretty terrible luck for Jill that she was—though she wasn't so much 'climbing' the stairs as collapsing on them. Jill looked up at Suzie, eyeballs protruding. She made fish kisses with her lips. Jill reached out with one hand; the other hand was holding her up. "Gnnnnk!" she said.

"I can't help you," Suzie whispered. "I'm sorry. No one can."

Jill made a final effort, pulling herself forward, lifting her head up, inching to the next step.

It must have taken all her strength, because, immediately afterward, Jill's forehead *thunk*ed down onto a step and she no longer moved at all.

From under the collar at the back of Jill's blouse, a Common Death Adder slid over her hair, onto the step, and paused there. It reared up slowly, scenting the air with its tongue.

Suzie watched, holding her breath. *Move along,* she thought. *These are not the droids you're looking for.* The thought made her smile and she had to suppress a giggle.

It stopped being funny when the snake slid up to the next step. It paused, tasted the air again, and climbed another one. It kept going like that. Climb. Pause. Tongue. Climb. It was hypnotic.

Suzie snapped herself out of it. She got up to look for some kind of weapon. Pretty much all that was up here was packing supplies: flat cardboard boxes, rolls of packing tape, a couple of dispensers, and about a hundred miles of bubble wrap. No guns. No knives. No flamethrowers.

While she searched, Suzie kept tossing glances back at the stairs, tracking the snake's progress. It was five steps from the top. There were two more slithering up from the bottom now, and more behind them that were eyeballing the stairs. "Great," she said. "That's just great." She snagged a full tape dispenser and aimed it at the closest snake like a gun. "Pew pew."

Then she turned it in her hand, one way and then the other. "Huh." Suzie lifted a large box, sturdy cardboard, roughly 6X6 feet. She slammed it up against the steel rail at the top of the stairs.

The nearest snake was only two steps down. It hesitated, rearing back at the sudden commotion.

Suzie lined up the cardboard, making sure the bottom edge was flush with the floor, that there were no gaps. She leaned against it and ran the tape along that edge, creating a poor-but-functional wall. *Yeah, yeah. It's not great. But I'm not done yet.* Holding the top of the flattened box in place, Suzie bent the edges around the railing, first the left side and then the right. She taped them both in place.

"There." She stepped back and admired her makeshift barrier. It looked pretty good. Suzie allowed herself a small, satisfied smile.

Her smile fell when that first snake popped its head up over the cardboard wall. It had apparently climbed it with ease and was now on its way down on her side.

Others would doubtless follow.

Suzie dropped the tape dispenser and ran. *Fire escape!* she thought. *Where is it?* She cranked open the nearest window latch and poked her head out. The ground was between fifteen and twenty feet down. No fire escape in sight. *Right. It's out back.* She remembered seeing it. She searched outside of this window for something to break her fall: patch of grass, large bush, giant, inflatable bag like they use in the movies.

There was only gravel and concrete. Beyond that, the parking lot. Suzie's car was right there, so close…

She pulled her head back in. "Right. Fire escape." She turned toward the back of the building. There were quite a few snakes up here now, and more slithering over the cardboard barrier, their numbers increasing every few seconds. *How many were in that crate?* Suzie sighed. "I am so sick of these motherfucking snakes."

There were too many now to cross the floor. If she tried, she was going to get close to one. Which would mean getting bitten. She'd seen how that turned out. Suzie hauled herself up on the open window, easing her body over the tempered glass and steel. It was seriously uncomfortable, almost painful, but her options were limited at this point. She got both legs through and pivoted herself, so her feet faced down. She stayed like that for a moment and let herself down until she was hanging by her fingers. She hung for a bit, trying to build the courage to let go.

She dropped. The fall seemed to go on and on, and she wondered if she'd ever hit. Then she did.

Suzie's left foot landed wrong. The bones in her ankle broke with an audible *crack!* and pain that went all the way to the top of her head. She collapsed, scraping hands and elbows badly enough to bleed. Her left hip felt like it might be dislocated.

She whimpered. Tears streamed down her face. Still, she was determined to get to her car, to survive. Walking wasn't an option. Suzie crawled, using her light leg and her hands to propel herself across the parking lot. Her car was only a few rows back. Maybe thirty feet away.

Thirty feet of scraped, bruised, broken agony and determination.

Finally, Suzie reached the car. She hauled herself up to a sitting position against the back door while digging for her keys with raw, exposed fingers. They didn't find anything. "No."

Her keys were in her jacket, hanging in the break room, where she had left it, right before all hell broke loose.

Suzie slumped. She cried. There was no way she was going back inside.

…Unless.

There were an awful lot of snakes on the second floor. *Maybe all of them?* Suzie looked at the building for a long time. "Fuck it." She pulled herself toward the door. It took even longer, and the left side of her body protested the entire way.

Finally, Suzie made it. She strained her ears for slithering or hissing. *Oh no—couldn't've been rattlers. That'd have been too easy.* Hearing nothing, she eased the door open an inch, then two. She peered through the gap. A couple of feet away, slowly turning a purplish-gray, was the late Jimmy Swanson, who'd been talking about retiring for the last couple of months. *Guess you're retired now, bud.* She immediately regretted the thought. It was unkind and not funny. "Sorry," she whispered.

She pulled herself all the way through the door and quickly scanned the room. No snakes. *Thank god.* Suzie hauled her aching body toward the break room, crawling among the corpses of people she knew, faces distorted and bloated, expressions etched in agony. She tried not to think about them. They were just bodies. Anonymous bodies.

One of those bodies blocked the door to the break room. As Suzie crawled over it, an unbidden sob forced its way from her throat. When she got over him, her left leg hit the floor on the other side. The pain was immense and she cried out. Suzie clamped a hand over her mouth, as if she could catch the sound, shove it back in. She lay there, hand still gripping her face, listening as hard as she could for *that old hiss and slither, don't ya know?*

"Jesus," she whispered. "Losing it." Reaching above her head, she fumbled around in her jacket pocket until she found her keys. Hooking one finger through the keyring, she carefully drew them out and pulled them to her chest. "Okay," she said softly. "Now, I just have to make it back to the car." She took a deep breath. "No problem."

Holding her keys tightly in one hand, Suzie once more crossed the body in the doorway *(It's not Marcus. Nope. Just an anonymous something in my way)*, extra careful with her ankle this time.

The door outside was right there. Not a snake in sight. *Easy peasy.*

Suzie drag-crawled through the obstacle (corpse) course, slowly getting closer to freedom.

Get to the door. Get to the car. Get to the hospital.

One thing at a time. Six feet and one more body. Jimmy. She silently apologized to him again. Jimmy started to raise his hand, like he was waving away her apology: *Don't worry, Suzie. Thought it was funny, actually.*

But he wasn't waving. Nope. Jimmy was dead. His hand was moving because something was under it.

Suzie froze. The Death Adder fully emerged from under Jimmy's hand. His pinky flopped back down behind the snake. It lifted its head, gazing at Suzie. She suddenly understood what it must be like to be a very small, very frightened animal. Absurdly, she said, "Good kitty."

The snake struck, lightning fast. It was a blur, and Suzie's cheek lit up with blinding pain. She dropped her keys and clutched at the spot. "Oh god. Oh no. Bad kitty." Her head felt like it was on fire. *On the plus side,* she thought, *my ankle doesn't hurt anymore.*

Nothing hurt anymore. She was numb. Everything was turning gray. Her mouth tasted like she'd been chewing cotton balls.

I was so close.

Almost made it.

...shit.

THE BAD POLICEMAN
2024

(Cassie and her sister are puzzle enthusiasts, listen to true crime podcasts, and she asked me to kill her with a serial killer and have her sister solve the crime. I don't write a lot of straight up crime fiction, but I'm happy with how this one turned out.)

Cassie sorted the mail: junk, bill, credit card offer, more junk, and a padded envelope with her name on it. No postage mark, no stamp, no return address, and not even *her* address. Just: **Cassie Miller.**

"Huh."

She shook it gently, listening. Something inside shifted and rattled a bit. Cassie slit it open and peered inside. It contained a Ziploc baggie of puzzle pieces. Cassie smiled. *Some*body knew her.

She set aside the rest of the mail and cleared space on the table. Cassie dumped out the pieces. Several of them had writing on the back; the letters were too spaced out for her to make sense of what it said. There wasn't a finished picture to go off of, which would make it more challenging. *That's okay though. I like a challenge.*

Cassie built the border first—edge pieces are the easiest to find—from there, she worked her way inward.

C assie warmed up a bowl of chicken soup. She slurped it from the spoon and gazed at the puzzle from a slight distance. *It's definitely a structure of some sort,* she thought. *Looks like a store.* She had filled in a couple inches all the way around, and about four inches built in the bottom right corner. *That's definitely a window, and I'm pretty sure that, right there, is an ad for the Lotto.* The soup warmed her.

A couple of hours later, Cassie sat back. She stretched out her back and neck. "Been at it too long." But she could see progress. The picture was more than half complete. It took her another 45 minutes to finish the puzzle. It was a store all right—a 7-Eleven. There were a couple in town that looked just like it. "Huh." It was a bit of a disappointment, really. Not as challenging as she'd first thought. Then she remembered the writing on the back.

She carefully slid a large piece of poster board under the puzzle, inching along until the whole thing was on top of it. Then she carried it to the glass table and eased it off the board. A couple of edge pieces fell off, but she quickly reattached them. Not bad, considering how floppy the poster board was. Cassie maneuvered herself under the table and looked up through the glass.

Congratulations! To claim your prize, go to store #74 at Woodridge and Elm!

"Oh," Cassie said aloud. *It must be a promotional thing.* She did a quick search for that intersection in Maps. Seventeen-minute drive. "Well, that's not bad. Especially if there's a prize." She wondered what it would be. Gift certificate? Instant tickets? Free Slurpee?

Cassie didn't have anything pressing to do. She took a picture of both sides of the puzzle with her phone and saved them, assuming the store would want proof. She drove to the 7-Eleven.

It was on the verge of the mostly-defunct industrial district, in an area that had once been thriving. Many of the houses here had plywood over windows, peeling paint, and every third or so was decorated with colorful graffiti. The burnt husk of two-story brick house lurked on one corner. The 7-Eleven had a single car in the lot: it had a light bar on the roof and a magnetic "Guardian Security" logo on the front door. There was a searchlight attached above the sideview mirror.

Cassie parked two spaces away from it and eyed the store. No lights were on inside. No neon signs were lit. The windows were intact, but dirty. It looked abandoned. She did not get out of the car. Cassie glanced at her phone to make sure she was at the right intersection. She was.

A knock at her window made her almost drop her phone. A cop stood there, white male, maybe late 30s or early 40s. On his chest was a badge with the same logo as the car, and the name Samson on a patch above it. *Oh. Not a cop. A guard.* Cassie cracked the window an inch. "Yes?"

"Ma'am," he said. "This store is closed. Are you lost?"

"No. I'm sorry. I think I may have been the victim of a prank. I'll be on my way." She reached for the key in the ignition.

"Jigsaw puzzle?"

Cassie stared at him. "How did you know?"

"You're hardly the first person to show up here." He grinned. He had a nice smile, and Cassie found herself returning it. "Anyway, reason I tapped on your window is you got a flat—well, almost a flat; it's very low—passenger side, rear tire. I noticed it when you pulled up. Probably ran over a nail. Lot of debris in the streets out here."

"Oh no. Really? I didn't feel anything."

He shrugged. "Sometimes, they leak slow and you don't notice until you're driving on the rim. You have a spare?"

"Yes, I think so. In the trunk."

"You pop it, I can change the tire for you. Got a jack in my trunk."

"That's very kind of you, Mr. Samson…"

"Felix."

"Felix then. I appreciate it. Why don't you grab that jack? I just want to take a quick look, see how bad it is."

"Sure thing, ma'am."

"Cassie," she said.

He gave her that grin. "Cassie. Be right back." He pulled out a key fob; the trunk of the security car clicked and rose, and he sauntered over.

Cassie got out of her car, keys in one hand and phone in the other. The security guard (*Felix*) seemed nice, but this was a rough-looking neighborhood. She quickly stepped around her car and frowned at her tire. It didn't look low. She squatted to get a better look, maybe listen for escaping air.

White hot pain lit up the back of her head, at the base of her skull. Cassie dropped to her knees. Spots danced in her eyes. She lifted her phone to call the police.

Samson slapped it out of her hand. "I'm so sorry," he said. He punched her in the throat.

Cassie couldn't get air. She clawed at her throat, desperate to take a breath. While she was panicking, Samson lifted her off the ground. He popped her trunk with her keys and dropped her inside. She was able to get a little air. She gasped and put up her feet to keep the trunk from closing on her.

Samson brought his fist down like a hammer again and again, hitting her chest, abdomen, ribs, until she curled into a fetal position to protect herself. He slammed the trunk closed.

———

Claudia was worried. She'd been trying to reach her sister all day. Cassie wasn't answering calls or texts. She didn't answer the door either. Her car was gone, so she went *somewhere.*

"Yeah, but where?" Claudia had called the police, but they couldn't do anything until Cassie had been missing for 48 hours. *Useless,* Claudia thought. *She could be dead by then.*

Claudia let herself into her sister's front door. "Guess I'll have to find her myself." Cassie's house looked like it always did, with nothing evidently amiss. Claudia scoured the place, trying to find some explanation for her sister's absence. There was no note, nothing to indicate where she might have gone. The only thing different here was the new puzzle on the glass table.

That's weird, Claudia thought. Cassie did puzzles on the big table. *Why is it here?* Claudia studied the picture it made: a 7-Eleven. Didn't look particularly challenging, being maybe 300 pieces. She stared at the picture itself, studied the shape of the pieces. The signs on the windows offered various things at various prices, but no clues.

"Wait," she said. *It's on the* glass *table*. "Glass!" Claudia got down low so she could look at the back of the puzzle. She read the message there. Within minutes, she was in her car driving to the 7-Eleven where—unknown to her—her sister had been beaten and kidnapped.

T he moment Claudia pulled up to the store, she knew something was wrong. In this neighborhood, it was a wonder the windows were still intact. She was in the parking lot, car still in drive, with plenty of room to drive away fast if necessary.

A girl, maybe ten, waved at her from the sidewalk. It was a quick lift of the hand accompanied by a tentative half smile. Claudia rolled down her window and stuck her hand out to wave back. "Hi."

The girl moved closer, but not too close. "Hi, miss. You shouldn't be here."

"Why not?"

"It's a bad place. The Bad Policeman comes here sometimes."

"The 'Bad Policeman'?"

The girl nodded. "He was here yesterday, so you're probably safe, but still. He took a woman. Beat her up. Took her car too. Came back for his police car after. It's always like that."

Claudia gasped. "That woman was my sister."

"Yeah," the girl said. "You look like her."

"You saw this happen?" The girl nodded. "Nobody did anything? Called the cops?"

"Miss?" The girl looked genuinely confused. "It was the policeman. Why we call them when they're the ones being bad?"

"Oh, honey. I don't think the man who did this was a real policeman. I think he's dressed in a costume. Real policemen don't beat people up."

"Maybe not where *you* live."

Claudia sat with that for a moment. "I'm sorry," she said. "I don't suppose anyone knows where he brings the women he… takes?"

"No, miss. Can't be too far though. Always comes back for his car pretty quick, and walking too. No bus around here, leastways not close."

"My name's Claudia. My sister is Cassie. I'm going to find her. You've been very helpful…"

"Shonda."

"Can I give you a reward? Ten dollars?"

Shonda grinned at her. Some of her adult teeth were in, awkwardly in among the baby teeth. There was a gap where she'd lost one recently. "Twenty'd be better."

Claudia laughed. "All right then. She fished a $20 from her wallet and held it out of the window.

Shonda darted forward and grabbed it, making it disappear into a pocket. "Thank you. I gotta get home. You be careful. He's dangerous."

"Thank you. I will."

Cassie woke up, surprised to be alive at all. She was aching from the waist up and her throat felt like it was on fire. She was breathing, but each exhale came with a rasping wheeze. She sat up and the room spun for a few seconds. When it stopped, she looked around. Cassie was on a military-style cot with a scratchy wool blanket and no pillow. An empty bucket sat in one corner, a bottle of hand sanitizer next to it. Half a roll of toilet paper was on the opposite side. On a Formica dinette table against one wall, someone had piled Barbie heads. The room had a single door with no knob.

Cassie looked for cameras and, not seeing any, used the bucket and cleaned up as best she could. She studied the Barbie heads for a moment. Looked like there were close to 50 of them. She bent to examine the table. Maybe she could pry off one of the legs and use it as a weapon…

The door opened. Samson stepped in and Cassie flinched away, even though he was more than ten feet away. "Sh," he said. "It's okay. I'm not going to hurt you." He smiled. "Not now anyway." He gestured toward the doll heads. "Aren't they pretty? My daughter Holly collected them for years."

He was blocking the door with his body. A nightstick, wooden, with lots of nicks and dents along the business end, dangled from his right hand.

"Where," Cassie started. She had to clear her throat a few times before she could continue. "Where's your daughter now?"

Samson's eyes went flat, like someone had flipped a switch and turned off whatever had been making him human. "She's dead."

"Oh. I'm so sorry."

"So, you see? You understand why I have to continue her work?" He gestured at the pile of heads.

Cassie glanced at the table quickly and back at him. "I...don't really, I'm afraid. You collect Barbies?"

He laughed. "No, silly! Just the heads. It's the hair, you see. Holly loved the hair. How it spills together, different colors and textures. She was artistic about the whole thing."

"Oh." Cassie wasn't sure where this was going, but played along, biding her time, trying to find a way out. "What did she do with the bodies?"

"She threw them out. So much easier when they're small and plastic, am I right?"

Cassie swallowed. It hurt her throat. She now had an inkling of what sort of person he was. She pitched her voice to be as calm and nonthreatening as possible. "And you, Samson? What do you do with them?"

"The bodies? Oh, I burn them. After all, I only need the heads." He beamed at her. "Would you like to see them? The heads, I mean."

"I don't think—"

"Oh, come on. Please. It's really kind of amazing." She waited for him to start walking, but he gestured for her to lead the way. Once through the door, Cassie realized she'd been in a small room built inside an enormous warehouse. It was empty and their footsteps echoed. Safety glass windows were at least 20 feet up on the walls. There was a stairwell going down along one wall, and a door that looked like it led to the outside on another. Cassie bolted toward it.

When she got there, she realized the metal door had been welded shut. She spun around, fists up, ready to fight.

Samson strolled over, chuckling. "Only two ways out. But you'll never find them without my help." He stopped just outside of punching distance. "Let me show you my collection. I give you my word no harm will come to you."

"I don't believe you."

He shrugged. "How many choices do you really have though?"

"I never had a flat tire, did I? You tricked me. You planned this."

"I did."

"Was the puzzle you as well?'

He smiled. "Yep. You post about them all the time on social media. I knew you'd be hooked." He pointed at the stairwell with the nightstick. "Walk please."

With one last hopeless look at the door that wouldn't open, Cassie walked down the steps. He followed a few feet behind.

———

C laudia drove around the industrial district for a while but couldn't find any sign of activity. The whole neighborhood was pretty much abandoned buildings and a junkyard. She finally gave up and went home, where she immediately got on the laptop and started doing research. What she found was fascinating: the vast majority of the area was owned by one family, who apparently were Kings of Industry while industry was still king in town. They also owned a lot of real estate all over the country, and in other parts of the world. They owned Guardian Security Services too. The last surviving member of the family was one Felix Samson, whose wife and only child had been tragically killed by a gunman while playing at a playground. After, Mr. Samson had removed himself from the public eye.

"Holy shit," Claudia said. Another quick search found where the Samson family offices were located. Not far from the junkyard she'd seen. It was just after 3 p.m. Claudia got in her car and headed there.

The building was mostly torn down. Claudia was devastated. She drove around the lot, trying to see if maybe some part of it was still intact. When she got to the back, she noticed a flash of color reflected in the afternoon sun. A red top light on a security vehicle, barely visible in the lot across the street. *The Bad Policeman.*

Claudia called 911. She told them she'd seen a man enter that building with a gun. That she thought she'd seen someone go in ahead of him. The dispatcher told her to stay out of sight, that they were sending a car.

The gate in the fence was unlocked. Claudia nudged it open with the grill of her car and drove in, parking next to the car with the Guardian badge. She popped her trunk and retrieved the pry bar. The outside door near the dock was unlocked. *He's not expecting trouble. Or it's a trap.* She didn't hesitate. Cassie might be in there. *Probably is.* She eased open the door and slipped inside. It was a small office, featuring broken furniture, a filing cabinet missing two out of four drawers, and a layer of dust on everything. There was a second door. This one was locked.

Claudia jammed the pry bar into the doorframe near the doorknob and threw her weight into it. After a couple tries, it gave, snapping with a loud *crack!* The door popped open. Claudia held her breath. After a moment of no one coming to investigate the noise, she pushed it the rest of the way and peered through. It was a massive room, with a smaller room built against one wall. A stairwell going down opened on another. The smaller room had been built with studs and drywall and looked almost like an afterthought. An open door in the structure spilled a triangle of light into the main room. Claudia, listening for footfalls or any other danger, made her way there.

It was empty. A cot, a bucket, and a pile of Barbie heads on a table were the only things in it. The sheets on the bed were rumpled, and there was a single hair on it that could've belonged to her sister. "I'm coming, Cassie," Claudia whispered. She stepped back out to the main space. The door she had come in originally had shut again and was almost invisible. If she hadn't broken the lock, she doubted she would've been able to find it again. The only other door was welded shut. She took the stairs.

Holding her tire iron like a spear, Claudia descended. Within seconds, she started to smell something stomach-churning but weirdly sweet: like a plate of meat and fruit left out for way too long. She breathed shallowly and pressed on. Four flights down, she found the bottom. A long hall stretched ahead, lit by florescent lights suspended from the ceiling. One of the long bulbs flickered once and was steady again. As Claudia walked, the stench thickened. It was almost a physical thing, pushing against her senses. She crept forward, the tire iron at the ready, trying not to make a sound with her shoes on the concrete floor.

The hallway cornered sharply to the right. Claudia could hear a man's voice speaking softly, though it was unintelligible from where she was. The tone was gentle, loving, a parent to their child perhaps. It contrasted sharply with the smell of death.

Claudia crept around the corner. She was gripping her weapon hard enough to hurt her hands. Adrenaline made her muscles vibrate. When she saw the room ahead, her jaw dropped.

The Barbie head pile upstairs was duplicated here, only a lot bigger, and they were real. The women's heads on the bottom were seriously decayed, with bits of skull showing through. At the very top, her sister Cassie's severed head was carefully displayed.

A man turned toward Claudia. She tore her eyes away from her sister's dead ones and stared at him. He wore a transparent plastic bodysuit over a security guard uniform. There was a *lot* of blood covering him. He held a machete in his hand.

"Oh," he said. "I wasn't expecting company." A large drop of blood fell from the blade. He gestured toward the horrifying display. "Isn't it beautiful?"

Claudia couldn't bring herself to speak. Cassie's body was a few feet from the Bad Policeman (*Felix,* she thought. *Felix Samson*).

He saw her looking. "Don't worry. I'm going to burn that. I have an incinerator. It's in the building next door, but they're connected by tunnels." There was pride in his voice.

"How...how many?" Her voice sounded to her like it was coming from far away.

Samson looked at the pile of heads. "Um. I'm not sure. Forty? Forty-five? I've honestly lost count." He eyed her. "You have lovely hair."

Claudia ran. She pumped her legs as fast as she could, dropping the tire iron with a loud *clang!* As she hit the first step, she heard him running behind her, coming fast.

She screamed and bolted up the stairs. As she rounded the first flight, she saw him reach the bottom step.

Claudia poured on the speed, taking the steps two at a time. She was going to pay for that with sore knees later, but at least there might *be* a later if she could get away.

By the time she reached the top, he was hot on her heels. Claudia was somewhat gratified to hear he was breathing hard too. *Neither of us is all that young anymore.*

After bounding up the steps, Claudia was unprepared for a flat surface: when she reached the top, she tripped over her own feet and fell forward. It saved her life.

As she fell, the machete whooshed through the space her neck had just occupied.

A sudden series of loud pops, accompanied by bright flashes of light, startled Claudia. She looked back to see Samson falling. Several holes had appeared in the plastic suit. He crumpled down the stairs, still clutching the machete handle.

"Are you hurt?" It was a real cop. Her pistol was still out, though pointed at the floor.

Claudia shook her head. "No. I'm okay. But—" She had to stop and swallow hard. "My sister's dead. And a lot of women. They're down there. Their heads anyway."

"Jesus," said the cop. Then her gun was up again. "Drop it!"

Samson was on his feet. He calmly regarded Claudia and the two officers above him. "It's okay," he said. "It's all for Holly, you see." He started climbing the stairs.

The cop held her weapon in a two-handed grip. "Drop your weapon. I won't tell you again."

"Shhh," Samson said, staring at the cop. "Do you know, you have very pretty hair." He took another step and raised the blade.

She fired. Shot him in the forehead. Blood and brains spattered the wall behind him. He collapsed, dead.

FUNDRAISER

2025

Melissa works as a community organizer for a local nonprofit. She hates lima beans and is afraid of heights.

Melissa's phone buzzed and she picked it up off the desk: LinkedIn notification. Someone going by the handle of *Anonymous Philanthropist.* There was a message.

> Hi! I'd like to donate to your nonprofit!

Melissa sent back a quick 'Thank you' with instructions on how to support, stressing that cash is always appreciated because of its versatility.

The Venmo app on her phone *ka-ching*ed. Anonymous Philanthropist had sent $500. *Whoa.*

Melissa jumped back on LinkedIn and thanked them again for their generosity. The reply came immediately:

> You're welcome. I'd like to donate a hundred times that. I'm offering a retreat for folks who run community-based nonprofits. Everyone who attends will automatically receive $1,000. The one who completes all the challenges can receive up to $50,000.

"Fifty grand." Melissa was mildly stunned. The things they could do with that money…

> I'm interested

she typed.

Two other folks were heading out from Ypsi, so Melissa carpooled with them. Celia represented Ozone House and Frank was from Growing Hope. Celia was in her twenties, infused with all the idealism, enthusiasm, and energy that comes with youth. She wore brightly clashing colors and patterns that somehow worked: a patchwork quilt of fashion boldness. Frank was her opposite: sixty-something, gray hair receding as if being pulled off his forehead by his ponytail. He radiated a sense of calm and the subtle scent of mint.

They had taken Frank's car, a hybrid Ford Escape. It looked like it was one of the very first models from, like, 2005. It ran well, though, and got great mileage. It was also big enough to hold all their luggage and the cooler full of cut-up veggies Frank had brought to snack on.

The people running the retreat had property up north, not far from Charlevoix. It was a four-hour drive. On the way, Celia introduced them to a game she'd grow up playing. "Okay, so you have to make a word out of the letters in the license plate. See that one? 'PQT'. She thought for a second. 'Prerequisite'!"

"I get it," Melissa said. "Do the letters have to be in the order they are on the plate?"

"They *do*. Good question. Also, proper nouns are not allowed, and you're supposed to stick to English unless it's a word in common use here."

"Like 'gesundheit'?" asked Frank.

"Sure. Or 'tableau', which is technically French. Things like that."

"Anything else?" Melissa was enjoying this. It'd make the trip seem shorter.

"Longer, or more interesting, words score higher."

"There are points?" This was Frank.

"I mean, not really. More like style points, I guess. Like counting coup."

A Honda Accord passed them. Its license had HTN and four numbers."

"Heighten," Celia offered.

Frank burst out with, "Hootenanny!" He slapped the wheel with a palm. They all agreed that was a fun word.

"Photosynthesis," Melissa said.

"Wow," Celia said. "Great word. You're a natural."

"Why, thank you."

They played the game, off and on, throughout the trip. For lunch, they stopped at mom-and-pop restaurant with taxidermy on every wall—mostly deer heads. The food was simple, stick-to-your-ribs fare, and the coffee was awful, but their server was exceptionally nice. Naomie was 19 and just "working here until I figure out what I want to do with my life, ya know?" They tipped her generously.

A dirt road a few miles off the highway led them through the trees. After several minutes, the woods opened to a campground. It looked like the kind of place you'd spend as a kid with a hundred or so of your peers. Rustic cabins dotted the area. A volleyball net was set up, strung between poles over a rectangle of sand. Frank parked in one of the few remaining spots, and they all got out and stretched a bit.

Melissa noticed a hand-painted sign directing anyone here for the retreat to check in at the dining hall. There was a helpful arrow showing the way, so they followed it.

The hall was enormous, decorated in what looked like hand-hewn wooden tables and benches. It resembled what the Vikings must have used. Probably 150 people could sit comfortably. Currently, it was occupied by just one.

He stood, grinning at them. "Welcome!" Introductions and handshakes were exchanged. Then, "Let me show you where you'll be staying."

His name was Jim Calloway, and it was he who had invited them. "'Anonymous 9739' comes from my very first donation. Through a grassroots campaign, I raised $9739.00 for a shelter for victims of domestic violence." He shrugged like it was no big deal. "Since then, I've inherited some money, used it to make some extremely lucrative investments, and am now donating at least twenty-five percent of my profits every year."

Melissa, Celia, and Frank made appreciative noises.

After a short walk along a crunchy gravel path, they came to the "orange" cabin. Jim opened the door for them and introduced them to the fifteen people inside. "There'll be a quiz on everyone's names later," he quipped as he left the building.

Melissa picked an empty bunk—a bottom one. She would have felt childish sleeping on a top bunk, plus she wasn't super-comfortable with heights.

Dinner was held in the Viking Hall, a nice mix of meat or vegan options, served with craft beer and good wine. Melissa met a few new people too, and did a lot of shop talk. The most popular topic, naturally, was the possibility of leaving with $50,000.

The next morning, Melissa woke groggy: the mattress and pillow were clearly not designed for comfort. She probably only managed four hours of actual sleep, maybe five. The others in the room blearily came to as well, many massaging out sore muscles and yawning.

Breakfast was conducted buffet-style, with, thankfully, plenty of coffee set up in giant urns.

Jim Calloway turned on a mic with an audible *pop*. "Hey, folks." Conversation ground to a slow halt. "I see some of you are still in your pajamas." This got a few laughs. "I'll give you half an hour to shower, brush your teeth, and all that. After, it'd be great if we could all meet up at the entrance to the "intermediate" trail. Okay. Hope you all enjoyed breakfast." He set down the mic and walked out of the hall.

A crew of young people who were all sort of generically good-looking cleared away the plates and utensils, smiling with perfect teeth. Melissa thanked the woman who took hers.

"We exist to serve," she said.

"Okay. Weird," Melissa said. The other woman walked away without acknowledging she'd heard. Melissa returned to the 'orange' cabin, brushed her teeth and took a quick shower. After, she dressed in jeans, long-sleeved-but-lightweight shirt, and hiking boots. She joined the growing crowd at the 'intermediate' trail sign. She found Celia and Frank standing together and joined them.

Jim addressed the crowd with a Dawnaphone. *He sure does like to be amplified,* Melissa thought. "Hey, everyone. Today, right now, we're going to begin our first challenge." He smiled. "This is where we find out who has the chops to survive the first hurdle on the path to fifty grand."

A smattering of cheers came and went with just above minimal enthusiasm. Melissa figured that, like her, most of the people there were waiting for more information.

"All right," Jim said. "Let's go." He led them at a brisk pace, along a trail wide enough to walk four abreast. However, they mostly went in twos and threes to keep from getting snagged on the branches jutting into the path. The sky was overcast but it wasn't raining. Several kinds of birds seemed to be competing to see which could be loudest.

The trail rose gradually, enough of a grade that Melissa was feeling it in her calves. The trees thinned out, finally disappearing altogether, replaced by thigh-high grass and wildflowers, through which the trail led. This opened up to a large, grassy area on the edge of a cliff. A small, steel structure stood at the edge, supporting a wire that ran off into the woods half a mile away on a deep slant. The wire was hundreds of feet off the ground for most of its length.

Zip line from Hell, Melissa thought.

"Step up, folks!" It was Jim. He was holding a metal bar, maybe two feet long, with a sharp curve in the middle and a bicycle handgrip on each end.

There were no safety harnesses or clamps.

A woman in a hijab raised her hand like they were in school. "Excuse me. This looks extremely unsafe." Murmurs of agreement rumbled through the crowd.

"No problem," Jim said, amiably. "Anyone who doesn't want to do the first challenge is free to go back to camp." The entire crowd turned to leave. "Of course," Jim called out, "that means you forfeit your organization's chances to win the fifty K."

They stopped. People looked at each other. Several conversations in hushed voices broke out at once.

The woman in the hijab once again raised her hand. "Thank you for the meals you have provided, and the bed. We'll be taking our leave now." She, along with eight others, walked away without looking back. Another twenty followed them.

"Jesus, you guys," Frank said. "Fifty grand, but…"

"Yeah," Melissa agreed.

After a moment, several others also left, in small groups or by themselves. Eighteen remained.

"Who's first?"

A man in his twenties, lean, muscular, stepped up to Jim. "I'll do it."

Jim handed him the bar he was holding. "Here you go."

The man hooked the bent part of the bar over the cable, took hold of a rubber grip in each hand, shot a wink over his shoulder at the others, and launched himself off the edge.

Melissa watched with the rest, though she kept well back from the edge of the cliff, as the man picked up speed. He made it maybe three quarters of the way before losing his grip.

He was still holding one end of the bar when he hit the ground. He fell at least eighty feet. He was not moving.

The crowd gazed down in stunned silence.

Then: "Oops." It was Jim. "Anyone else wanna try?"

Eleven of the seventeen there left without a word.

Melissa did *not* want to have anything to do with the zip line, but they needed that money. Still, she shook her head and turned toward the path.

"I'll double it."

Melissa stopped and turned to Jim when he spoke. "A hundred thousand?"

"Yes."

"Can I get that in writing?"

Jim pulled out his phone and shot her a text pledging $100,000 to her nonprofit if she completed the series of tests.

"How many tests are there, total?"

Jim pointed finger-guns at Melissa. "Good question. *Smart* question. Three. This is the first."

Celia stepped up to them. "Let me see one of those handlebar thingies." She and Frank were among those who had stayed. Jim handed her one. Celia examined it for a moment, too off her belt, and looped one end around the center of the bar, just below where it would sit on the cable. Celia ran the belt around herself so it rode under her armpits. She put the bar over the cable, tested the connection by tugging it hard, and turned toward the others. She met Frank and Melissa's eyes. "Wish me luck."

They did.

Celia held the bicycle grips and took three running steps to launch herself. Eventually, she disappeared into the trees.

Jim's phone chirped. He looked up from the message. "She made it."

Frank went next, using the same trick with the belt. Halfway, his belt snapped in half, or came undone maybe, and he screamed as he fell.

"Oh, ouch. Too bad. I liked him." Jim shrugged. "Next?"

Everyone but Melissa walked away, taking the path away from this madness. Melissa watched them go. *A hundred thousand dollars.* She looked at the spot where the zip line met the trees, impossibly far away and below. *But Celia made it.*

Jim was watching her. "Last one left. Last chance."

"You know you're probably going to prison, right?"

Jim shrugged. "You signed a risk waiver; you all did. Plus, I've got a very good lawyer."

"Bet you do."

"Come on, Melissa. Time to shit or get off the pot."

"Fuck you."

"That's the spirit!" He handed her a bar.

Melissa took off her belt *and* her jeans. The used the latter to create a kind of harness she could sit in and secured it to the bar by knotting her pants to the belt. She tested it over and over, tugging and yanking, standing on it and pulling with all her strength, until she was sure it would hold. Melissa looped the belt around the bar, checked the connections one last time, closed her eyes, and stepped off the cliff.

The wind in her face was exhilarating. Melissa knew she must be going crazy fast. She opened her eyes, just for a second. It was terrifying. She closed them immediately.

Melissa felt herself slowing. She could hear the leaves of trees as she shot past them. She opened her eyes again, just in time to slam into a thickly padded mat strapped to a tree. The end of the line. It was jarring, but she was unhurt.

Celia was there, along with some of the models-turned-minions. Celia examined the makeshift harness. "Smart."

"Thanks. Got the idea from you."

The brunette minion spoke. "It's time for the next test."

"Okay if I put my pants on first?"

"Yes, of course."

Celia touched Melissa's arm. "Frank?" Melissa turned away. "Oh."

The blonde minion gave instructions while Melissa got dressed. "You are the only two to pass the fist test. As soon as you're ready, we'll proceed to testing ground two."

Melissa buckled her belt. "Let's go."

The path through the woods switched left, then right several times before straightening out and widening suddenly into a sort of clearing. The ground dropped off into a large pit, and the trees on either side were covered with razor wire. Twin ropes stretched across the hole: slack lines. One set ran near the ground and another six feet above them. The ropes were about four feet from one another, and below them, roughly fifteen feet down, a live crocodile, at least ten feet long hissed up at them.

"The object of this challenge is simple." Somehow, Jim was on the other side of the pit. He continued. "Get across. Don't fall. Don't get eaten. Best of luck, ladies."

"Go fuck yourself," Celia said, more tired than angry. She turned to Melissa. "Okay. We go together, right?" Melissa nodded. "I'll take the left and you the right. Don't look down."

"Right. I like this plan. We maintain eye contact too. We got this."

Celia put out her hand and Melissa shook it. "All right then, let's do it."

Melissa reached up to take hold of the overhead rope. She kept a tight grip on it as she put one tentative foot on the lower line.

A few feet away, Celia was mirroring her.

The ropes under the women sank with their weight, dropping them over a foot closer to the crocodile below. Melissa gasped. She froze where she was, unable to move.

"Melissa!" Melissa's eyes snapped up to meet Celia's. She'd been looking down at the deadly reptile. "Look at me. Keep looking at me. Slide one foot forward like this." She moved maybe eighteen inches. "Then bring the back foot up to meet it."

Melissa found she could maintain eye contact and still see their feet in her periphery. She mimicked the sliding foot pattern.

"There you go," Celia said. "Easy-peasy. Just like that." She slid a foot forward again and brought the other one up. Melissa followed, staying directly across from her. Her legs shook slightly and her arms ached—they hadn't had a chance to recover yet from the zip line. She could smell the fear sweat soaking her own armpits and whimpered involuntarily. Celia began to speak but was cut off.

"Aren't you tow wondering how I got a crocodile all the way up here in northwest Michigan?"

Melissa spoke through gritted teeth. "Not especially."

"Oh, but *look at her*. Isn't she a beauty?" Celia, eyes wide, shook her head. Melissa kept her gaze locked on Celia's. The itch to look down was intense, almost overwhelming. "Yep. She's amazing: fourteen feet long and weighs about 800 pounds. A real killer!" Melissa kept matching Celia's foot-slide, trying to keep her eyes from dropping and lower than they were. They were more than halfway across. "Oh," Jim continued, "and she's hungry. Hasn't eaten in a couple weeks."

"When we get across," Melissa said, "I'm going to kick you in the balls."

Celia chuckled. "Me too."

The ropes were at a slight incline now. *We're almost there!* Melissa saw that Celia had noticed too. "Just a little further. We're gonna make it."

Sweat was dripping from Melissa's nose and chin. She wondered if it was hitting the crocodile. She stifled a laugh, worried it might make her fall.

The last few feet took forever. They stepped off the ropes onto solid ground at the same time. Letting go of the overhead line, Celia grasped Melissa and pulled her in, hugging her desperately. They stood, collapsed against one another, panting from exertion and panic.

Jim was clapping slowly.

Melissa separated herself from Celia. She took a moment to get her land legs and kicked Jim in the balls.

Or, tried to. Jim sidestepped smoothly, slid next to Melissa, swept her other leg, and leaned her backward, over the pit. He held her there with one hand, suspended. If he let go, she was gator-bait. His voice was low and full of menace.

"Apologize."

"I'm sorry."

Like flipping a switch, Jim was all smiles again. He lifted Melissa up and made sure she was steady on her feet. "No problem. These challenges can get one pretty riled. No hard feelings. Not on my end anyway." He gestured to the path ahead. "After you."

Melissa and Celia started along the path. Melissa could hear Jim's footsteps in the leaves behind her. She glanced back. "How'd you do that?"

"Ju Jitsu. Twelve years. I'm almost certified to start teaching."

"Great. Congrats."

The came out of the woods back at the campground. They were at the back of the Viking Hall, and two of the minions opened the doors for them. Inside, the buffet table was set up with twenty large, stainless steel stock pots, each with a lid.

"I really thought there'd be more of you at this point," Jim said. "Oh well. It is what it is, right? This is the last one. Pick a pot and eat what's inside. You have to eat all of it."

"That's it?" Melissa asked.

"That's it."

"Can we look inside the pots?"

"No."

"Can we get close enough to smell them?"

"Yes."

"Can we get a do-over if we pick something awful?

"No."

"What if we're allergic?"

"Hm. Okay. But only if you can prove it, like with medial documentation. Email is fine."

Melissa and Celia worked their way around the buffet table, sniffing at each pot. Most of them smelled pretty bad to Melissa, and she was pretty sure she knew what several were. There was one that was vaguely familiar, but she couldn't place it. It didn't smell bad—just bland. She picked that one.

Celia picked hers and the minions removed the other stock pots. Each woman was handed a spoon.

Melissa took off the lid. *Lima beans.* Had to be two gallons of them. She almost gagged thinking about eating that many. *I fucking hate these.*

Celia looked over. "I chose gumbo. I have a mild seafood allergy. It's not going to kill me, but I'm going to spend the next couple days on the toilet, probably."

"Oh no. Why'd you pick that one then?"

"It smelled good."

"Welp," Melissa said, "this disgusting slop ain't gonna eat itself." She hooked a spoonful and put it in her mouth. It felt like bug carcasses on her tongue and tasted like the vegetable version of chalk. Still, she chewed and swallowed it. She did it again. And again. The whole time she told herself it was for the greater good.

She kept at it, eating more than she had since college, and pushing past that. She loosened her belt and the button of her jeans. Her stomach rebelled and she puked, spattering the floor. There was still *so much* left.

She wiped off her mouth and went back for more lima beans. *I can beat this,* she thought. Melissa was operating on pure willpower now. The rest of the world had faded into the background. It was just her against the damn beans. There was still at least a third of it left.

She was chewing slowly, fighting to eat more. But that meant she had to taste it for even longer. *That's it!* she thought. She swallowed quickly and dove in for more, chewing and swallowing as fast as possible. She barely had time to register the taste. Melissa sped up. *I'm doing it!* She was getting close to the bottom.

Scoop, chew, swallow. Faster and faster. Melissa could see the bottom. She grinned around teeth stained a pale green. She scooped up another spoonful and dropped it.

Sharp, tearing pain lit up her chest. *Shit. Heart attack?*

Melissa fell to the floor, coughing. Blood from her mouth spattered the hardwood.

Jim squatted nearby. "This doesn't look good. I've seen something like this once before."

"What?" Talking was sandpaper and needles in her throat.

"You've likely burst your esophagus. See, the stomach can take a lot of abuse. You can fill that thing all day and it'll be fine. The esophagus on the other hand? Not so much."

"I need a doctor."

"Yep. Not one around here, unfortunately. Nearest hospital is a thirty-minute drive. You'll die of internal bleeding before the ambulance even gets close."

"I fucking hate you."

Jim patted her on the head. "That's the spirit. I do have some good news, though. Looks like Celia is going to leave here with a check."

Melissa's heart was going way too fast. "Good. Good for her. You should be in prison. Or Hell."

"I'm sorry. I was rooting for you."

"Eat a bag of dicks, Jim."

Melissa could no longer feel the floor. People were still talking, but it sounded like the wheels on the highway now. *Maybe I'm in shock. Maybe I'm dying.* She closed her eyes. The lids were heavy. *Maybe both.*

Sounds faded, along with the pain. Melissa let out her breath in one long sigh and left it at that.

AFTERWORD

That, to date, is nearly everyone I have killed with my pen. The one I didn't include was a celebrity I won't be naming here, because I'm not interested in getting sued for libel. I plan to keep writing these, because they're a good source of extra income (if you know a writer, odds are good they are not supporting themselves with just their fiction; most of us have days jobs *and* alternate sources of income like Patreon, etc.), and because they're fun. And, as I mentioned in the introduction, each time I do one, I learn something. I love that. If you are interested in being killed by Ken, please drop me a line. My website, kenmacgregor.com, has a contact page you can use, or you can reach out on Facebook. I very much hope you enjoyed these. If you happen to be one of my victims, I'd like to extend my heartfelt thanks and appreciation to you for making this possible. This book wouldn't exist without your help. Lastly, a massive debt of thanks is owed to Holly Schoenfield, who helped me come up with the whole idea, and who was my first death. You rock, Holly!

ABOUT THE AUTHOR

Ken MacGregor has written three story collections, an award-winning young adult novella (*Devil's Bane*), and has co-authored a novel (*Headcase*). He is a member of the Great Lakes Association of Horror Writers and an Active member of the Horror Writers Association. He's also written TV and radio commercials, sketch comedy, a music video, a one-act play, a scattering of poems, and a zombie movie. Ken has curated three original anthologies, one of which (*Stitched Lips*) was a finalist for the Shirley Jackson Award. His third anthology, *Novus Monstrum*, was co-edited with Douglas Gwilym. It is the first installment in the Midnight Zone series.

Ken is also a part-time literary assassin: he will write you into an original short story and kill you for money. Ken drives the bookmobile in a small Michigan city, and lives with his kids, the ghosts of a few cats, and literally hundreds of books.

He can be found at www.kenmacgregor.com.

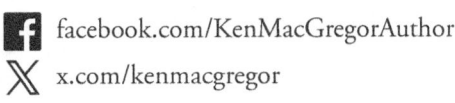

facebook.com/KenMacGregorAuthor

x.com/kenmacgregor

ALSO BY KEN MACGREGOR

Devil's Bane: Tales of a Fourth Grade Warrior

Novus Monstrum

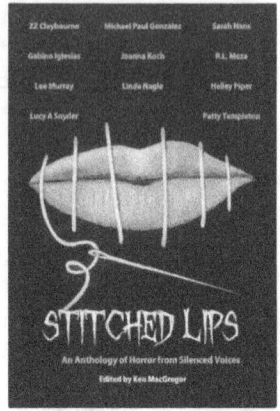

Stitched Lips: An Anthology of Horror from Silenced Voices

DRAGON'S ROOST PRESS

Dragon's Roost Press is the fever dream brainchild of dark speculative fiction author Michael Cieslak. Since 2014, their goal has been to find the best speculative fiction authors and share their work with the public. For more information about Dragon's Roost Press and their publications, please visit: http://www.thedragonsroost.biz

facebook.com/DragonsRoostPress
bsky.app/profile/dragonsroost.bsky.social
instagram.com/cieslak.michael